UNDER TOW

UNDER TOW

A KARI SHARPE THRILLER

K. T. KONKOLY

Published by Thomas & Mercer, Seattle

www.apub.com

Amazon, the Amazon logo, and Thomas & Mercer are trademarks of Amazon.com, Inc., or its affiliates.

EU product safety contact:
Amazon Media EU S. à r.l.
38, avenue John F. Kennedy, L-1855 Luxembourg
amazonpublishing-gpsr@amazon.com

ISBN-13: 9781662526893 (paperback)
ISBN-13: 9781662526909 (digital)

Cover design by David Drummond
Cover image: © zhengshun tang / Getty Images; ©Aliona_25 / Shutterstock

Printed in the United States of America

To my husband, Steve, whose unwavering support, encouragement, and love made every page of this journey possible. Your belief in me never faltered. Thank you for being my greatest cheerleader.

The winds and waves are always on the side of the
ablest navigators.
—Edward Gibbon

Chapter 1

Greg Stadt sat in the corner of Dry Dock's bar, nursing his seventh beer for the night. The well-worn thick wood table felt smooth against his arms, the sticky surface as familiar to him as the kitchen counter in his childhood home. Glancing around, he knew he needed to start heading back to the boat to tuck in for the night, yet he remained. He barely recognized his friend Rod as he approached with their fourth round of shots. Greg's eyes came in and out of focus as he tried to concentrate.

"Hey, man, I figured we'd go out in a blaze tonight! One last shot before closing time," said Rod. He placed the whiskey shots on the table with a thud and slid into the booth across from Greg.

They clinked glasses, sloshing the liquid, then knocked back the shots in unison. "Dang, that felt good! Especially after the night I had. Damned woman really knows how to get under my skin," said Greg. He wiped the line of whiskey that trailed down his chin with the back of his hand, then clasped the sweaty, cold glass of beer to stabilize himself.

Rod leaned back into the booth, eliciting a hiss from the vinyl. He laughed so hard Greg wondered if he had said something funny but forgot. Booze always made him forget. The more he drank, the less he understood things around him. Tonight he clung to wisps of under-standing, trying to steady his mind.

"You two have been fighting like alley cats for as long as I remem-ber. Geez, half of your fights played out right here." Rod knocked on the table for effect. "Remember that time in high school when you and

Stacy broke up and Pam Metser started hanging around? Holy hell, I thought Stacy would rip Pam apart." Rod laughed so hard, spittle sprayed across the table, peppering Greg's hand.

"Oh yeah, and I made the mistake of playing darts with Pam. Nearly got her beaten up when Stacy came in that afternoon," said Greg. He picked up his beer. The glistening glass slipped slightly in his grasp as he tried to down it. The beer spilled over the rim as his hand shook. The front of his shirt darkened with cold pilsner. He slammed the thick pint glass down and uttered a loud "Ahhh."

"That's it for me, man. I've gotta get back to my boat before I forget where I've moored it," said Greg. "You headed out?"

Rod looked around the bar, seeming to consider his options. The place had become nearly empty except for Marsha Sterns, who sat at the bar with her friend Alice. Occasionally Marsha gave a side-glance to the two of them. Apparently sensing an opportunity, Rod said, "No, man, I think I'll hang back for a while." He gave Greg a mischievous smile, then jutted his chin toward Marsha.

Greg followed his gaze, seeing the women at the bar. Normally he wouldn't mind being Rod's wingman. But tonight the fight with Stacy had dampened his mood. He just needed to get back to his boat and sleep off the buzz, then deal with Stacy in the morning. Assuming she wasn't waiting for him on the boat. Maybe they'd screw it out. Wouldn't be the first time.

"Okay, see ya, Rod, and don't do anything I wouldn't do," said Greg as he slid out of the booth. His feet became tangled, nearly causing him to spill out onto the floor. He placed a steadying hand on the table hard enough to wobble it sideways. "Yeah, I need to get back."

He yanked the heavy wood door to Dry Dock open to the night. The porthole in the door was a gimmicky addition the new owners had installed about ten years ago. The blast of cool air felt great on his sweat-slicked face. He hadn't realized just how stuffy the bar was until the air hit him. Despite the indoor-smoking ban, everyone smoked in Dry Dock, which made the place intolerable at times.

The waterfront in Portland, Maine, was deserted at this time of night. None of the boat traffic moved, no tourists popped in and out of shops, no locals tried to get to their offices. Just the cobblestones, brick buildings, and working waterfront. The navigational buoys chimed audibly in the distance. He and Stacy had decided to purchase a sailboat and moor it in the Old Port section of town. They figured it was like having their own little slice of the expensive city. They'd spend weekend nights eating and drinking with friends in Portland and then crash on the boat to sleep it off. On numerous occasions several of their wasted friends had crammed themselves on the boat, too drunk to make the journey home. A gaggle of hungover, grouchy people would awake when the hot sun blasted its rays onto them. They'd walk down to Becky's Diner for a tall stack of pancakes and strong coffee. Nothing had been better to Greg than those mornings with Stacy and their friends.

The toe of his flip-flop nudged against one of the raised red bricks, causing him to fumble forward and grasp at the air for purchase. He fast walked, tumbled and fumbled forward until finally landing hands first onto the bricks, scraping his knee and palms in the process. Standing, he brushed himself off and tried to act nonchalant as his mind continued to spin and tumble. As he turned down the pier toward his boat, a blond head came into focus. Was someone on the boat? Stacy? Had she waited for him?

He walked down the pier to where his thirty-two-foot Sabre sailboat sat tied to the dock. As he approached, she came into focus, a beer in her hand. A large bottle of Tito's next to her.

"What are you doing here?" The pathetic words the only thing his tired, drunk mind could muster.

"I thought we'd spend some time together. We're always so rushed," she said.

He grabbed the stanchion and pulled himself on board, nearly falling over the side as he navigated himself onto the cushion of the settee across from her.

"I brought you a bottle of Tito's, I know how much you like it. Thought I'd get the party started while I waited." She poured shots for them from the open bottle and handed the booze to him.

Despite his reservations he eagerly took the free drink. Something about free stuff made him throw caution to the wind. She had been right, he loved Tito's. Tito's and Fritos, the stuff he and Stacy had built their turbulent relationship on. He knocked back the warm, clear liquid and thrust his cup toward her for a refill.

Maybe tonight would be interesting after all, he thought, glancing at her. The second and then third drink hit his head fast. She talked endlessly about something. He struggled to concentrate on her words. What was it? Casinos? The town? What the hell was she talking about?

He stood, ready to make a move. Maybe get lucky? Why the hell not? He inched his body closer to her, then changed his mind. He needed to take it slow or risk rejection. He stood on the settee and then stepped up onto the brightwork. His legs wobbled under his weight. Then his mouth and face began to feel numb. Booze never made him feel numb. A heavy feeling spread its way from his face, down his neck.

"No! Don't . . . you need to sit back down?" she said.

"I'm fine, do this all the time. Just adjusting the line to stop the maddening banging," he said. Everything on the sailboat clanked, rocked, or squeaked. Normally he wouldn't have noticed, but he was going for romance tonight, not nautical noise. As he staggered toward the center of the boat, his left foot caught the cleat. He stumbled hard toward the deck, grasping air as he flung sideways into the lifeline. The pressure of his weight against the line, combined with the momentum from falling, flipped him over. He went headfirst into the harbor with a loud splash. His open mouth caught seawater as he pierced the surface, screaming.

The cold ocean instantly sobered him up. The jeans and T-shirt he wore suddenly felt like lead weights pulling him down. His heavy body slipped below the surface as his arms and legs kicked in an awkward attempt to tread water. Struggling, he saw her looking over the side at him, yelling. Then she moved away. His hands clawed at the smooth side of the hull, grappling for something to hang on to or to use to pull himself out. Gasping precious mouthfuls of air as he tried to save himself. He started to feel tired. A heavy weighted feeling crushed his chest. He looked toward her. The light-blond wisps of her platinum hair hung around her face as she peered over the side toward him.

"Grab it!" she yelled. She pushed the boat hook pole toward him. His hands slipped off the metal, sliding down its length as he attempted to clasp it. The numbness moved from his face to his hands and legs, making it nearly impossible to tread water. She pushed the pole toward him, grazing his face with it. The wound barely registered through the fog.

Swimming had always been something he did well. Even drunk he could swim, yet tonight his body refused to work properly. What the hell was happening? He gathered enough strength to push his hands out of the water one more time to grab the hook as she thrust it toward his open palms. He could feel the metal, but his hands refused to close around the hook.

She leaned over the side a little farther, shouting something at him. Her garbled words unclear as he sank under. She shoved the hook at him, jamming his shoulder in the process. The sting of it traveled up his arms like a shot of fire.

A searing pain burst through his chest. He curled inward reflexively, unsure how to help himself.

The final thing he saw was her looking down at him. The moon shone over her shoulder, giving her an ethereal appearance. The last face he would ever see. He gasped involuntarily, filling his lungs with cold seawater. Sinking. Soon the struggle ended and everything faded to black.

Chapter 2

Kari Sharpe stood in line at her favorite local coffeehouse, the Chill Bean. This morning they had been cooking a fresh batch of coffee. The machine made a soft whirring sound as it turned the beans, heating them to perfection. The small, crowded café filled with an intoxicating scent. Their java always tasted amazing, but once a month on roasting days, their brew was next-level fresh and delicious.

She had intended to treat herself to a cup of café mocha, the chocolaty, decadent treat she allowed herself only once per month. However, when inside, she knew her coffee needed to be enjoyed unadorned. No chocolate to distract her taste buds from experiencing the nuanced flavor.

"What'll you have?" asked the barista. The tattooed, bearded man bounced slightly side to side as he took her order. Distracted, he darted his eyes behind her to the ever-growing line. Jimmy Buffett's "Margaritaville" played in the background, competing with the loud chatter of customers.

"I'll take a double espresso and a bear claw," she said.

"Good choice. The bear claws just came out of the oven; it'll still be warm for you," he said with a slight smile.

"Perfect, I could use a sugar hit today," Kari said as she paid with her phone.

Last night she went on yet another first date with a man she'd met through an online dating app. He talked incessantly about himself. His accomplishments. His work. Even as she tried to deftly shift the topic, the boring man managed to focus on himself. At this point, using the dating app had resulted only in frustration and far too many wasted evenings out.

"Kari," shouted a barista, announcing her order was ready.

The tiny cup of espresso and her pastry each felt warm to her touch. She had moved back from New York City over a year ago to be with her brother Jimmy. Resigning her position as a partner at the law firm of Barnes & Smith had been far harder than earning it. She found herself going from her vaunted, high-prestige position in New York City to the bottom of the pile once back in Maine. The Sharpe family name had become synonymous with alcohol, drugs, and jail time. Initially she felt as though she would never break into the legal community as cases trickled into her office slower than she could have ever imagined. Then her break came.

The navy had asked her, as a Navy JAG reservist, to represent Youseff Ahmed, a young sailor, during a murder investigation. She had worked her tail off to find the real murderer and free Ahmed. The press and other lawyers had finally seen her as a competent part of the legal community. From the day she gave her first press interview about the case, work had flowed into her office. Mostly criminal defense matters. Something she'd wanted to move away from after her time in the navy. However, the money had been good enough to support her financial needs, the office rent, and her assistant. Finally.

She walked along the redbrick sidewalk that hugged Portland's working waterfront. Numerous wooden piers jutted out from the land. Sailboats, fishing boats, and various motorboats bobbed in the receding tidewater. During low tide many of the boats floated so low that they could barely be seen. Those days also brought a sharp briny, fishy smell of the sea and rotting seaweed, which overtook the more pleasant salty sea air that normally blanketed Portland.

Turning down the pier to her office, she smiled at the building. She rented office space on a floating dock. The redbrick building rose and fell with the tide. It felt magical to her every time she walked down the pier. A far departure from the glass-and-steel skyscrapers of New York or the gray haze of a navy ship. The office was entirely hers. Something to be proud of even if she chose to come to Maine for less-than-glamorous reasons.

She unlocked the door to the office, balancing her espresso and bear claw. The warm beverage wafted its aroma through the opening on the lid. She could hardly wait to crack into it. Walking past the reception desk, she recalled Ruth had mentioned she would be a little late this morning. Something about a doctor's appointment.

Her office sat upstairs from the reception area and conference room. The separation of one level allowed her to be alone, away from Ruth and any clients who waited to meet with her. Because of this feature, the office cost considerably more than others she had looked at. However, despite the money, her mental health and privacy depended on the separation.

The lid to her coffee moved with a slight plastic creaking sound as she lifted it off. The first sip of espresso had been all she hoped for. The smooth, strong elixir slid across her taste buds, enlivening them. She pulled the bear claw out of its paper wrapper and shoved it in her mouth. The barista had been right—the decadent pastry still felt slightly warm from the oven. Pure heaven. She sat at her desk, enjoying her breakfast and the still office. Each day brought its own assortment of chaos as she navigated her numerous cases, but for now she would take an extra minute to herself.

Finally, she felt ready to turn on her desktop and start her day. Her full inbox contained various client questions; opposing counsel had sent documents for review; and one of her law school friends, Jill Sayer, had sent her a lunch invite, which she readily accepted. Jill had moved to Maine for school. As a transplant, she had no knowledge of Kari's family's transgressions. She had not grown up seeing the Sharpes mentioned on the news for their crimes. Instead, Jill had taken Kari as she'd presented herself, an ambitious, scrappy Maine kid who worked hard, earning excellent grades and a prestigious Navy JAG position.

Over the course of the year since she'd moved to Maine, her professional successes had become more public thanks to the media coverage. Eventually other law school classmates had started to warm up to her. She no longer sat alone on counsel bench in court as other lawyers chatted. Instead, the once-distant attorneys greeted her and sat nearby. Kari hated their fake warmth. She knew damned well that if she had not won several high-profile criminal cases, none of them would be bothered with her, except Jill.

The door to the office slammed shut just below her. "Good morning, Kari," Ruth yelled from downstairs.

After a few minutes Ruth appeared in her office doorway, looking excited. "Do you know what's happening?" she said, out of breath.

"Happening? With what? I'm not following."

Ruth clamped her hands together and looked past Kari to the harbor just beyond the window. "There are cops and the fire department everywhere. Didn't you hear the sirens?"

She hadn't heard a thing. The thick double-paned windows protected her from the harsh winter wind blowing off the ocean but also prevented her from hearing anything outside.

"Really? Where are they?" Kari asked as she stood up.

She unlocked the window closest to her and heaved the heavy double-hung pane up a few inches. Sounds and humid ocean air immediately flooded the small office. Several different sirens competed with one another as police and an ambulance sped down the pier outside the offices. The police parked anywhere space allowed in a jumbled tangle of official vehicles.

"Holy crap, I can't believe I didn't hear any of this. What do you think is happening?" Kari asked Ruth.

"I have no idea, but I want to walk outside if you don't mind. I know I had a—"

"I don't mind at all," Kari said. "I'll join you, but first I need to call Jimmy to be sure he's okay. You go and I'll catch up."

Kari grabbed her phone off the desk and hit Jimmy's number on her favorites list. The line rang several times before he answered. "Hey, Kari. What's up, Sis?"

"I'm just checking in on you. There's something big happening on the waterfront. I wanted to be sure you're okay," she said with relief.

An ocean navigational buoy sounded through his line. A deep horn from a tugboat blasted close to his lobster boat. "Everything's fine. I'm pulling my traps. Just doing my thing. I haven't heard anything."

She walked to one of the other windows in her office and leaned her head against the pane, trying to see down the pier.

"Okay—I'm going outside to check it out. I'll let you know what I find," she said and hung up before he could reply.

He sounded sober, thankfully. At ten in the morning, she should not have to worry about his drinking, but with Jimmy she never knew what to expect. His rapid descent into alcoholism was what had finally yanked her back to Maine. She'd given up not only her position in New York for him, but all her friends and the practice she'd built in the prestigious firm. Thankfully, after several shaky months together, Jimmy had returned to his AA meetings and sobriety.

Kari took two steps at a time as she bounded down the stairs and out the door to the pier. The sun blinded her when she first stepped out. After she blinked a few times, her eyes started to relax. Walking behind her office, she saw Ruth watching everything unfold. At least ten Portland Police officers, an ambulance, and a fire truck crammed onto the small pier.

"They found a body," said Ruth as Kari approached.

"Oh crap. Where?"

"I'm not sure. I've been trying to listen in. From what I can gather, I think it got tangled under the dock near those sailboats." Ruth pointed to the end of the dock. Several divers sat on the side of it, dangling their flippers into the ocean as they prepared their masks. A minute later they jumped into the salty, cold water.

"Geez. I wonder if it was a drunk tourist? Wouldn't be the first time," said Kari.

Tourists and locals alike came to the Old Port to drink, hang out, and eat. Over the years several inebriated people had gone into the water and died. Some of the lucky ones were fished out by their friends. During high school Kari had been out with a few people partying in the Old Port. The group had left the bar to smoke weed on the pier when one of the guys toppled over into the water. The loud splash and yelling had sobered everyone up quickly. The smashed group had struggled to yank him out of the water, finally succeeding.

Something floated to the surface; then a diver popped up and out of the water, clearing his mouthpiece. He held on to the arm of the floating man whom the divers had freed from a watery grave. Several of the firefighters moved into position. They lassoed the dead man and pulled him toward the dock. It took several firefighters plus both divers to finally pull the body from the water.

The ambulance drivers stood close by, waiting with a gurney and a body bag. Once the body had been heaved onto the pier, they lifted it into the bag, then wheeled it down the wooden dock to the waiting truck. Several times the squeaky wheels of the stretcher got stuck in the warped wooded planks. The men had to shove it hard to keep it moving, nearly toppling the body off with the effort.

"Well, that's a lot of excitement to start our day. I'm heading back inside," said Kari to Ruth.

"Seriously, that was a lot."

The women walked silently side by side past the back parking lot and into the office, the air-conditioning a welcome relief to the summer humidity.

Kari walked up the stairs. Sitting in her comfortable chair, she spun toward the window and let out a long exhale. She took the last sip of her now-cold espresso, jammed the rest of her bear claw into her mouth, and began to work. After a minute she turned on the small desk radio, curious if the local news would cover the death in the Old Port.

Chapter 3

Stacy Marcs Stadt stretched her thin frame across the bed and yawned. She glanced at Greg's side of the mattress, realizing that he hadn't come home last night. Not unusual. They started the night drinking at Dry Dock, as they had done on so many evenings. However, instead of staying on the boat with him, she went home because of another loud, public fight. Not the first nor the last. It didn't mean anything.

They had been together since middle school. The two of them had navigated so many things together—school, friends, braces, puberty. He felt like her second skin. The second skin that always had an itchy rash. Marrying him seemed predetermined. The sort of thing that just happened because everyone expected it to happen.

She pulled the cozy, thick comforter up to her shoulders and grabbed the remote. Clicking on the morning news was a luxury she would allow herself this morning. She didn't have to rush to their office, she told herself, just relax awhile. Enjoy the quiet house.

A journalist was interviewing Kari Sharpe about a case she'd recently won. "You seem to have a knack for finding the innocent clients, Ms. Sharpe," said the reporter.

"Well, everyone is innocent until proven guilty. I just hold the prosecutors to their task of proving each case beyond a reasonable doubt," Kari replied.

Stacy rolled her eyes and yawned. Stupid Kari Sharpe. She could hardly believe that rough kid had made something of herself. They'd grown up together, spending the first decade and a half of their lives in the same school system. Stacy and Greg had married two months after graduation, while Kari apparently went on to get her college and law degrees.

She probably wishes she had my life, Stacy thought. She looked around the well-appointed bedroom. The four-poster bed, expensive thick bedding, matching dresser, and nightstands all a testament to the success she and Greg had built together. They'd worked tirelessly to establish themselves as premier housebuilders in Sweetwater, Maine.

Their toy poodle, Ginger, jumped up onto the bed and licked Stacy's face, dancing with her back legs, tail wagging. "Hello, baby girl! You about ready to get up?" she asked the little dog. Ginger turned her head side to side in a quiet reply. "Okay, I can't be lazy all morning." She kissed Ginger's soft nose, ruffled her topknot, and got up.

The adjoining en suite had been every bit as luxurious as the rest of the bedroom. She and Greg "went big" with the entire house. For the primary bathroom, they'd chosen the best marble Bald Billy's Flooring offered. They'd also installed the biggest soaking tub they could find and stately gold-finish hardware on the sinks. Ginger followed Stacy into the bathroom, her nails clicking on the smooth floor.

Once downstairs she let Ginger out into the expansive yard and poured herself a cup of freshly brewed coffee. The coffee percolated on its own each morning thanks to the timer she had set. Somehow having a cup of steaming coffee waiting for her made each morning feel like she woke in a fancy hotel, instead of their garrison house in Maine.

She picked up her phone and checked to see if Greg had contacted her either last night or this morning. Nothing. *That's odd,* she thought. It was already 10:00 a.m. Typically she would have heard something from him. The fight had been bad but not call-the-cops bad. At least not this time. She tapped her long, manicured nails on the granite countertop, wondering if she should call him. She didn't want to appear weak or grovel, but she did need to know his plan for going into the office today.

She used speed dial to call his cell phone and waited. The phone rang without answer until it finally went to voicemail. *Maybe he's still mad?* Or maybe he went to the office already and was too busy to pick up the phone. She looked at his location on the Find My iPhone app. From what she could tell, he appeared to still be on the boat. *Odd.*

Ginger barked and swiped at the glass door just off their sunny yellow kitchen. The little dog stood on her back legs and scratched the clear glass, trying to get Stacy's attention. Stacy walked over to the door and let her inside. "Sorry, girl. Mommy was distracted. Let's get you some yummies." Ginger wiggled as she walked excitedly with Stacy toward her treat closet.

Stacy checked her schedule. She needed to get moving, no more lazing around. Payroll had to be done today, or their seven employees would not be paid on time. After dashing upstairs, she dressed quickly in a pair of skinny jeans and silk blouse. Turning around in the mirror, she glanced at her behind and said to her reflection, "Damn, girlfriend! You look good." She flicked her light, bottle-blond hair and walked out of the bathroom. Smiling, she went downstairs, kissed Ginger goodbye, and left their house for the morning.

The office of Houses by Stadt was a mere three miles away from their home. Perfect for dashing back to the house when she wanted lunch or just to nap. She parked her car in front of the door and glanced around the lot. Greg's truck wasn't there. Maybe the location service had correctly pinned him on the boat. She wondered what he was doing. Despite his drinking, he always showed up for work early, before the employees arrived. He considered greeting his employees in the morning an essential management duty, setting the tone for the day, making everyone more productive. Today for the first time ever, she arrived at the office before him. A sinking feeling of dread started to claw at her, twisting her empty stomach into a knot. Had something happened?

She yanked the glass door open and entered the office they'd established ten years earlier. "Good morning, Shirley," she said to the receptionist.

"Good morning, Stacy," she replied a little too chipper.

Once she settled into her office, she pulled up Greg's schedule on their shared drive. From what she could tell, he had a meeting with a prospective customer this morning. She glanced at her watch and realized the customer would be in the office in less than twenty minutes. Where the hell was he?

Tapping the desk with her fingernails, she looked out the window toward the parking lot and Route 1. Was last night's fight so bad that he just wanted to stay away from her? The sinking feeling of dread returned as she sat wondering about him. Her knee bounced as her mind shot around to the various possibilities. When she'd left Dry Dock, he had been just as inebriated as she was, maybe more so. Rubbing and pinching her nose, she shot up from her chair like a caged animal needing to flee. "Where the hell are you?" she whispered softly to the empty office. Swallowing hard, she readied herself to greet the potential client.

Chapter 4

Beth Thornberry splashed cool water on her tired face and stopped for a moment to look at herself. The deep lines of worry etched across her brow. Her chocolate eyes drooped in a tired, sad sort of way. At least her short pixie cut remained the same, even if her hair color changed from a chestnut to a salt-and-pepper gray. Despite taking care of herself, time had passed, changing her into the midlife woman in the mirror.

She stood at her kitchen counter, drinking a steaming cup of black tea, her first of many she would have over the course of the day. A gentle breeze fluttered the simple white lace curtains. The muffled sounds of chickens clucking in the yard drew her attention. The chicken coop sat a short distance off her kitchen door. After her tea and a fresh homemade scone, she and her dog, Max, went outside.

"Come on, Max! You ready to get outside?" she said to him.

The small mutt of a dog wagged his tail excitedly to join her. They stepped out of the dark-brown ranch and onto the stone patio. She had installed the Vermont slate patio a few years ago when Sweetwater Downs, her family business, had been doing well. Now she looked at the patio, wishing she could trade the beautiful multicolored stones for the fifteen grand she'd paid.

The wooden block holding the chicken coop door closed turned with a loud creak. "Good morning, ladies!" Her words were met with a loud cacophony of excited clucking from the seven chickens. Max pushed his way between her legs to get a sniff of the coop and each chicken as they marched down the little plank, heads held high. The tawny-colored birds clucked loudly as they passed, oblivious to Max's inspection.

She held her egg basket in one hand as she stretched her arm inside the coop. The smell of chicken feathers, excrement, and hay nearly made her gag as she scooped up the still-warm eggs from each of the little nests. Her seven chickens produced enough eggs that she'd started a small farm stand at the end of her driveway. One weekend she'd built a table with a little wooden roof and then painted the entire thing white. A sign read "Farm Fresh Eggs. 30¢ Each. Honor System." Every morning she left the "daily catch," as she called it, in a cooler on the table. At the end of the day, the cooler was empty, but the wooden box had been filled with money.

As the racetrack started to flounder, she wondered if her neighbors bought eggs as a form of charity. Seeing five-dollar bills in the box made no sense given the cost of the eggs. Of course, she had no way to prove it. The thought of anyone feeling sorry enough to give her a handout really annoyed her. It bothered her so much that she considered stopping the egg sales, then thought about the alternative. What would she do with the eggs? Eat all of them? Impossible. Throw them away? No. The practical, frugal Mainer in her would never waste good food. Instead, she used the money from the stand for the chickens. Chickens don't have a sense of pride, she reasoned.

After finishing her morning chores and getting dressed, she headed out of the house for the day. "Come on, Max!" she yelled to the dog as she patted the side of her thigh. She held the door open to her fifteen-year-old dark-green Chevy pickup truck as she waited for Max. He went with her to the racetrack every morning. On days when she felt like sitting at home, not wanting to face the problems presented by the business, his excitement to go motivated her. He bounded over to the gravel drive, jumped inside the cabin, and waited for her to get in.

"All right, let's go." Living in inland Maine placed her close to the racetrack but far enough away that she felt like she had her space. The modest ranch house had been her grandmother's home. Growing up, she'd spent most of her summers at the house as her parents worked long hours building the racetrack business. Her grandmother hated the track. She would say, "Nothing good will ever come of that place. Nothing but drunk men betting their lives away on nothing."

"Nothing" had been Grammy's favorite word, except she pronounced it "nuthen." Maybe her grandmother had been right? Who knew. Things hadn't been great at the track for a while now. The financial decline threatened to shutter its doors. If that happened, she risked losing her grandmother's home, because she had used all the collateral in the property to keep the business running. Her fingers tightened on the steering wheel as the stress of being homeless clawed at her. Where would she go?

The Chevy's wheels crunched as she pulled into the "Owner" parking spot with the same spark of pride she felt the first time her father allowed her to do it. Something about being labeled the owner of the racetrack gave her a sense of purpose. Her steel-toed work boots scraped the dusty gravel as she walked toward the barn. Pulling the heavy wooden door, she slid it all the way back on its rails to the fully open position. Walking into the dark, cool stable she clicked on the overhead light.

Long rows of wooden stalls sat on either side of the main walkway. In total, they had enough stalls in the barn to house thirty-seven horses. Over the years, the number of horses staying in the barn had ebbed and flowed. Some years she thought she would have to build more stables; other years, she considered using the empty stalls for storage. Currently, only eighteen horses lived there, despite her efforts to find new tenants. Ten of those horses belonged to Beth. Revenue from the rest was not enough to keep the lights on.

The sweet smell of hay mingled with the heady aroma of the horses in a pleasant, almost homey combination that she loved. She stopped by one of the stalls to greet her favorite racer. The chestnut mare extended its long, thick neck over the worn half door to greet her. She ran a hand over the mare's warm, muscular neck, pulling on the soft mane as her hand traveled, finally resting on Royal's velvety nose. The mare brayed a welcome to her and leaned into Beth's hand. Royal opened her thick, soft lips to nibble Beth's fingers as they came close to her nose. "I didn't bring any apples today—sorry, girl. But how about if I get you out first."

She lifted the wrought iron peg and slid it back to open the stall. Grabbing Royal by the harness, she walked with her side by side down the length of the barn to the opposite end to the paddock. Royal's large hooves clomped in tune with Beth's boots on the solid earthen floor of the barn. Once she put Royal outside, Beth made her way through the barn, escorting each horse to the paddock. The horses spent their day outdoors, each getting exercised on the track by their in-house trainer. After the exercise, the stable hand groomed them and then returned each to their stalls for the evening. She had always had a few stable hands, but now the exhausting tasks fell on her shoulders. Along with everything else.

"Morning, Beth!" yelled Joe Spencer. He had been the racetrack's primary horse trainer for as long as she could remember. Even when she was a kid, Joe had been out in the paddock with the horses. He had coaxed winners out of numerous horses.

"Morning," she shouted with a wave.

The owner's office was in the corner of the barn. The locked door ensured she could keep money and valuables inside the little space without worry. She trusted her employees, but everyone had a threshold for crime, as she'd recently discovered. Even honest people could at times do the wrong thing for what they considered the right reasons.

She unlocked the door to her office and stepped inside, softly closing it behind her. The wood-paneled room contained a desk, a couple of chairs, and a small couch in the corner. Pictures of the winning horses lined the walls. Each horse wore a stack of ribbons and stood proudly next to their smiling jockey. The horse's owner stood on the opposite side. Frank Nash had been in many of the pictures. He'd run his horses at the racetrack for decades, never caring about the horses or the track, only the money. The man made her sick. She wanted to rip the pictures of his overstuffed face off her walls but knew she couldn't. Displaying the pictures had been expected. Besides, the last thing she needed would be to piss him off.

The two new slot machine casinos in Maine pulled business from the racino. The number of people coming to spend the day at the track had dropped significantly since they opened. Every aspect of the business suffered with the reduction of foot traffic. The restaurant ran at a loss, the grounds maintenance projects remained unfinished, and even the barn maintenance needed to wait. The only thing she never skimped on was the health of the horses.

The bookshelves, the desk, and the tops of the filing cabinets were strewn with papers, files, books, brochures, and other things. Some of it belonged to her late father. She had never bothered to clean the messy office when she'd taken over. A week after he'd dropped dead in the barn, she'd just walked into the office, rolled up her sleeves, and started to manage things.

The phone rang right on time. The guy from the bank told her he'd be calling at 10:00 a.m., and sure enough, right at ten the phone rang. Damn him. She bit her lip and shook her head, irritated. Then she stood, snatching the receiver off its cradle.

"Hello. Sweetwater Downs," she said with a chipper tone, despite how she felt.

"Good morning, Ms. Thornberry, it's Rick from Sweetwater Savings and Loan. How are you today?"

"Everything is just wonderful, thanks for asking." She tried to sound normal as she pushed the panic down, away from her throat, away from her voice. Her leg trembled with nerves as her fingers fidgeted with various things on her desk. The dusty rock, the crystal paperweight, the ballpoint pen. She picked up and put down each item in turn.

"As you know, the track has defaulted on its loan, once again. At this juncture, we will need a substantial arrears payment to stop us from proceeding against the collateral," he said. His stale voice so blasé, so normal, despite everything she felt. He talked at her as though he spoke about the weather, not selling off her family business.

"What does that mean?" She was stalling for time. Her mind turned over trying to come up with a solution. Her eyes darted from the paddock back into the office, then around the office, settling on a picture of her father—young, enthusiastic, smiling, and full of life. She jerked her head away from the picture, and tears welled in her eyes as she struggled to listen to the loan officer.

"As we discussed, it means the bank will have no choice but to start selling the property, including all assets. All grounds maintenance equipment, the horses, and any feed or small items will be auctioned off. Finally, we will sell the property."

Her wind caught in her chest. She found herself panting shallow breaths. She needed to calm herself down or she would pass out. The chair creaked as she collapsed and looked back out the window. Joe rode one of the horses around the paddock. Rex, their maintenance man, mowed the grass behind the track, as he had done for over a decade. What would happen to them if she closed the track? She rubbed her tired eyes and tried to focus on his words. Her sweaty hand trembled.

After a minute she said, "I have a plan to raise the funds. I just need a little more time. Can I have thirty more days? Please? This is my family business. It's an important part of the Sweetwater community. I just need thirty days, and I know I can sort all of this out." She said the lie so effortlessly and with so much passion that she almost believed it herself. However, her plan depended on more than her efforts. It depended on the board of the Town of Sweetwater voting to allow slot machines at the track. The slot machines would ensure the track could compete with the other casinos in Maine.

"What's your plan? I need specifics or I simply won't be able to sell the idea to my superiors," he said dryly.

She wanted to shout, "Bullshit! There's only three of you in the damned bank. Everyone knows you don't have to 'sell' anything." Instead, she looked down at her boot as she tapped the edge of the scuffed desk with her toe and said, "The Town of Sweetwater is voting on the issue of the slots in the next couple of weeks. This time the measure will pass, and we'll get an infusion of money from the New Jersey casino people. Everything will work itself out. They've even promised to refresh the paddock."

She tried not to sound desperate as she spoke. *Remain calm,* she told herself, even as the panic rose again. If the bank started their process of selling off her assets, everything she had done, every shady thing, would have been for nothing. Huffing a ragged breath and stiffening her back, she waited for his reply.

She had made a deal with the devil. Come what may. Her misdeed had been done.

"Okay, I'll give you one week after the town vote. Not a day more," he said. Then the phone clicked dead.

She threw the phone down and held her head in her hands. The folder in front of her contained so many past due notices, she didn't even know where to begin. She was desperate for the New Jersey casino slots to be installed. Everything depended on it. Nothing else would save them. Gamblers wanted to play the slots. Plain and simple. Compared to the other casinos, Sweetwater Downs appeared quaint, old-fashioned. Tired.

She shuffled around the past due notices and the utility turnoff letters. An unopened envelope sat among the bills. The envelope promised immediate cash and a zero percent introductory interest rate on balance transfers to the new credit card. Did she dare? She had been playing a shell game of credit card roulette for some time now. It never helped the situation. Instead, she found herself getting deeper into a financial hole with every new card she opened.

Joe Spencer stood in the paddock next to a large bay-colored male standardbred horse. He walked around the horse, inspecting the beast, checking each hoof as he moved. Damn it. She knew his careful inspection could only mean one thing, an expensive veterinary bill. She ripped open the credit offer envelope and picked up the phone to call the company. One last time. Once the casino money started to roll in, everything would settle down.

Chapter 5

A few days later Jimmy Sharpe eased the throttle on his Back Cove lobster boat as he pulled up to one of his lobster pots. He had been lobstering in one capacity or another since high school. After long years as an apprentice, the State of Maine had finally allowed him to obtain his own lobstering license. He leaned over the side of the *Magpie* and yanked the lobster pot out of the deep, cold sea. The weight told him another one of his traps had scored big. Enough lobsters had walked into his traps for the past week to give him a sense of financial ease.

He opened the hull to dump the crustaceans into the hold. The black eyes of the numerous lobsters he'd caught that morning stared up at him. He hated seeing the eyes. Despite him never feeling anything about killing the lobsters, their eyes freaked him out. What were they thinking? he'd wonder. He rubbed his tired face and looked to the horizon to clear his head.

His mind had been drifting into dead-end, disturbing tangents since the body had been pulled from the harbor. He threw the wooden trap overboard, then stood to watch as it slowly drifted back to its resting place in the depths of the sea. The colorful buoy marked the location.

He hung on to the lifeline as he worked his way to the rear storage hold. The damned eyes looked at him. The brownish-green crustaceans crawled over each other, seeking an exit that did not exist. The futility of their efforts poked him somewhere deep. "We're all crawling around in our own traps! You guys aren't any different!" he yelled as he slammed the cover down hard, rattling the boat.

Back at the helm, he held the metal wheel with one hand, the other on the throttle, and paused. He needed to take the edge off. In the past he would have easily had at least one drink. His eyes darted to the small, now-empty compartment where he had always hidden his stash of booze. A year ago, he'd left the boat in neutral while he'd snatched a bottle of whiskey from the storage cubby. His fingers had shaken with anticipation as he'd twisted the metal cap off the bottle. Knocking back one drink meant something different each day. That day, he'd held up the bottle and taken a long, deep pull. The brown liquid had flowed down the back of his throat, burning as it went. He'd needed the punishment. He'd needed the relief. After several gulps, he'd screwed the cap onto the bottle and opened the compartment. Alcoholics Anonymous had helped him to see the patterns in his behavior. His sponsor had kept him on track between meetings.

Suddenly his boat shook violently from the starboard side.

"What the hell?" he muttered as he looked around. The unexpected rocking nearly toppled him over as he daydreamed.

His friend and fellow lobsterman Chet pulled alongside his boat.

"Hey, Jimmy! How's the biz this morning?" asked Chet.

"I can't complain. The day is clear, traps are full. It's all good. You catching anything?" he asked.

"Oh yeah, my traps have been full. If this keeps up, we'll all be able to relax in the winter. Put our feet up like the suits do!"

"After the lean summer we had last year and the hard winter, a quiet season would be amazing," he said, running a calloused hand through his hair.

Chet stood for a moment, assessing Jimmy. His eyes trailed down Jimmy's shirt to his jeans. Jimmy shifted from side to side, uncomfortable under his gaze. He ran a hand over his chest, trying to figure out why Chet stared at him. Did he know? Had Chet seen him drinking in the past? Jimmy stood straighter. Those days were over. For good.

"You hear who they fished out of the drink?" asked Chet.

"No," said Jimmy.

"Greg Stadt. He grew up in your area. Maybe you or Kari knew him? I saw him around, mostly at Dry Dock, but never really knew him. They think his wife offed him. Threw him skunk drunk over the side! Just like that! Dang. It's cold as hell. So cold I could see Sissy doing the same thing to me," said Chet, laughing.

Chet reliably had the best gossip on the waterfront. If something went down, Chet knew about it. Then he made sure everyone else knew as well.

"Oh crap . . . Seriously? I wonder if Kari heard," said Jimmy.

"Beats me. Okay, man. Gotta go. I'm about halfway through pulling. Then on to the fun stuff."

Chet released the lassoed line from around the cleats on Jimmy's boat and engaged his powerful engine. The bow of Chet's lobster boat lifted out of the water as he moved away. The *Magpie* rocked side to side from the wake Chet had created. The force of the movement made Jimmy sway as his sea legs automatically stabilized him.

He pulled a water bottle out of the side pocket near the helm and chugged the cool water with a loud gulping sound. Looking over the colorful lobster buoys scattered through the bay, he exhaled slowly. The long, ragged breath left him with urgency as though not even it wanted to accompany him any longer. Abusing his body for so long had been second nature. It would take time to heal. His water bottle clanked the sides of the compartment with a rhythmic tapping sound. A crisp, salty wind blew hard against the side of his face, like a cold slap.

He tightened his grip on the steering console and fished his phone out of his back pocket. A motorboat with a smiling family whizzed past him toward a beach or island to the north. Lucky kids. They grinned from ear to ear and threw their heads back with laughter as their dad zoomed over the swells, bouncing the bow up and down hard. The racket from their engine trailed as they passed. After dialing Kari, he waited as her line rang. He glanced at his large athletic watch and wondered what she would be doing at ten in the morning. Probably at her office. Or in court. Finally, just as he thought it would go to voicemail, she answered.

"Hey, Jimmy. Everything okay?" she asked without skipping a beat. A simple question laced with nuance.

"Why do you always assume something isn't okay? Geez."

"Do you really need me to tell you?"

"Fine. Have it your way," he said. "Talk to you later."

"Wait . . . okay. Sorry, I'm always worried about you. Let's start over. What's up?"

He could hear the rhythmic sounds of her tapping away on her keyboard as he spoke. She always did that when he called. Never giving him her full attention while at work. He shook his head, trying to clear his thoughts.

"You remember the guy they pulled out of the water, near your office?" he asked.

"Yeah—of course I remember. Why?"

"Chet told me it was Greg Stadt. Remember him?"

She stopped typing. Silence.

"Kari? You still there?" he asked.

"Yes, sorry, I'm here. He was such a monster. Of course I remember him, the douchebag. I hated him and his girlfriend Stacy. They were so brutal to me when we were kids," she said softly.

He knew reviving the name of her childhood bullies had been unkind. At least he could have waited until the end of the day. Or let the news pass without mentioning it to her. He grimaced as he realized how insensitive he had been.

The sun had moved over to the side of the boat near the helm where he stood. The searing-hot summer rays burned his skin despite the breeze. He pushed the throttle upward, engaging the powerful engine. The deafening sound rose as he moved. The next lobster pot sat closer to land. He navigated to the pot, then returned the boat to neutral.

"Stacy? You mean his wife. Those two married after you guys graduated from high school. Remember?" said Jimmy, shouting over the racket.

"Oh my gosh! That's right, I do remember now. The unholy alliance is what we labeled them. They deserved each other."

"Yep. According to Chet the cops think Stacy pushed his drunk ass into the harbor, drowning him."

Her only reply was a full, loud belly laugh. After a few seconds she finally said, "That's too good. Thanks, Jimmy. That made my whole day."

He could hear her office line ringing as she spoke. Their time had come to an end. The tapping of her fingers on the keyboard started again.

"I aim to please. See ya, kid," he said, then disconnected, feeling like less of a jerk.

Turning the smooth surface of the phone in his hands, he glanced at an incoming text. Got a minute? asked his sponsor, Wes.

Yeah, I'll call you in about thirty, he typed back. He needed Wes. He needed the sanity of AA. Probably always would.

He hoisted the last pot of the day onto his boat. Opening the hold, he tried not to look at the doomed catch. Once finished, he surveyed the bay for boating traffic. The loud horn of the Casco Bay Line blew, announcing its departure from the pier. The blast caught him off guard and made him jump in surprise. His legs were unable to catch him. Instead of righting himself after the jump scare, he tumbled backward onto the deck, nearly splitting his head on the hold lock as he fell flat out. Not the first time, nor the last. The men who made a living on the water were covered with an assortment of bruises and scars. He was no different. His abused body carried the visible badges of the profession.

Righting himself took considerable effort as the sea bounced him around. "Damn it," he muttered. Once vertical, he clung to the railing and coughed heavily. The deep rattling of his chest forced his body into a curved shape as he hacked uncontrollably. He wiped his mouth of spittle with the back of his hand and looked around. Several lobstermen worked the area, but none seemed close enough to see his embarrassing fall. Thankfully.

Chapter 6

Mack waited impatiently behind a loaded car full of tourists. The white license plate read Ohio. The delay at the light meant they were lost. He tapped his fingers on the steering wheel, trying to remain calm as the light changed from green to red. The summer months had always been his least favorite in Maine. The damned tourists filled the restaurants, the roads, and everything in between. During the summer months, getting around seemed impossible for the locals. Finally, they started to move. Suddenly a mom and her bratty kids dashed in front of his car, causing him to slam on his brakes. She didn't even notice how close they'd come to becoming roadkill.

He was cranky from a lost night of sleep. He'd stayed up well past midnight last night shooting pool with Debbie, an on again, off again woman he dated. If it could be called dating. Mostly they fooled around and drank too much. That morning he'd done the walk of shame on his return home. The only thing he'd wanted from Debbie had been a distraction. It seemed to suit her just fine too.

Finally, he made it to Kari's office. Pulling his LeSabre into a very tight spot on the pier took some maneuvering. Nothing he couldn't handle.

It had been a couple of weeks since Kari had asked him to come to the office. Despite racking his brains for an excuse to stop by to flirt with Ruth, nothing believable had come up. Ruth might still be griev-ing, because despite their brief but heady dalliance, she was keeping him at bay. He needed to be careful about how he turned on the signature Mack charm. *Just bide your time, big guy,* he told himself.

Running a shaky, nervous hand down the front of his shirt, he almost laughed. That morning after his shower, he searched desperately for a clean shirt. Not wanting to see Ruth wearing one of his usual stained shirts. The only thing he could find had been an ill-fitting, slightly frayed button-down in the back of his closet. Good enough.

He glanced at his reflection in the rearview mirror, double-checking for crud in his teeth. Slicking his hair back, he attempted to get out of the car.

The car door banged loudly against the truck parked next to him. Crap. It was closer than he thought. His foot clanked on the pier before he lifted himself out of the seat, desperately squeezing between the door and the frame of the car. He risked a glance toward Kari's office. The windows reflected the shapes of the boats docked at the pier. He had no way of knowing if Ruth had witnessed him trying to suck in his gut to get out of the car.

Finally free, he dashed to the office, trying not to be too transparent even though he rippled with excitement to see her.

"Good morning, beautiful!" he said to Ruth. The door slammed behind him, causing her to jolt slightly.

"Oh, Mack, stop!" she giggled and blushed.

He placed his forearms on the reception counter and leaned into her space. The proximity allowed him to experience her delicate floral perfume. Her signature scent had always lingered in his bed long after she returned home.

"I'll bet you're tired from a weekend of fighting off suitors. A beautiful woman like you probably gets asked out all the time." He smiled.

"Please, that would be the day!"

He walked up the stairs, needing to get away from her before he really embarrassed himself. Maybe he'd struck the right chord with her? Once she started dating, he intended to make his move before some other guy swept her away.

Mack's loud footsteps clomped as he walked to Kari's office. Usually his noisy arrival announced him. Not today. Kari sat looking out the window.

"Hey there, anyone home?" he said softly.

She turned to him, pale and exhausted.

"Geez, you okay? Someone take away your birthday?" he asked.

"I don't know, Mack. I just talked to Jimmy. He told me that Greg Stadt had been the guy they pulled from the harbor. I hate to admit it, but I was amused at first. But then I started to think about Greg and was flooded with horrible memories." She rubbed her tired eyes for several seconds. Dispensing a tissue, she wiped them and then blew her nose loudly.

"Greg Stadt? Why do I remember the name?" he asked. He rubbed his chin, lost in thought.

"He's the guy who brutally bullied me for years. The one Jimmy had punched out in the cafeteria."

"Oh geez. Sorry. How could I forget?" he said. "Man, those were crappy years for you."

"Worst time of my life. I hadn't appreciated how much pain I still hung on to from the bullying. Just hearing his name blew me back about fifteen years."

"I'm sorry, Kari. I had no idea. Well, I did, but I didn't. How did Jimmy know?"

"Chet. Same way he always knows things," she said with a soft smile. She returned her gaze to the sea. A dead stare into nothing.

Mack settled onto the chair across from her. The cheap, olive-green faux leather chair groaned as it accepted his weight. He shook his head and exhaled a long breath. A familiar tightness in his chest found him again. The weight of Kari's and Jimmy's problems had been something he'd dealt with for years.

"I'm so conflicted. Greg's death should give me closure, yet somehow I feel robbed. Like shouting at him or standing up to him and Stacy would have been better for me. It might have felt like I could let go of the pain they caused me," she said softly. Grabbing another tissue, she swiped at her eyes.

"You might be right, but you'll never know. My advice? Just let it go as best as possible. Fighting back means not doing this anymore because of them. It means not allowing them to yank you around. Dead or alive."

Mack's favorite uncle drank himself to death when Mack was fourteen. The family tried everything to help him. He'd watched his mom as she helplessly begged her brother to stop drinking. He never did. The experience gave Mack a cold, hard dose of reality and the realization that no matter what we do, changing another person or the past was impossible. He had learned the hard way to let go and move on. He hoped Kari could do the same.

"I know. I know. I feel like I should've never come back to Maine. I should've stayed in New York, where no past crap smashed me in the face unexpectedly. What have I done to my life?"

Mack got up and walked around her desk. "Come here," he said, extending his arms for a hug. She got up, hiccuping as she stood. He pulled her into a gentle hug and held her for a moment before he spoke again. Her slim body heaved up and down with her breaths. Just like when she was a kid. "What you did was return to the only family you have. Then you built a very successful law practice and helped your clients navigate the criminal justice system. I'd say your life is going just fine."

He held her by the shoulders and took a step back to look into her eyes. "I'm prouder of you than you could possibly imagine. You've done good. Real good. Greg and Stacy are the past. You're winning right now, champ." He pulled her in close for a second hug and then released their embrace.

Kari blew her nose and grabbed the glass of water off her desk, gulping the liquid quickly.

"Slow down," he laughed.

"I didn't realize how dehydrated I became. I just couldn't stop myself." She smiled. Grabbing a folder from the corner of the desk, she turned to him. "Thanks, Mack. I feel better. Nothing like a cry and a hug. I know you're right. I need to let the past go once and for all and focus on building my practice."

"Yep. You ready?" He moved out of her way and extended his hand toward the door, then followed her down the stairs to the conference room.

"Would you please hold my calls, Ruth? We need to work on the Shaffer file and a few others," she said.

"Sure thing," Ruth said. Then she turned to Mack, smiling. He nodded and winked at her.

Is she blushing? he thought. Dang, maybe he would get another chance with her sooner than expected. He tried not to smile as he settled into the conference room.

Kari closed the door softly and said, "Okay, lover boy, you sure you want to work today? I feel like I'm interrupting the two of you."

"Hey, you can't blame a guy for trying."

They discussed several cases she needed help with. Typically, she hired his private detective services for wayward spouses, credit checks, and to serve papers on those who thought hiding would somehow make things go away. He enjoyed the work she gave him, even if he had yet to charge her his usual rate. It had been only a little over a year since she had hung her shingle in Portland. During that time, she'd been in the news numerous times for winning high-profile cases. Little by little she became known in the legal community as a winner. By his estimation, the only thing that could tank her success would be her brother Jimmy or the memories that haunted her. Today had been a painful reminder of the rough past she'd endured to get here.

Glancing at Kari, he really hoped for her sake she could keep things together.

Chapter 7

Stacy Stadt stood at her kitchen sink and stared out the window to the large private backyard she and her husband, Greg, loved. Over the years they'd painstakingly planted each tree and shrub. The landscape architect they'd hired had designed numerous large islands of perennials. They'd planted lavender, hydrangeas, rose hips, and sage in the beds. During the summer the delicate floral fragrance of the flowers wafted through the open windows of their home. Greg had tirelessly tended to every aspect of the yard's care. On the first warm day of spring, he power washed the Maine granite stones ringing each perennial bed as well as the three granite birdbaths until they sparkled. Who would do all the yard work now that he was gone?

She ran her hand across the smooth, cold, black granite of the kitchen island. It had been three weeks since Greg died. Three weeks and she remained a basket case. The well-wishes ended, the flowers died, the food had been eaten or thrown away. All that remained was her grief and anger.

"Damn him! What an idiot! Who dies like that?" she said. She slammed her fist onto the countertop.

Ginger cocked her head side to side, listening intently from her round bed in the corner of the kitchen.

"Now I'm stuck dealing with everything!" Stacy took her ponytail out, pulled her platinum blond hair back, and put it up. "Get a grip," she muttered. Vacillating between staring off into space and blurting out angry thoughts wouldn't keep her life moving forward, something she desperately needed right now.

Her cell phone rang. She picked it up and looked at the caller's name: Rod Pieters. She almost put the phone down but then decided to speak with him rather than isolate herself.

"Hey, Rod. How's it going?" she said softly. She rubbed her forehead and looked down at the clean floor.

"I'm okay. Hanging in. Probably the same as you," he said with a somber tone.

Rod and Greg had been friends forever, the two of them like brothers. He grieved for Greg in many of the same ways. She walked down the hall to the stairs, passing their wedding pictures as she ascended to the second floor. Their smiling, youthful faces had been so full of love. They'd chosen to have a traditional Maine lobster bake immediately following an outdoor ceremony. She lingered at one of the pictures of Greg. He stood in front of a backdrop of thick, dark-green pine trees, looking handsome in his tux. She touched the picture gently and then dashed up the stairs.

Stacy let out a long exhale and replied, "Yeah, I get it. I'm going into the office today for the first time since . . . well, you know."

"Already? Why not take the rest of the week off? I'm sure everyone will be fine. I'll pick you up, and we can go for lunch in the Old Port. Maybe kick back a few at Dry Dock."

She stopped halfway into the main bedroom, stunned.

"Why the hell would I want to go to Dry Dock? Greg drank himself to death there. With you. Of all the insensitive crap you could ask me to do. Seriously?"

"Stacy, I just—"

She moved the phone away from her ear and hung up.

Damn him. What the hell was he thinking? She'd just move on? Was Rod trying to make a move on her? Everyone knew he'd had a crush on her since high school, maybe even middle school. She walked into the bathroom and eyed herself in the mirror. She wore her workout clothes from this morning's aerobics class. The skintight yoga pants and jog bra clung to her slim, muscular build. She worked hard to keep her figure and was proud of it. *Damn Rod, what the hell was he thinking?* she thought, shaking her head.

The shower knob creaked as she turned it on and waited for the glass door to steam. Greg had installed heated floors in the bathroom so her feet would stay warm even on the coldest winter mornings. Now she stood alone on the warm floors, tears welling in her eyes, the sound of the water creating a cocoon in the well-appointed bathroom.

Ginger barked loudly, jolting her away from her thoughts. The little dog jumped off the bed and onto the window bench, barking feverishly at something outside. Maybe a squirrel or the mail truck?

"Ginger! Geez. Cut it out," she yelled over her shoulder.

Steam fogged the bathroom mirror. Ginger barked and pawed at the window.

"Okay! I'm coming," she said to Ginger.

Rounding the four-post cherrywood bed, she padded on the thick carpet to the excited dog. Three police vehicles sat in front of her house. A gaggle of officers stood in the driveway, chatting.

What the hell?

A loud banging on the front door followed by three hits of the door chime shook her. She scooped up Ginger. The loud banging and door chime continued as she made her way to the front door.

A tall man in a suit stood on the front stoop. He banged on the door again just before she opened it.

"I'm here! Stop banging. My dog is going nuts," Stacy said as she opened the door.

"Ms. Stadt?" said the man.

"Yes," she said.

"I'm Detective Mareak from the Sweetwater Police Department. We have a warrant to search your house and business," he said in a brisk, crisp matter-of-fact way.

"What? Why? I don't understand," she said. Panic rose in her chest with a tight gripping force.

Detective Mareak pushed past her, shoving papers in her hand as he moved. The papers looked official, but she could not understand all the fancy words on the pages. She glanced at them for another second and then lowered her hand.

"What are you searching for? My husband just died. I'm grieving. Can't this wait?"

"No, Ms. Stadt. It cannot wait. We are here because you are the prime suspect in the murder of your husband, Greg Stadt."

Murder? Her legs became wobbly as the force of his words settled into her body. Ginger squirmed in her arms, intent to bark the men away. She gave up trying to hold the dog as her muscles went limp, and Ginger jumped to the floor.

"Greg was murdered? What? I . . . I don't understand."

The officers who'd stood on the driveway flooded the house. They went everywhere. The den, kitchen, and living room. Everywhere. One took pictures off the walls. Others went through Greg's desk. Then someone in plain clothes walked in carrying boxes.

"I want everything bagged and tagged. All of it," shouted Detective Mareak.

"You can't do this! I didn't do anything wrong!" she shouted.

None of the men even turned in her direction. No one cared. They continued to search as she stood watching. The lives she and Greg had built tossed around like trash. She struggled to breathe as the edges of a panic attack touched her.

Yanking her phone out of her pocket, she called Rod.

He picked up on the first ring. Before he could say anything, she said, "Rod! I need you!"

"What? Geez, Stacy, what's happening? Calm down."

"The cops are here. They're searching our home. Taking everything. I don't know what to do."

One of the officers pushed past her into the kitchen. Neighbors came out of their houses, looking toward her as she stood in the hallway, locked in place by her panic. Nosy jerks. Of course the neighbors all wanted to witness her shame, she thought. They'd been jealous of everything she and Greg had built. The money, the relaxing life without the chaos of kids.

"Holy crap! Why the hell are they there?"

"They said I'm a suspect in Greg's murder. A suspect. The prime suspect. Can you believe it? What do I do?"

"Murder? I thought he drowned. You need a lawyer to stand there with you. You shouldn't be alone right now. Let me think."

A cold chill moved over her shoulders. She needed to get dressed, out of the still-moist jog bra and yoga pants. The outfit made her feel naked, exposed. One of the officers stopped her as she went upstairs.

"We need you to step outside or stay right where you are until we're finished."

"Rod? They won't even let me go upstairs to grab a sweatshirt. Rod? You there?"

Did he hang up on me?

"I'm here. I'm here. Just thinking. Didn't you guys use someone for your business? Maybe we should call that attorney? Get a lawyer to stop them or something?"

"Bob Sellers? No way. That guy was Greg's choice for the corporate stuff. He's like a million years old. Besides, I don't think he'd know what to do."

"Yeah, okay. Hey, I know. On our last night at Dry Dock, Greg and I saw Jimmy Sharpe. Do you remember him from high school?"

"Oh yeah, I do. He's a real loser."

"Totally. But his sister, Kari, is that hotshot attorney who got the Black navy kid off last year. Remember? I see her name everywhere. Apparently this is all she does, and she's good at it. We need to call her."

"Hell no. I'm not asking stupid Kari Sharpe for help. I'd rather deal with this myself than talk to her after all these years. No way."

One of the officers carried a box out to a waiting patrol car. Box after box their lives were taken. A clanging in the kitchen caught her attention. One of them dumped the junk drawer onto the floor. Damn them. They'd scratch her Brazilian hardwood.

"You can't do this alone. You need a lawyer. Don't you ever watch TV?"

"I've got something up here!" yelled one of the officers.

"They're taking boxes of stuff. Damn it. What the hell is going on? They told me he drowned and now this." Her shoulders hunched as she heaved dry sobs.

He was right. She needed a lawyer, but Kari Sharpe? Anyone else but her. Their past had not been great. Stacy and Greg hated Kari and made sure she knew it.

"Look. She's the best idea I have. Call her right now. I've texted you her office number. I'm going to hang up. Do it right now. I'm on my way over."

With those words he disconnected the call. *The coward.* She huffed and looked at the phone, stunned. Of course, when he was asking her out to lunch, he took time with her, trying to sweet-talk her. Now that she needed help, he just hung up on her. Nice.

His text chimed. He'd sent the link. This is bad. Call her right now. I'm on my way over. Be there in fifteen.

Fine, she thought as her hand closed tightly around the phone. Her eyes scrunched as she clicked the link, then dialed the number. *I'll call stupid Kari Sharpe.* She leaned against the wall and let out a long exhale, waiting for an answer.

"The law offices of Kari Sharpe," the pleasant-sounding woman said.

"I need to speak with Kari. Now. The cops are searching my house. Look, I need an attorney, right now."

"Okay. I'll need a little information before I can put Attorney Sharpe on the line."

"Look, I don't have time for information. Didn't you hear what I said? They're searching my house. Right now. Get her on the damned phone," she screamed.

"What's your name?" The woman remained calm despite being yelled at. Usually Stacy got her way by yelling and pushing people to bend for her. Over the years she had honed her skills. The right combination of angry words and sickly sweet sentiments always worked.

"Stacy Marcs Stadt. She knows me. Look, I need to speak with her. Now. I don't have time for your nonsense."

"One moment, please."

Acoustic elevator music played as she waited. Waited too long. The great Kari Sharpe kept clients waiting? Nice. She isn't all that professional.

"I'm very sorry, Ms. Stadt. Attorney Sharpe is unavailable right now. I can refer—"

"Bullshit! We both know she's sitting right there. Look, you get her on the damned phone or else I'll . . ."

"I'm very sorry, but she is unavailable," the woman repeated.

Then she hung up. Stacy looked at her phone, then toward the uniformed police crawling around her home. Their dirty shoes had soiled the entire house, something she never allowed. Her mind spun out of control as her breathing hitched in her chest, causing her to pant shallow breaths. Heat rose along the skin of her back, beading in sweat. She dropped to her knees in a low squat and leaned up against the wall. Her blue eyes remained open, but she could barely register her surroundings as the panic attack gripped her.

"Stacy? Stacy? Are you okay?" asked Rod as he ran through the front door, past the police.

He rubbed her arm and then shoulder. She could feel his hand on her but somehow couldn't connect with him through the brain fog of panic. Her eyes etched the pattern of the grains of hardwood.

"Breathe. Stacy, you're holding your breath. You need to breathe. Do it with me. In and out," he said.

He tapped her on the shoulder and then shook her, repeating his words.

"Long, slow inhale. Come on. Do it with me. Long exhale."

Her stomach lifted and fell with his words. Breath found its way into her belly. After a few more rounds of deep breathing, her body temperature decreased.

"Better now?" he asked. He grabbed her elbow and lifted her up. Her back slid along the wall as she stood, leaving a slick of sweat behind.

"Yeah, a little. Look at what they're doing," she said. She waved her hand around. They had created a mess of her perfect home. Normally everything had a place, and everything had been in its place. It would take her hours to put everything back in order.

"I know. I see it. Did you call Kari?"

He grimaced at her. His eyes narrowed; brows knitted together to form an eleven. The normally casual, flirty Rod looked worried. She had never seen him like this before.

"Did you call her? Stacy?" he demanded. He shook her shoulders again, harder this time.

"Yes. I did it. I did it but shouldn't have. I think the stupid jerk refused to take my call. Can you imagine? Who the hell does she think she is? Too good for me? Nice. Look, I told you calling her was a mistake. Now what do I do?"

Rod shook his head. He looked around at the police and rubbed his goatee. Finally, he said, "Let me give her a try. Can't hurt. I don't know who else to call."

"Fine."

After a second he said into his phone, "Hi, I'm calling to speak with Kari Sharpe."

She listened to his words as she eyed two of the officers huddled in the corner of the living room.

"Rod Pieters. Yes. Thank you."

Rod poured the politeness on thick, making her feel like gagging. Why be polite to stupid Kari Sharpe?

"Hi, Kari, this is Rod Pieters. I'm here with Stacy Stadt. She needs to . . ."

A second passed and he said, "She really needs to speak with you. Yes. The police are here right now. About Greg's death. Yes, I know."

She twirled her hair as she listened to the one-sided conversation. A door slammed upstairs, making her jump. The muffled voices of several officers laughing angered her.

Rod handed Stacy the phone and mouthed, *Take it.*

"Kari? Come down here. I need you. The cops are searching my home."

She started sweating again. Her breath rose in her chest. She felt Rod's hand pushing her back down the wall. Her bottom hit the gleaming hardwood with a thud.

Panicked, she yelled, "Are you coming? I need you here now."

After a moment Kari said, "No. Stacy. I will not be coming down there. I am unable to take your case. You'll need to hire a different attorney."

Her mind spooled up, as it did whenever she got very angry. It always felt the same way, like a rush of energy was hitting her head.

"Look, you can't do that. I need you to get down here, right now. You have no right to refuse me," she yelled into the phone.

Rod nudged her arm and shook his head at her, trying to slow her down. He mouthed *Stop* as his hands went out side by side.

"Stacy, I'd rather pluck out my own fingernails than come over there to save your ass. Get someone who cares. And I'll give you a piece of free advice, shut your damned mouth for once in your life before you incriminate yourself."

"What? How dare you speak to me like that. Who do you think you are? Look, I need help. Apparently you . . ."

The phone went dead. The ringing in her ears got louder and louder. Sweat poured from her body. In the distance, she thought she could hear Rod telling her something. His words sounded garbled, waterlogged.

The phone clanked to the floor, and the world went dark as her head hit the hardwood.

Chapter 8

Kari slammed the phone down onto its base and rubbed her eyes. She knew Greg Stadt was the man pulled from the harbor but never expected Stacy to call her for legal help. That took nerve. Her hands shook slightly. Stacy and Greg had tortured her for years. The relentless bullying and cruelty had made her deeply dread going to school.

Ruth's footsteps clomped on the wooden staircase as she walked up to Kari's office. A second later she appeared in the doorway. "I'm so sorry. I would have screened the call from Mr. Pieters if I knew he was calling on her behalf. Geez, what a jerk. Why not just call a different firm?" Ruth shook her head angrily.

"Seriously," Kari said. "But then again, Stacy had always been a bully. She probably thought she could yell at me until I gave in and drove over there to deal with the cops. She was a real terror in high school and middle school. Who am I kidding, she was awful even in grade school."

Kari rubbed the back of her tense neck. She faced a mountain of work today. The last thing she needed had been a confrontation with Stacy Marcs Stadt, of all people. The blast from her past left her mind blunted, dull.

"Oh really? Like one of those mean girls you always see on TV?" Ruth's face lit up with the prospect of gossip.

"Exactly like that. In high school she was the leader of a little pack of rot. The four of them mercilessly picked on everyone, but I was their favorite target. She made life miserable for me for years. Now she calls me for help? That took guts. I'll give her that."

Kari rotated in her chair to stand. She needed air. Unlocking the window with a creak, she lifted the heavy double-hung into place, propping it open with a book. Cool, briny ocean air flooded the small office. The screeches of seagulls filled the void of their momentary silence.

"Maybe you should think about representing her? If they own Houses by Stadt, then they're loaded. Well, she's loaded now that he's gone. Charge her double your usual rate." Ruth smiled. "You know. A little payback."

Kari sat back into her chair and inched herself close to the under-mount keyboard. She moved her mouse to wake up her computer and then said, "Hmm . . . interesting. I haven't kept up with them, but you might be right. It's tempting. Although after I told her I'd rather pluck out my nails than represent her, I'm not sure she'll be calling back."

"Probably not, but you never know. She certainly sounded desperate. Sorry again, Kari. I try so hard to screen the nonsense calls."

"You're doing a great job, Ruth. No need for an apology. They took us both by surprise."

After Ruth left, curiosity took hold of Kari. She glanced at the clock. Thirty minutes remained before she needed to grab her file and walk the four blocks to the courthouse for a hearing. She navigated to the Registry of Deeds website and searched for Stadt. After a few seconds she found their home address, noting that they owned the property free of a mortgage. The satellite map offered her a glimpse of the house from the road. A large, three-story colonial on an extensive wooded lot. The landscaping looked immaculate, and expensive. The entire house looked perfect. Just like Stacy.

Next, she opened the Secretary of State website and searched for *Houses by Stadt*. Sure enough, Ruth had been right. Greg and Stacy Stadt had been listed as officers in the corporation. They formed the business after graduating from high school. She glanced at the clock one more time. Ten minutes remaining. From what she could tell, the business had been doing very well. It held title to various large plots of land in and around Sweetwater, Maine. *Interesting.*

Her calendar alarm chimed, alerting her that she needed to leave for court. She had previously packed the files she needed into her rolling briefcase. Despite resisting the rolling bag for the first few months in Maine, she'd finally decided to give her body a break. The fashionable bag she'd sported in New York City had crushed her shoulders as she trudged uphill to court. In New York, the offices of Barnes & Smith had prime real estate directly next to the courthouse. Because she'd never had to carry her files far for an appearance, looking chic had been easy. After the first winter in her hometown, she'd changed back into the Mainer she'd been before she left.

Gone were the fancy high-heeled leather boots in favor of rugged L.L.Beans. Even her pretty crimson long wool coat, with the oversize black fur-trimmed hood and wide belt, had been replaced by what could only be described as a sleeping bag for walking. Giving up the more stylish coat had been hard but necessary. As the wind whipped and the snow flew, she went into survival mode with the rest of the Mainers. No one cared what others wore or judged. Cold days demanded warmth.

"Hey, Kari!" someone said from behind her.

She stood in line at the courthouse to go through security. She hated that the marshals required the lawyers, officers of the court, to go through screening. By her estimation, officers of the court should be allowed to walk through without emptying their pockets.

Turning, she saw Jerry Getz, a fellow attorney. "Hey, Jerry."

She waited for him as her bag, watch, and phone all moved through the airport-style security screener. He reassembled his belt after taking it off for security. She hated removing a belt for security so always wore beltless outfits on court days.

"What do you have going on today?" she asked him.

"A final mediation on a very cantankerous divorce," he said. He stood back and allowed her to walk past him to the stairs.

"You think it'll settle?" she asked.

"Who knows. I represent the husband. He has no interest in yield-ing to her at all. It's been one of the harder cases to move. They're so angry with one another. Hard to believe they loved each other at one point in time." He chuckled.

"I seriously don't know how you do it. I'll take criminal work any day of the week over family law cases. Good luck," she said with a wave as she turned toward her designated courtroom.

Kari's shoes clicked along the marble corridor as she walked. A little window into the courtroom allowed her to peer inside. Standing on her tippy-toes, she viewed the two lawyers standing behind the counsel table, nodding as Judge Robins spoke. She'd wait until they finished before going into the room. At the top of the hour, attorneys and their clients flooded from various courtrooms into the main hallway, chat-ting, animated. A woman in jeans and a T-shirt sobbed softly, wiping her eyes with one hand and holding a little boy's hand with the other. An older couple in their Sunday best walked out of a different court-room. The husband looked stricken. The wife seemed to hold herself together with sheer force of will.

Finally, the door to the courtroom swung open as one of the attor-neys walked out into the hallway. She stood to enter, nodding to him as she passed. Her mind returned to Stacy Stadt. Curiosity chewed away at her better judgment as she wondered what it would be like to represent the woman.

Her mind sluggishly returned to the courtroom when the bailiff said, "All rise."

Chapter 9

Lori Spec inched her body out of bed, careful not to wake her daughter. The sound of the sleeping toddler's deep rhythmic breathing filled the still, nearly empty room. The shabby apartment in New Hampshire had been theirs for a few weeks. Nothing about the place felt like home. Memories of their luxury colonial in Maine dogged her as she tried to chart a new course for herself, away from her husband, Bruce.

Her mind returned to the day she and Mary had fled. She'd woken early, her husband lying next to her, snoring loudly. Again. The nightly racket made her crazy, ruining her sleep for the past eleven years. She had never dared to say anything to him. Never dared to leave the room for a quiet place to sleep. She'd feared he would view her actions as a criticism, giving him another reason to hit her.

She had always gotten up early to take care of their two-year-old before she could wake and start yelling or, worse, crying. If Bruce heard the morning crying, it would set him off, guaranteeing a punch to her stomach or face.

That fateful morning, she had winced from the bruising a recent beating had left on her ribs. Pain had become her constant companion, as though a third person had entered their relationship. Once in the bathroom she'd lifted her T-shirt to look at her ribs. The bluish, yellow-green marks had started to heal. Experience had taught her that he hadn't broken a rib, this time. Warm splashes of water on her face comforted her momentarily. Her reflection looked nothing like the woman she'd been.

The deep circles under her eyes mocked her. A reminder of her exhaustion and poor choices.

She padded across the quiet bedroom just in time to hear Mary calling for her. "Shhh . . ." She willed the little girl not to start crying. *Just give us time before he gets up,* she silently prayed. Mary's room sat at the end of the hallway of their large, traditional home. "Hi, baby girl," she whispered to the toddler. A night-light illuminated the space in a soft golden glow. The room smelled of baby powder and clean baby hair. She sat on the side of the small, low bed, breathing in the freshness of the room and Mary.

"Mommy, lay with me," said the little girl softly. The garbled words had been said so many times, Lori understood.

"Not today, baby. We need to get up and have our pancakes. You want those, right? Or maybe waffles?" she said playfully as she rustled the girl's soft light-blond hair.

"Pancakes!" said Mary. Her little mouth made the word sound like "fancakes." Lori scooped Mary's slim body into her arms, breathing in her heavenly scent. They held each other in silence, their last quiet moment together before Bruce woke. She told herself everything about their lives would change today. Everything. She just needed to keep her cool until he left for work. Just a few more hours. She could do this, and then everything would be okay for them. Lingering another minute, she rubbed her hand against Mary's warm back.

Once downstairs, she set Mary in front of the television and pulled out the frozen pancakes; then she made Bruce's coffee. Everything had to be perfect when he rose, or she faced showing up to work with fresh facial bruising. An embarrassment she desperately wanted to avoid reliving. The expressions of her colleagues at Maine Medical always told her everything she needed to know. Not one of them ever believed her story of another "fall." They'd look at her with a combination of pity and compassion, making her feel small for being a victim.

She quietly walked toward the staircase, listening for movement. Had he woken? Did she have another minute to herself? Maybe enjoy a cup of coffee in peace? The upstairs looked dark. He hadn't turned on the bathroom light or made any noise. She padded back to the kitchen, poured a steaming cup of coffee, and inhaled its heady aroma. If everything went as planned, this would be the last cup she drank while living with Bruce.

She and her sister had set up a separate checking account without Bruce knowing. Over the past year she'd quietly sold small personal items to anyone willing to pay cash. She'd deposited the meager amounts into the account until she had enough to escape.

Bruce controlled everything about their lives, including their finances. Leaving depended on her getting her own funding, something she had never been able to do despite working full-time. He noticed every penny she spent. One time he canceled her credit card privileges, accusing her of spending too much at the pharmacy on "unnecessary things" like pantyhose and deodorant. She was told to "make do" with less while he flashed new clothing, a new car, and all the golfing equipment most men could only dream of purchasing.

The loud stomping of Bruce's footfalls shook the house, startling her. Mary cried. Scared. "Mommy? What was that?" she whimpered. Warm, salty tears streamed down her small round face.

"It's okay, baby. Daddy's awake. That's all."

She kissed Mary and held her for a moment. Cartoons played in the background, distracting the little girl from her pancakes and the scary noise. The sweet scent of maple syrup laced Mary's gentle face.

"Lori! Where the hell are my green chinos!" boomed Bruce's voice from upstairs.

Lori tensed, scaring her daughter. She hugged Mary tight and silently said a soft prayer for the strength to get through the morning, then she set her daughter down, smoothing the little girl's curls. "I'll be right back. Finish eating so we can get dressed. You want to wear your mermaid top today?" she asked.

"Yay!" said Mary, distracted by the cartoon. She clapped her little hands, smearing syrup from one to the other.

Bruce clomped down the stairs loudly, then stomped into the kitchen. The glass doors on the kitchen cabinets vibrated with his footfalls. She rotated her shoulders, shielding her face from his gaze. "Your coffee is ready, and I made some eggs for you," she said. Her voice shook slightly. A bead of sweat rolled down her back.

"Eggs look cold. You need to do better," he mumbled.

She shrank at his words, though she was grateful that he wasn't yelling. Small parts of her died each time he screamed at her.

The daily shouting, blaming, and beating started shortly after they'd married. Her sister Brenda had tried to warn her about him. Brenda had heard rumors that his father had acted the same way. "How different could Bruce be from his dad?" Brenda reasoned. But Lori's love had blinded her to the obvious red flags. She'd never admitted to Brenda that one of his ex-girlfriends had confided in her about his abuse. At the time, she'd dismissed the warning as coming from a gossipy, jilted ex-girlfriend. Of course, in retrospect, she realized the help his ex-girlfriend had tried to render, and the risk she must have taken to do so. If Bruce knew they had spoken, there was no telling what he would have done. Finally, she'd realized that not even her love would make the situation better.

She walked into the family room to check on Mary. "You about done, peanut? We need to get dressed for school." The toddler sat, distracted by *Dora the Explorer*. Mary hummed the words to the familiar song Dora sang about her map. "Okay, baby. It's time for us to find your backpack for school." Lori scooped up Mary in her arms and squeezed her tight. *Just a little longer,* she told herself. Her legs felt shaky as she carried Mary upstairs.

As she dressed Mary, Lori attempted to be cheerful, despite the gnawing anxiety she felt in the pit of her stomach. Keep everything normal. She bit her lip hard, pushing back tears for the end of her marriage. Despite choosing to leave, she grieved the loss of the fantasy life she had hopelessly clung to for far too long.

"See you! I'm going to be late tonight. Don't wait up," shouted Bruce. The door to the garage slammed shut, shaking the house and rattling her frayed nerves. She peeked out the front window to watch him zoom down the quiet cul-de-sac. Numerous neighbors complained about his excessive speed, to no avail. He simply did whatever he wanted irrespective of the impact on anyone else. Must be nice.

She let out a long breath, realizing she had been holding it. Giddy with anticipation, she allowed herself the luxury of believing the plan would work. Dashing down the stairs into the kitchen, where she tidied up from breakfast. Then she stopped, laughed out loud, realizing the dishes were now his problem. Not hers. Her legs ached with anticipation, and she wanted to bolt as quickly as possible, but Brenda had told her to wait, just in case he returned. The digital clock on the coffee maker moved slower than she thought possible. Only ten minutes had passed since he'd left. She had to wait another five minutes. Leave at her normal time, no matter how tempting it would be to leave immediately.

Finally, the time had come. She held Mary's smooth, tiny hand as they walked out of the house for the last time. She loaded the little girl into her car seat, kissed both of her cheeks, and rubbed their noses together. Laughing, Mary said, "Mommy, Mommy. Silly." Mary patted both of Lori's cheeks and the side of her head softly as she giggled.

Her car roared to life, then rolled down the driveway of the home she thought would be hers into their old age. The disappointment, the fear, the hope for something better accompanied her as she took one last look at the slate-blue colonial. The pretty pink doors and flower wreaths made the house look cheery, despite everything. The sage and lavender she had lovingly planted swayed in the gentle morning breeze. The pang of regret touched her heart again. *Do I really have to leave?* she thought as she fought back tears. Brenda had told her nothing would work but leaving. Thanks to a therapist, she finally knew Brenda had been right.

She had seen her therapist, Joanne, steadily over the past year, giving up her lunch hour every Wednesday for the appointment. Brenda had paid for the appointments so as not to alert Bruce that things were changing. Her feelings had gushed out of her during the weekly cry sessions. "Why is this happening? If I only could do better everything would be fine," she'd plead as she turned over a crumpled tissue in her shaky hands. Over time, she'd begun to see that Bruce had been the problem, not a bad meal, crying baby, or messy house. Just Bruce.

The turning point had come one day when Joanne suggested that she tell Bruce, "I'm scared. Just tell him 'I'm scared' when he rants and intimidates you, and see what he says."

Later that night, when Bruce had stomped around screaming at her about his latest grievance, she'd said the words "I'm scared."

Without skipping a beat, Bruce had shoved a finger in her face and shouted, "You should be!" Joanne had told her if he said "You should be scared," then she needed to leave immediately. Things would only get worse, and her life was in danger. For the first time, she'd seen Bruce as others had seen him. As a monster. She'd known she needed to take the advice for herself and Mary.

Brenda and a women's shelter in New Hampshire had helped her establish the apartment where they now resided. The run-down, sparsely furnished place felt safe and clean. The two things she needed most.

"Mommy?" Mary called from the bedroom.

"Coming, baby," she said, putting down her coffee mug. She walked out of the kitchen, leaving the memories of Bruce behind. Intent to survive. One day at a time.

Chapter 10

The next morning Ruth's alarm chimed. She hit the button on the digital clock hard enough to nearly topple it and the water glass off the side table. "No. Just a little longer," she moaned as she pulled the covers over her head, sinking into the smooth white cotton sheets.

After a few moments she swung her feet over the edge, pulling herself upright. A quick splash of cool water on her face made her feel human again. Coffee. She needed caffeine. The small ranch house she had shared with her husband had been their home for decades. Each wall and floorboard as familiar to her as her own hands. Their kids had grown and left Maine, as so many of Maine's youth had done.

Once their kids had moved out, the three extra bedrooms had been used in various capacities. When she'd taken on sewing, she'd created a room for her new hobby. When on a health kick, suddenly an exercise room appeared. Then, after years of dealing with David's snoring, she'd finally told him to make the den his permanent bedroom. He'd reluctantly agreed. Eventually the sleeping arrangement suited both, allowing each to stay up late or sleep in without worry of disturbing the other. After he died, she'd wondered if she should have allowed him to stay in the bedroom with her.

She walked past the den; the door remained closed. Despite the passage of nearly a year since David's death, she had kept the door shut, just as it had been the morning of his aneurysm.

The day had begun as it always had, with her going to the kitchen for coffee. Instead of being greeted by the aroma of freshly brewed hot java, the pot had remained cold. Looking back, she probably knew something had happened, but just didn't want to face it. The memory made her smile in a sad way. She knew she had clung to the last few moments of their life together before facing the inevitable separation.

A few days after she found him, he'd died alone in the hospital, without her or their kids by his side. She had been in the cafeteria, grabbing a snack, when it happened. The kids had been en route to Maine. Ruth's eyes teared as she recalled sitting on the edge of his bed, holding his still-warm hand. Touching David's face, she had brushed his hair neatly and then placed her hand on his chest. Despite death, he'd felt warm, like himself.

The nurse had consoled her by saying, "Most people prefer to pass without their family members present. We always tell caregivers to take breaks to give the patient a chance to let go. Trust me, honey, this worked out for the best." Her kind words had barely touched Ruth's heart.

The funeral had come and gone in a blur as guilt consumed her. He'd died alone while she went in search of a snack. In that moment the stories she'd told herself about their life had crashed around her. She had cheated on him with Mack. The infidelity only enhanced her grief, making her wonder if she had a right to grieve. The deep pain of loss seemed the province of faithful spouses, not adulterers.

The microwave beeped, distracting Ruth from the memory. Sitting at the small kitchen table, she clicked on the morning program as she ate her oatmeal. The wall clock clicked the time; the morning sunlight softly lit the room. Life went on.

Her spoon scraped the bottom of her bowl. She had been so absorbed in beating herself up that she had barely noticed her food. "What am I doing?" she muttered as she stood. Replaying every detail of David's death had become a way of hurting herself. A misguided atonement for the affair.

Kari had reassured her when David had first gone into the hospital, saying, "Everything will be okay. He's in good hands. The doctors at Maine Medical are the best." Her tone had been such a comforting balm to Ruth.

Kari had come to Maine full of a big-city edge that never really settled down. At moments like that, when she spoke from the heart, Ruth saw a glimmer of the deeply sensitive person she was.

Ruth took her time dressing for work. She surveyed her extensive jewelry collection, choosing just the right accessories for her outfit. Then she took an extra minute to style her hair. After the grief lifted, she began to wonder if Mack would ask her out again. Their affair had been brief, lasting only a few months. Yet she had relived the memory repeatedly. They had an undeniable chemistry, something she and David always lacked. Mack made her feel beautiful, young, and full of laughter. Being with him had been a joy, laced with guilt. Like licking honey off a razor's edge.

Surveying herself in the hallway mirror, she said, "What are you doing, Ruth? You don't deserve this. Quit acting like a teenager with a crush. Geez." She shook her head at her own silliness, all the while wondering if Mack would be in the office today.

Chapter 11

Kari hustled around her office to get it ready to receive clients. Normally Ruth made the fresh pot of coffee and tea, setting out a nice tray in the conference room ahead of each meeting. Today she needed to step in for Ruth to accommodate a client's request for an earlier meeting. Standing straight, she glanced over the room, satisfied with her efforts. The heady aroma of fresh-brewed coffee chased her up the staircase to her office.

She turned her wrist to check the time. The delicate gold wristwatch had been a purchase when she'd lived in New York. Normally a thick banded athletic Timex graced her slim forearm. As a young associate fresh out of the Navy JAG, she continued to wear the watch even after she switched her uniform for a tailored suit. One of the nastier partners at her firm, a grumpy old man who had been with the firm forever, had said to her, "Ditch the watch. It makes you look cheap."

She pulled out the file for the first meeting and read through her notes. Parents of a twenty-five-year-old had hired her to handle a case against their son, Trevor. Despite his age, Trevor had been showing up at various parties on the campus of Southern Maine Community College, mostly to sell drugs. One night, after making a tidy sum, he had used the remaining stash of X to further inebriate a young, drunk coed. Days later, when pictures of him violating her while she lay unconscious floated their way across social media, the victim involved the police.

Her desk phone rang. "The law offices of Kari Sharpe. Attorney Sharpe speaking," she said.

"Good morning, Attorney Sharpe. It's Rod Pieters. We spoke yesterday while I was with Stacy Stadt. I think we got off on the wrong foot." He cleared his throat.

Kari rolled her eyes and stood. *I never should have answered.*

"Wrong foot? Is that what you call it? I already told Ms. Stadt I will *not* represent her." Her hand shook as she poured herself another cup from the hot teapot on her desk. The pit of her stomach had clenched as soon as Rod mentioned Stacy's name. She rubbed the back of her neck.

"Yes. I get it. Stacy can be a handful. Believe me. You and I never really hung out together—I was in Greg's class. He and I were best friends." His voice cracked as he spoke.

"I'm sorry for your loss, but I—"

"Please. Stacy needs the best. They've arrested her and charged her with murder. There's no way she did it. No way. Would you at least look at everything and then let us know your answer?" His voice sounded desperate. Nothing Kari hadn't heard before. She looked down as she rubbed her forehead.

"Fine. I'll make a call later today to the Portland Police Department and see what they have. I'm not guaranteeing anything, just a look. No advice. Got it?"

"Thank you, I really appreciate it, and I know Stacy does too. And she was charged in Sweetwater. Not Portland. Not sure it makes a difference."

Kari preferred not to engage in a protracted explanation about policing mutual aid agreements. Instead, she quickly said, "Okay. I'll be in touch," then hung up the phone before he could draw her in even further. She dropped the phone onto its cradle with a clatter. *What the hell am I thinking?*

The outside door chimed, announcing the arrival of her first of many clients lined up for the day. Gathering her things, she headed down the stairs to meet with them. She chewed on her lip as her mind swirled, thinking about the case against Stacy.

Chapter 12

Beth Thornberry hitched Rocky, a young black standardbred, to a post. The two-year-old horse had run his best race over the weekend, exceeding everyone's expectations. He'd flown over the course as his jockey urged him on from the sulky. The horse had trotted his way to his first win. The crowd had roared to life as Rocky nudged past more experienced racers to victory. Beth had stood in the owner's box as she cheered with the excited crowd. She had taken a chance when she'd purchased him. The cost had set the track back financially, further driving it into the dirt.

She ran her hand over his smooth, muscular flank and patted him gently as she moved across his shoulders. The warmth of his body soothed her frayed nerves. He nibbled on the little treats she had given him as she assessed his powerful hind legs. Picking up the currycomb, she brushed in circular motions to loosen any dirt or matted hair he had accumulated during his morning exercise with Joe, their horse trainer.

The sun shone down on them as she tended to each quadrant of his strong body. Heat radiated from the dry earth, stinging her nostrils. Joe walked back toward the barn with the next horse that needed grooming.

He stopped next to her. The mare he walked with leaned her tawny neck toward Rocky. Rocky just nibbled away, oblivious to her flirtations. "That's okay, girl," said Joe sweetly to the mare. The horse shook her head, whipping her mane side to side against her neck and Joe's hand.

"Beth, why don't you let me handle these next two grooms? Brushing down each horse and picking their hooves. It's too big of a job for one person," he said. His voice boomed loud enough to break through the wheezing of the Weedwacker the gardener used to tidy up the beds.

Beth stopped brushing and looked to him. She stretched her aching back and rubbed her side. "It's okay, I've got it. Besides, you've got your hands full with training. I can get the rest," she said, trying to remain chipper, despite how she felt.

Joe stopped walking. He stood looking at her with a grimace, then moved closer. "You can't keep up this pace. No one can. You'll exhaust yourself," he said. Concern etched on his wrinkled face. Even under the shade of his large, brimmed cowboy hat, she could see his sincerity.

She looked at the ground, kicking her boot. Dust swirled around Rocky's front hooves. Inhaling sharply, she fought back the urge to cry. After her father died, Joe had become a stand-in for him in so many ways. He'd taught her how to be hard, and he'd taught her how to yield when needed. "Come on, Beth, let's grab a much-earned cone," he would say. Eventually she'd begun to count on their ritual Sunday-afternoon ice-cream cone to celebrate the end of the week, something her father had always done. She'd confided in him about the financial health of the track, drawing him into the complexities of running a failing business. "I just don't know how much longer I can continue to run the place," she'd told him.

"Let me spot you some cash. An old-timer like me has more lumps under his mattress than good sense. I've got it and want to help you and the track," he'd said to her. Eventually she'd agreed to accept his generosity. He had already given her $10,000 without knowing how she used his savings.

She cleared her throat and said, "Thanks. I appreciate the offer." Looking toward the empty track, she added, "I really do, but I can't ask you to take on more than you already do, and I won't accept charity. You already gave me a loan, which I'm trying to pay back. Adding unpaid labor to the debt I owe you will just make me feel even worse about everything." She threw down the currycomb and picked up the brush. Clearing her throat, she hoped he didn't notice the tears in her eyes.

"It's not charity. You're like family to me, you know that. And this place . . ." He paused and looked around. "This place is like my home. I don't know what I would do with my wrinkled old ass if I couldn't come here every day. It's all I know." He looked away from her with a quick chin jerk.

The sound of a vehicle on the gravel drive ricocheted off the horse barn, drawing their attention. She had not expected to see anyone today, which could mean only one thing. "We'll talk about this later. I need to see who's coming," she lied. She knew who drove onto the property. She had hoped to delay the meeting another week.

The barn smelled of horse manure baking in the hot afternoon sun. Each stall had to be mucked out before the horses returned for the night. Another task she had been forced to take on. Standing in the threshold of the barn, she watched the black Cadillac Escalade with New Jersey plates pull into the first parking spot. The driver didn't even bother turning off the truck. He kept it idling, then opened the back door.

Ryker Jones took his time getting out of the vehicle as his driver stood waiting. Her heart pounded hard in her chest, urging her to run. Finally, he swung his long, slim legs down onto the gravel drive. Her fists balled tight as her arms crossed protectively around her abdomen. She felt like she was going to her execution as she walked to him.

"Hi, Ryker, I wasn't expecting you today," she said with a slight wave, desperate to act casual.

His dark eyes narrowed as he assessed her. Rubbing his neatly groomed black beard, he smirked and said, "I'm sure you weren't, little lady, but here I am."

She shuffled from side to side on her heels, trying to keep the panic at bay. Flipping off her baseball cap, she smoothed her hair back, then cleared her throat. "What brings you to us today?" The question sounded even more ridiculous after she spoke the words. They both knew why he was here.

He chuckled and moved in close to her. His hot breath touched her face. "Don't play coy. You owe me." He leaned back and snorted, then said, "Heard you had an exciting win this weekend, enough to keep people betting. I want some of the haul as a show of gratitude."

She'd made a deal with the devil to save the track, and she knew it. His eyes bored into her as he waited for her reply. Taking a slight step back from him, she turned her body to give herself a break from his intensity.

"I've used the money to pay some debts, then I thought—"

She hadn't finished her sentence when he pounced on her.

"Debts! How dare you pay anyone ahead of me," he shouted in her face.

Spittle and hot breath peppered her skin. She tried to hold herself in place as her legs shook.

"Can I help with something? Would you gentlemen like a tour of the barn?" said Joe. The butt of a pistol peeked out of the waistband of his jeans.

Ryker stepped back from her, turning to Joe. "That won't be necessary. We are almost done here. Why don't you go back inside. This doesn't concern you, horse man." Ryker glanced down at the pistol and chuckled, unfazed.

Joe didn't move. His eyes trailed from the men to Beth and back. "It's okay, Joe. I've got this. I appreciate it. Maybe you could finish grooming Rocky?" she said. Her voice sounded gravelly as she croaked out the words.

She willed Joe to leave. The last thing she wanted would be to get him tangled into the mess she'd created. Ryker didn't seem like the sort of guy who took a threat lightly.

The kind old man studied her face for a moment and said, "Okay, I'll finish him up for you. I'm just a shout away if you need me." He glanced back at them a couple of times as he walked into the barn.

"I can give you a thousand. That's all I have," she pleaded.

Ryker put his hands on his hips and narrowed his eyes at her. "Just a thousand? I think you can do better than that."

She had a plan to get out of debt, and they both knew it. "The town is voting soon. Once they do, you can bring in your slot machines, like we planned. Everything is waiting, the space has been cleared, a few of our regulars have been told. Everyone is very excited about playing slot machines at the racino."

"You've been promising me that for a while now. Looks like you have a problem with the town board of Sweetwater. Doesn't seem like they want me in their shabby little corner of the world. If that's the case, the three hundred thousand I loaned your pathetic business needs to be repaid. Immediately. We both know how this works." He leaned closer. "And I'm not a patient man."

"The town will clear it, you'll see," she said. "Greg Stadt, the remaining member who held up the vote, died in an unfortunate accident. The alternate member will have to stand in for him. It will pass."

As she said the words, she knew she had said too much. Giving Ryker anything he could use against her had been stupid, and she knew it. Damn it. What had she done? Her fists balled, open and closed as she chewed her lower lip.

He chuckled and said, "An accident? Wow. Missy—didn't know you had it in ya. I'll take that thousand and be on my way for now."

Beth jumped away from him, hardly able to control her legs from bolting. "I'll be right back," she said as she sprinted to the office.

Once inside, she shut the door behind her and leaned against it. She closed her eyes for a moment, sweat pooled on her brow. She brushed the salty liquid off her face as she composed herself.

After a second, she knelt at the safe under her desk. Her shaky hands could barely punch in the number her father had told her. Finally, on the third attempt, she yanked open the lead door. The cash sat in a neat stack on top of old documents that had been in the safe for as long as she could recall.

She grabbed the money and counted it. One thousand three hundred, the entire sum of her available funds. She shoved the three hundred back into the safe, slammed the door shut, and spun the lock. The money had been earmarked for the gardener and Joe. Now what would she do to pay them? The last thing she needed was a complaint from an employee for not paying wages. The state would be all over her, charging fines she could never pay. She straightened and forced herself to concentrate on the issue at hand. Ryker.

She pinched her nose, then rubbed her eye. A nervous tic she picked up along the way. Hesitating, she stood with her hand on the doorknob unable to move. *Come on. You can do this,* she thought as she willed her hand to open the door.

Ryker walked through the barn, looking at the empty, manure-filled stalls. He looked up at her and said, "Would really hate for anything to happen to this place, but you understand. Business is business."

He stood waiting for her to pay him. Her hand shook as she handed him the meager profit. "Everything will work out. Once the town approves the slot machines, we'll be in great shape. We'll be the most popular place in southern Maine for gambling."

Ryker looked around the barn and said, "For your sake, I hope you're right." He turned from her, shook the fistful of cash overhead, and said, "Thanks for the cash. I think I'll enjoy a nice lunch in the Old Port."

She watched his thin frame move through the barn. The bright sun outside the barn made him look like nothing but a dark, shadowy shape moving into the sunlight. *What have I done? What would my father do?*

"Look at all those cars, Bethy," her father had said one afternoon. "All these people are here because of our family's business. Someday all of this will belong to you." He'd glanced at her lovingly. "I'm trusting you with my legacy," he'd said firmly with a hand on her shoulder. A few weeks later, he'd died. At the time, she hadn't understood what a legacy meant. Now "legacy" only meant guilt, shame, and stress.

The business had been different when he ran it. People had flocked to their establishment every weekend in the summer. It had been so busy, they'd decided to start racing on Thursday evenings to accommodate the demand. People had ordered food and drinks nonstop, only adding to the profits. It had been a heyday for the racino and her family. Then, over the years, two casinos had opened in northern Maine with casino-style slot machines. Suddenly harness racing looked like an antiquated pastime. The slot machines had drawn her customers away at a clip she'd never expected. Then Ryker had come to her, offering a lifeline to the dying establishment.

Beth slumped, exhausted from what had become of her life. Her stomach tightened at the thought of another town meeting. Another vote. More angry stay-at-home moms showing up to voice their concerns about turning Sweetwater into Las Vegas. "What will happen to our children?" they'd say. "Gambling is the beginning of this town's decline. We'll have drunk drivers, crime, and child molesters." Somehow the angry moms had forgotten that the town already allowed gambling at the racetrack.

What will happen to me? Beth thought as she walked back into the cool darkness of the barn.

Chapter 13

Ryker leaned back into the cushion of the leather seat, then adjusted the dial on the air-conditioning vent. He hated the stench of horse manure. The odor clung to the inside of his nasal passages, making him queasy hours after exposure. Once he managed to blast the air on his face, he inspected his shoes and pant legs. Lifting and turning each foot, looking for straw, manure, or anything else gross he might have picked up in the barn.

He quickly counted the cash Beth had given him. He had no intention of crediting her account for the payment. Instead, he'd treat himself to something nice. His phone rang as he considered the possibilities.

"Hello?" he said as though not knowing who called.

"Hello? Is that all you say to me? I expected an update from you first thing in the morning. Where the hell have you been? And how dare you make me search for you," the man said.

"Sorry about that, sir. I had to make my rounds. It took slightly longer than expected this morning," he lied. Ryker chose not to call the man with an update because he had nothing to report about the southern Maine casino project.

The man chuckled softly and said, "Rounds? That's a nice way of putting it. So did you get my money?" he demanded.

"Not yet, sir, but I believe the racino is close to getting a green light from the town. Once that happens, the slot machines will be installed, and the cash will start to flow."

"You've told me that before, but nothing happened. Why are you so certain things will change?"

Ryker cleared his throat. "The last holdout on the town board died in an unexpected accident."

"Hmm. And you think *that's* going to break this thing open? How incompetent are you? That death will only bring a new member onto the board. A person full of fresh ideas. Now you'll need to deal with a new player. Sounds like you didn't think this one through. Like so many things about you, this is sloppy."

Ryker's jaw clenched as he tried desperately to not shout at the dangerous man. "I've already laid the groundwork with the first alternate. He's a lock in favor of the slots," he said with more certainty than he felt. "It's the second alternate that I'm not so certain about." As soon as he mentioned the second alternate, he shook his head and mouthed, *Shit.*

The man pounced. "You're telling me that the guy you've been working on to change his vote is dead, and you're essentially hoping the first alternate will be the one to replace him. Do I have the gist of it?"

Ryker rolled his eyes. "Well, I'm fairly certain—"

"Just shut it. I don't want to hear anything else from you. This is how it's going to go. My partners and I will wait for one more vote. If the measure is rejected again, you'll pay. And by the way, I expect you to drop off the wad of cash you picked up from the Thornberry woman. Don't even think you're going to skim off the top."

Ryker's eyes darted to the back of his driver's head. The man had snitched on him. Rage shot up his back, bringing heat to his face.

Before he could say anything in response, the man hung up. Ryker threw the phone down into the footwell. The driver continued to navigate the roads of Maine, unaware that he'd just sealed his death warrant.

Chapter 14

Kari tapped her pen on the desk, finally tossing it down. She picked up her phone. Distracted. The app told her Jimmy's location. It also told her how she would feel for the day. If she saw him moving along Casco Bay, everything was fine with her brother. However, if his boat seemed to linger in one location on the water for too long, then she started to panic. Even worse? When his location indicated he never made it to work. She always assumed the worst. Lobstering was dangerous work. Many in the profession had been seriously injured or went overboard, never to be seen again.

She closed the location app and opened her dating app. Scrolling through its roster of men made her feel slightly sick. Dating had become a chore. She had been on more first dates than she cared to think about. Yet despite meeting plenty of eligible bachelors, she couldn't let the memory of her last significant relationship go.

Her mind toggled between current dates and memories of a past lover. Each man failed to measure up.

She stood to make a second cup of tea, delaying the start of another grueling day. She had a lot on her plate and needed to focus. Not check on Jimmy or the dating app. The cold water rushed out of the tap into the kettle. The kettle soon whistled, then gurgled as she poured the piping-hot water into her Museum of Modern Art mug. The modern-designed MoMA logo mug had been a parting gift from one of her colleagues "so she wouldn't forget the cool stuff about New

York." Smiling, she returned to her office, holding a small piece of her former life.

The line on her phone rang. *Damn it.* She hustled to get to her desk in time to answer. Ruth hadn't yet arrived for the morning.

"Law offices of Kari Sharpe, this is Attorney Sharpe."

"Hi, Kari, this is Attorney Kevin Radcliff over at the public defender's office. I have a file I'd like to send you, but thought I'd give you the heads-up first."

She grabbed a pen and fresh legal pad. "I wasn't expecting a file from your office. Can you tell me a little about it? Maybe it's getting routed to the wrong firm?"

She leaned over to turn down the light classical music playing on her small radio.

"Sure, it's the case against Stacy Stadt. She's been charged with murder. The victim is her husband, Greg Stadt. The police in Sweetwater picked her up yesterday. A couple of days ago the Sweetwater PD searched her home. The evidence they acquired gave them enough confidence in the case to justify arresting her. She was arraigned this morning, then released on bail pending trial. The prosecutor pushed hard to incarcerate pending trial, but our offices managed to get her released with electronic monitoring and a hefty bail sum."

"Congratulations. What turned the tide in favor of her being released? What was your argument based on?"

"Ms. Stadt and her deceased husband own Houses by Stadt. She handles payroll processing, accounts payable and ordering supplies for their builds. She is an essential component to the business. If she were incarcerated for three to five months pending trial, then their employees, home buyers, suppliers, etc. would all be left hanging. Without her working, the business is in jeopardy of collapsing. Then there's the standard things we always argue. You know the drill, no criminal record, she doesn't pose a threat to herself or others, strong ties to the community, the usual."

"I guess she's no threat to herself or others. But wow. You met her. She's tough to be around. Or at least she was when we were kids," said Kari.

"She still is tough to be around. I walked her through the arraignment process. After she pled not guilty, she told me to send everything to your office because you're going to represent her."

Kari laughed out loud despite herself, then said, "Well, that's news to me. Initially I took a hard pass on the case but then agreed to at least look at the evidence."

"Yeah, well, I can understand why you'd walk away from this one. She's a real handful. Getting her through the arraignment was difficult, to say the least. Frankly, I thought she'd start screaming at the judge. And you know how well the bench responds to a criminal defendant having an angry outburst."

Kari whistled after he spoke. The thought of Stacy trying to scream her way out of a courtroom had been almost too delicious. "I can only imagine. I knew Stacy and Greg growing up; they were real pieces of work. While I have you on the line, do you mind giving me a thumbnail sketch of the case against her?"

She rubbed her eyes and waited for his reply. The pollen had been tough on her this morning. Her eyes felt grainy and dry.

"I don't mind at all. Initially the cause of death had been accidental drowning. However, once toxicology came back, they discovered bute in Greg's blood, along with a lot of alcohol. The bute gave him a massive heart attack. Between the alcohol, bute, and heart attack, he never stood a chance."

She grimaced and nodded her head. "Still sounds like an accident. Why charge her? Maybe Greg had a drug habit?" She glanced down at the picture of her brother Doug.

Rustling on the other end of the line sounded like he was flipping through pages. Finally, he said, "Yes, it's plausible, but you add the defensive wounds, and now it starts to look bad."

"Defensive wounds?"

"Yes. He had fresh bruising and scratches all over his palms and face. Someone was with him when he went into the water. It looks like that person either tried to help or had tried to hold him under the water or at least prevent him from getting out. Who knows. Could go either way. And there were bite marks on his abdomen."

Kari dug the bottle of eye drops from her drawer and said, "Bite marks. Geez. That's odd. Why are they pinning it on Stacy?"

"Apparently she and Greg were at Dry Dock the night of the incident. The cops have several eyewitnesses who'll testify that the two of them fought like alley cats. Plus they nailed her on surveillance camera heading to the boat, the location of his death near the time he died."

"Interesting." Kari thought about the evidence and how to defend against the charges.

The door chime interrupted her. She peered toward the parking lot. Ruth's car sat in one of the slots. Finally.

"Kari? You still there?" asked Kevin.

"Yes, sorry. I was just considering everything." She paused again and said, "You know what? Sure. Send the file over. I'll have a look at it."

The loud sound of chatter in Kevin's office broke through; then he said, "Okay. It'll be brought over to you by courier. Should have it in a few hours."

"Does the courier crab walk across town? Our offices are only a few blocks apart."

Kevin laughed and said, "You know how it is, do less with more and all that government-efficiency stuff."

"I get it. Believe me. Thanks for the call. I'll be on the lookout for the file."

Ruth's footfalls fell heavy on the wooden steps outside of Kari's office. Moments later Ruth stood in her doorway with a mail folder.

"Here's your mail," she said flatly.

Normally Ruth made herself up for work. Her appearance always looked carefully crafted. Neatly done makeup, curled hair, and a rotating selection of broaches and scarves were her daily staples. Today, however, she looked terrible. Dark circles under her eyes, no makeup, and her hair lying flat against her head.

"Are you okay, Ruth? Sit for a minute," said Kari as she stood. She gently took Ruth's elbow and nudged her to the chair across from her desk. The Casco Bay Liner's horn blared in the harbor outside of her windows.

Ruth sat on the offered chair, saying nothing. A blank expression on her face.

Kari felt unsure of how to proceed. Finally, she said, "What's up? Can I help you with anything?"

Ruth shook her head, finally meeting Kari's eye. "Today is David's birthday. I went to the cemetery this morning to place fresh flowers. That's why I needed to come in late." She pulled a tissue from the box and blew her nose. "I just can't believe he's gone. Sometimes his death is so raw, other times I feel like it happened ages ago."

Ruth had sat in the same chair almost a year ago when she told Kari David had died. A minute later, Ruth stood up and walked over to the corner window. Several powerboats floated pierside, waiting to be taken out for a day of fun. Her eyes glistened with tears yet to fall. Ruth absently poked her finger into the pot of the closest plant, checking to see if it had been watered.

Kari walked over to her and circled her arms around Ruth in a warm embrace. Ruth's legs buckled slightly, and then she started to sob again.

"Please, Ruth, you need to go home and be with family. I'm okay here, just take care of yourself right now. The first birthday is rough."

Kari knew people made funeral arrangements for their loved ones but had never been part of the process. She and Jimmy had been on their own when news of Doug's death reached them. They had barely made ends meet as it was. Adding the cost of a casket, funeral, and burial site had not been an option for them. "We need to let the prison take care of him, Kari," her brother Jimmy had said to her. He had spent the better part of an hour combing through their finances, trying to find a way to give Doug a proper burial. In the end, Doug had had to be buried by the state as an indigent person. She pushed the painful memory aside.

"Yes. Yes. I know. I just thought coming in would get my mind off things. I don't know if I can face any of this right now. I really underestimated how I would feel today. I'm so sorry, Kari."

"Don't give it a second thought. Call your kids. Spend the day reminiscing. You'll feel better," she said, not knowing if it was true.

"Are you sure? If you want, I'll come over later today."

Kari took Ruth by the arm and led her back down the stairs. She gathered Ruth's bag and keys.

"Come on. I'll help you to your car."

They walked in silence to Ruth's waiting car. Kari finally said, "Please don't even think of coming in. You need to be with family. Everything here is moving along at a manageable clip. Just take good care of yourself." She hoped Ruth wouldn't notice the white lie. Everything had been moving along well, but managing things without Ruth would add a load to an already full day.

"Okay, Kari. Thank you," said Ruth softly.

Kari closed the car door and stood back, the warped wooden planks of the floating dock uneven under her feet. The chime of a navigational buoy sounded in the distance. Tourists walked past laughing as they discussed where to get a good Maine lobster roll.

Ruth pulled away. Stopping at the corner, she put on her left blinker and then turned right, making Kari wonder if she should have driven Ruth home. Then she remembered the mountain of work waiting for her. She rubbed the back of her neck, feeling like she carried the weight of the world on her shoulders.

Chapter 15

Chet sat on his favorite barstool at Dry Dock, nursing his second draft beer. Someone selected "Born to Be Wild" to play on the jukebox. The music ricocheted off the walls loudly in the mostly empty establishment. A couple sat at the end of the bar, discussing their plans for the rest of the week. From what he could gather, the tourists had planned to hike the famed Mount Katahdin but then chose to stay in Portland a little longer because of the stormy weather. The dark interior of the bar contrasted sharply with their bright, optimistic attitude.

The door opened with a loud bang, letting a ray of light into the Dry Dock's dim interior. Seth Moyer stood in the doorway, giving his eyes a second to adjust. "Geez, Marty, I can't see anything. Do you need to keep it so dark in here?" he complained to the bartender. Even on a rainy day, nearly everyone had to wait for a second for their eyes to adjust to the cave-like interior of the bar.

"What can I say? People expect a certain amount of ambience when they come to my establishment," said Marty with a wave of his hand. He'd run the bar for a little over ten years but would always be called its "new owner" by the locals.

Seth patted Chet's shoulder as he sat on the stool next to him. "Hey, man. I didn't expect to see you here today, given the rain."

"Yeah, me neither, but I managed to hit a few of my pots before things turned bad out there. Now it's so nasty in the bay you can't see your nose in front of your face," said Chet. "Makes it tough but not impossible to lobster. I thought about hitting a few more, but then figured the hell with it. I'll take a nice long lunch instead." Chet held up his pint glass and gave Seth a nod.

"What'll you have, Seth?" asked Marty.

"You got any of the Banded IPA on draft?" asked Seth.

"Sure do."

The pint glasses clinked as Marty picked one up. He held the glass at an angle to get the perfect amount of foam on the cold IPA. Chet watched as the golden elixir poured from the tap. Marty set a paper coaster in front of Seth and then the beer. "Can I get any food started for you?"

"Nah, I'm sticking with my liquid lunch today. Gotta watch my figure and all that," said Seth, smiling. Marty placed a small bowl of salty nuts in front of them and returned to washing glasses.

"Banded? Isn't that the brewery in Biddeford?" asked Chet. Chet always drank a Blue Ribbon. Always had. Always will. He never understood the lure of anything else, despite watching nearly everyone he knew drinking more exotic beers. Over the years Maine and Portland, in particular, had seen a boom in the craft beer industry. Now it seemed that everyone brewed their own. It had gotten to the point that Chet wondered if he'd still be able to get his Blue Ribbon with so many fancy beers on tap.

"Yeah, it's good too. Not like some of the local swill they pass off on the tourists as Maine craft beer," said Seth.

The song on the jukebox ended, prompting the woman at the corner of the bar to ask her husband to start a new one. "Go see if you can play our song," she cooed. Chet turned away from them, then braced himself for whatever sappy love song the dude played. Poor guy. Can't anyone just sit in silence? Moments later "Love Stinks" rocked Dry Dock as only a song by the J. Geils Band could do. Chet smiled to himself at the choice. The music was so loud, he barely noticed when the door opened and Jimmy Sharpe walked in.

"This is the last place he needs to be," said Chet, jutting his chin in Jimmy's direction. Chet eyed him suspiciously, wondering if he had stayed sober. In the past, Chet had noticed Jimmy looked buzzed when out lobstering. He had become increasingly concerned for Jimmy's safety as well as the safety of the entire boating community. An impaired boater could get a lot of people killed. He'd spoken to Jimmy about his observations and given him a stern warning—either he sobered up or Chet would report him. Over the past year, he had watched Jimmy navigate a new life of sobriety.

Jimmy sat next to Seth. "Hey, Marty, can I get a Coke and burger with fries?"

He sounded sober enough. But then again, he just might be one of those drunks who can sit in their cups without tipping over. At least until they eventually tipped over. Chet had seen it with his wife Sissy's mother. She'd secretly drank for years. No one had had a clue until one holiday when the weather had taken a turn, necessitating a stay over for Christmas Eve. That night he, Sissy, the kids, and Sissy's brother had watched Lara drink more than he thought humanly possible. And that said a lot.

Marty placed Chet's burger on the bar in front of him, bringing with it an aroma of grease and warm bread. He could hardly wait to dig in. His stomach had been rumbling all morning. Moving the plate closer, he turned to Seth and said, "You still working at Sweetwater Downs?"

"No, man, I wish. Beth laid me off. Can you beat that? After twelve years on the job. I barely saw it coming," said Seth. He took a sip of his beer. "I'm starting my own handyman company. Bought a truck and everything. I'm tired of relying on others for money. There's no loyalty anymore."

Chet wiped the ketchup off his lip and shoved several fries into his mouth. "You getting any jobs yet?" he asked.

"Yeah, it's slow, but everything is in the beginning. Once word gets out, referral business will pick up quickly. It's only a matter of time."

"You worked at Sweetwater Downs? Isn't that the place that's trying to bring slot machines to the area?" asked Jimmy. He cupped his Coke as though he held a baby. Taking a few gulping slugs at a time. His gaze rarely left the bottles lined up on the back wall behind the bar.

Same as my mother-in-law, Chet thought. Her eyes had always been trained on whatever bottle was closest. Like a kid eyeing a bag of candy, just waiting to grab some. Chet turned away. Why was Jimmy torturing himself by having lunch in a bar?

"Why'd she lay you off?" asked Chet before Seth answered.

"As soon as those damned casinos opened in Oxford and Bangor, the Downs just dried up. Overnight it went from doing well on the weekends to a ghost town. Beth's cutting corners where she can."

Chet took a large bite of the burger. Marty had cooked it perfectly. The juices from the rare patty dripped down his cheek onto his jeans. He brushed his thigh with his dirty palm.

"You think she'll have to close? Be a shame to lose the place," said Chet between bites.

Jimmy turned toward them. "Yeah, it's been around for as long as I can remember."

Seth sat up straighter and ran his fingers over his jaw, scraping his stubble, then said, "I'm not sure it'll be there much longer. I know Beth's been trying to get slot machines in the place so she can compete with the other two casinos. I just don't know if it'll happen."

"Why not? Seems like a no-brainer to me? Can't she just buy a bunch of them?" blurted Jimmy.

"The Town of Sweetwater needs to vote to allow casino gambling at the track. So far, the measure hasn't gone through because of Greg Stadt. He's one of the town board members who always votes no. Who knows what'll happen now," said Seth. He looked down at his beer and shook his head from side to side. He grimaced and took another swig.

"Oh no!" Jimmy said. "You mean *the* Greg Stadt? The one they pulled out of the drink?"

"Yep. That guy. I hate to say it, but maybe him dying will clear the way to save Beth's business? I feel terrible even thinking it, but who knows, could change everything."

"You think it'll pass now?" asked Chet.

"Beats me. The alternate will vote in place of Stadt. I have no clue who that person is or how they'll vote. But for Beth's sake, I hope it goes through. She's had a hard life, running that place. She needs a break. Maybe she'll hire my handyman services."

The couple at the end of the bar rocked their heads in unison as their song played. The man leaned in for a kiss during the chorus of *yeah, yeah*.

Seth took the last swig of his beer and placed a ten on the bar. He tapped it and said to Marty, "Keep the change." Then he turned to Chet and Jimmy. "See you guys."

After Seth walked out, Chet moved to a stool closer to Jimmy, shoving his nearly empty plate across the bar in one smooth move. "You doing okay lately?" he asked Jimmy.

"Living the dream. You know how it is. At least this summer we've all had full traps. It's a big relief."

Chet considered him a moment and then said, "How's your sister? I hear her name everywhere. A real hotshot attorney. You must be proud of her." Chet needled Jimmy for dirt on Kari. Maybe the two of them had fought? Or she had some secret love affair? Chet liked to be up on everything happening with everyone around him.

"You got that right. She's the talk of the town. Former Navy JAG, partner in a big firm in New York. Then she solved the case against the Ahmed kid. Yeah, she really earned her place here." He beamed with pride as he spoke about his kid sister.

Jimmy glanced at the clock behind the bar and threw down a small wad of cash. He shoved the last few bites of his burger into his mouth. "That's it for me. I've gotta run." He elbowed Chet as he stood to leave.

"See ya, Jimmy!" said Chet over his shoulder.

After Jimmy left, Chet waved Marty over to his side of the bar. "You been seeing him a lot lately?" he asked.

"Not really. When he does come in, it's always the same order. A Coke with burger and fries."

Chet dragged the last french fry across the plate into the remaining ketchup pool. "You make damned good fries, man. Jimmy's been through a lot. All the Sharpes have, between their parents dying of drugs and booze, then Doug getting killed in prison. It can't be easy."

"I hear that," said Marty as he walked away.

Chet sat for a few more minutes, not feeling like leaving just yet. Once he went home, Sissy would hand him her "honey-do list." Damned woman never gave him a break. His barstool scraped the wooden floors with a loud clatter as he stood.

"Catch you on the flip side, Marty," he said.

Yanking the door open, he stepped out into the pouring rain. Conspiracies about murder, slot machines, and harness racing swirled in his head as he ran to his truck,

Chapter 16

Kari Sharpe walked the short driveway up to her brother Jimmy's house. Weeds poked through the numerous cracks in the concrete drive. The garden beds sported more tall milkweed plants than perennials. The backyard had not been mowed in at least two weeks. Its long grass swayed in the breeze. Jimmy had never been a good homeowner. Once the neighbors complained, he'd do something about the mess. It was just a matter of time.

"Knock, knock! Special delivery," she yelled into the darkened house. The warped frame of the screen door creaked loudly as she pulled it open. "Jimmy?" she said again, hesitantly.

The side entryway and the kitchen were dark, but she could hear the television from his den. His truck sat in the driveway. Walking down the hall to the back of the house, she felt her mind spinning toward anger. *I better not find him passed out.*

The television blared a commercial for the local mattress company. Although the sun had not completely set, the gloom of the day and the fact that Jimmy's house faced north made it much darker inside. Jimmy yawned as he opened his eyes and rubbed his face vigorously. "Kari? What are you doing here? I wasn't expecting you." He sat up, yawned loudly, and then stood to stretch.

"Well, you might've known I was coming if you answered your damn phone," she said with an edge.

"Yeah, sorry. I saw you called, just been working. You know how it is."

"I brought us a couple of pints of Ben & Jerry's. I get the Chunky Monkey first."

Kari followed Jimmy into the kitchen. His silverware drawer clattered as he shoved the loose utensils around, looking for two spoons.

"What's the other flavor?" he asked over his shoulder as he walked into the living room.

She took a seat on the plaid sofa across from him and said, "You have to ask?"

She tossed him the pint of Super Fudge Chunk, his favorite. He tossed her a spoon. The two of them cracked open the sugary treats in unison. Jimmy scraped the sides of the pint first, gathering up the melted portions before nudging his spoon into the interior. Taking a mouthful and then another, he shoved down the ice cream with gusto.

"Hey, slow down, save some for round two," she protested.

They sat in silence, eating for a few more seconds, when Kari said, "Today was Ruth's husband's first birthday since he passed."

Jimmy stopped eating. "Poor lady. That's tough."

Kari wiped her face with a napkin and said, "I know. She looked like a wreck. I sent her home for the afternoon. Sometimes I can't believe he died of an aneurysm like Mrs. Rush, my seventh-grade math teacher. Remember her?"

Mrs. Rush had been the best math teacher Kari had ever had. She had a glass fishbowl on her desk filled with candies. She would toss a candy to anyone with a correct answer. Somehow she made math fun, cracking jokes and taunting the class. If no one answered her question, she provided the class an answer and said, "Looks like I'm getting another chocolate." On particularly hard lesson days Mrs. Rush's face and fingers were smudged with chocolate.

"Yeah, I remember how sad you were when she died. One day she was there, the next, gone. That was hard."

Kari shook her head, trying to clear the memory. "Yeah, Mrs. Rush was the only bright spot at school. The loss was hard on everyone. Poor Ruth, I feel for her."

Jimmy scratched his face with the side of his hand and then said, "Ready to switch before I devour this one?" He held up the pint.

"Sure am."

They swapped pints and kept eating; then Kari interrupted them. "In other news, Stacy Stadt has been charged with murder in connection with the death of her husband. I'm thinking of taking her case."

Jimmy closed his recliner with a loud bang as he leaned toward her. "What? Stacy Stadt? Are you out of your mind? Why would you deal with her? Let that witch go to jail."

Kari paused for a moment before she answered, unsure of herself. She pinched the corners of her eyes and then said, "I know. I know. I refused the case at first but then reconsidered."

"Why? You're flooded with work. Everyone wants you; you're the hotshot attorney on the waterfront. People want a piece of the Kari Sharpe magic. Let this one go." He batted the air as though swatting a mosquito away.

She stood and walked across the room. Stacks of old papers sat in the corner. Jimmy had a habit of reading the Sunday *Portland Press Herald* and never throwing it away. The dusty pile merely grew with each passing week. Her mind kept returning to images of Stacy's twisted, beautiful face as she taunted her. Despite her efforts, Kari couldn't let the images go.

She glanced out of the front window at the gloomy evening. "You're right. Work has been coming in. It's been great. I certainly don't need more, but I feel like I need to do this for myself. Stacy and Greg Stadt made my life a living hell for years. Even mentioning their names caused me to panic. I want to face this, face her, or I won't be free from the past. Besides, seeing her afraid of going to jail is priceless. In fact, I've relished so much in knowing she's terrified, I've thought I couldn't ethically represent her," she said with a slight laugh.

"Can you? Represent her, I mean? She was terrible to you growing up. You don't have anything to prove. Not to her or Greg or anyone else."

Kari sat back on the couch and leaned into the worn cushions. "Yeah, she was a monster, even when we were in grade school. I can't count how many times she shoved me or tripped me just to make everyone laugh. It got to the point that my bruises never healed. Not that Mom or Dad ever noticed." A shadow of sadness veiled her face. Her mind returned to revenge.

"Doug and I noticed. We noticed every bruise. We wanted to beat the crap out of her and that smug turd Greg. You never let us."

She shook her head. "I thought it would end. Magically. I felt that I just needed to make it through the day and then they'd move on to someone else."

"Yeah, but they never did."

"No. They never did. It only got worse."

"Stay away from her, Kari. Dealing with her is too heavy. Just let it go."

"I know. But I can't. I'm not running from anything anymore. Never again."

She considered her decision again, thinking about Stacy Stadt. "Yeah, I need to face this."

"I think you're making a mistake," he said, breaking her concentration. "Remember what she did to your project? The one in the shoebox? You were devastated. You came home looking like you'd cried for half the day. She's a monster and we both know it."

The memory haunted her. In the third grade she had worked tirelessly on a social studies project. She had created a diorama of the Oval Office by collecting little scraps of material from discarded items, because she knew asking her parents for art supplies would have been met with nothing more than a huff of disgust. Jimmy had given her one of the shoeboxes he stored in his closet with little things he collected. "Kari, you can use this one," he'd said, excited.

"But I'll ruin it. Are you sure?" she'd asked.

"Of course, you need it. I just had some feathers and a few sticks for whittling in there, no big deal."

Over the course of two weeks, she'd transformed the little shoebox into what she considered to be a masterpiece. Her face had shone with excitement on the day she brought it to school. She had carefully wrapped the little treasure in plastic wrap to keep it safe and then proudly trudged with it in her hands to the bus stop.

She could barely get herself onto the high step of the waiting bus, not wanting to free her hand to use the rail. Instead, she cradled her treasure, thinking about the excited smile of her social studies teacher, Mr. Groth. As Kari moved to the back of the bus, Stacy spotted her and couldn't resist the temptation to once again dig into her.

"What is that crap? The box is old and dirty. Are you really handing that in today?" She laughed in disgust.

Kari held her breath. She just needed to make it to the back of the bus, to her usual seat. Her hands shook as she neared Stacy. She tightened her grip on the project as she approached her nemesis.

She had almost made it past when Stacy's hand jutted up and knocked the little box from Kari's grasp. Her project went flying, rotating over itself, then landing with a slight clatter. The little pieces of homemade furniture went everywhere. Then Stacy stood and kicked the box under a seat.

Kari leaned down, scrambling to grab everything. Maybe she could arrange the items again? She just needed to get the pieces back. She clawed the floor, desperately picking up the fragile items. The air brakes on the bus hissed as the driver left her stop. She had tumbled backward onto her butt to a loud round of laughter, led by Stacy and her minions.

Kari glanced at Jimmy. His worn face looked tired and worried. "Yeah, she ruined my little project." She slurped up the remaining ice cream straight from the pint. The cold liquid ran down her chin. Gathering the last clean corner of her napkin, she swiped it across her face, then said, "In any case, I need to face this. Let the fears of the past go. I refuse to allow the past to control me, you know, all that therapy crap."

"I guess, but if you ask me, people rarely change from who they are at their core," he said. Jimmy yanked the lever on his recliner, putting his feet up and leaning back. The old recliner wheezed in protest at the effort. "I was at Dry Dock today for lunch and ran into Chet and Seth Moyer. I don't know if you remember him. He's a little older than you."

She shook her head. "No, the name doesn't ring a bell. And Dry Dock? Really? Don't you think you need to stay out of that place?"

Jimmy waved his hand and said, "Don't worry. I order a soda and a burger. Anyway, Seth was laid off from Sweetwater Downs. He thinks the place is going under. The casinos up north are pulling business away from the Downs. Apparently everyone wants to play the slots."

"What does that have to do with Stacy?"

"That's just the thing; Greg was a Sweetwater town councillor. According to Seth, the town needed to pass a measure allowing the slot machines. Greg was the only one to vote against it. Went through a couple of rounds of votes too. I'm sure Chet's got all sorts of conspiracies about Greg's death. Who knows? He's not always wrong."

"Not Chet again," she said with an eye roll.

"Yeah, yeah . . . he's a little crazy, but who knows?" he said. He shrugged his shoulders and then drank the remaining ice-cream milk from his pint. "He knows just about everyone in the state and talks to people all the time."

"True. It's an angle I can think about, maybe explore when I meet with her tomorrow."

"I hope you know what you're doing. This might be harder than the case is worth for you," he said.

"I know," she admitted softly. A thin smile caressed her lips as she savored the jolt of sugar.

Facing Stacy Stadt was something she had never expected to do again. Facing Stacy as an attorney tasked with defending her may prove far more difficult than she could ever imagine.

Chapter 17

Kari prepped the conference room for her meeting with Stacy Stadt. Spraying cleaner on the large wooden table, she glanced out the window at the pier next to her office. Several boats bobbed gently with the movement of the water. High tide caused the boats to be fully visible, nearly even with the dock. It gave her a chance to get a good look at the toys other people possessed. Maybe someday she'd get herself a boat. Who knew?

The coffee percolated in the small butler's pantry just outside of Ruth's workstation, filling the office with a pleasant, slightly burned aroma. Stacy requested the early meeting so she could get to her office on time.

Once the conference room had been prepped, Kari prepared herself for the meeting. She had not seen Stacy since they had graduated from high school, a day stained by public ridicule. She could feel the embarrassment of that day as though it had just happened.

Their graduation had taken place in the high school gymnasium. The small graduating class of roughly two hundred kids had sat on folding chairs, while their proud parents had been seated on the metal bleachers. When Kari's name had been called, she'd stood proudly, wearing her cap and gown and walking the short distance to receive her diploma from the principal, Ms. Lordes. Just as she'd made her way to the wooden platform, Stacy had yelled out, "Loser!" Their fellow classmates had erupted in laughter, as had several adults. Kari had continued to walk forward on wobbly legs despite wanting to run. She hadn't been able to help but notice that even Ms. Lordes was smirking.

She shook off the memory, running a jittery hand through her clean hair. What the hell was she doing? Maybe Jimmy had been right. She needed to pass on this one. Let Stacy crap out her case with any other attorney. Then she remembered the extensive properties Stacy and Greg had amassed over the years, and their business. She could afford Kari's rates, her New York rates. Not the meager amount most Maine lawyers charged for their services. *Why not price gouge the witch?* she thought.

The outside door chimed, announcing the arrival of someone downstairs. With shaky hands Kari scooped up the file she had received. She squared her shoulders, lifted her head high, and proceeded down the stairs.

"Hello? Anyone home?" yelled Stacy to the empty office.

The sound of Stacy's voice jolted Kari. It had not changed since high school. Kari inhaled sharply. She caught the handrail to steady herself as she continued walking down the stairs. *What the hell am I doing?*

"Yes. I'm here. Come in, Stacy," said Kari cooly.

Stacy popped her gum and huffed. "Such a hotshot attorney doesn't have staff to answer her door? Geez."

Kari bit her lip, willing herself not to respond to the barb. She had seen the behavior before. Nothing new.

Stacy stood in the threshold of the conference room, staring out the window. Greg had been pulled out of the water near Kari's office. Stacy stood in place, stunned. Her jaw flexed as she vigorously chewed her gum.

"Have a seat, please," said Kari as she sat at the head of the table. Kari motioned to the seat next to her, placing Stacy's back to the docks. Leaving the shades to the murder scene open had been both cruel and intentional. She willed her face to remain still, not registering the satisfaction she felt.

As though in a trance, Stacy moved slowly toward the table. Sliding the chair out for herself, she said, "I hadn't expected to meet so close to where . . ."

For once Stacy looked humbled. Yet despite the look on her face, her perfect tipped nails, professionally colored hair, and pink Louis Vuitton Pochette Métis East West bag screamed confidence and success. Kari twisted in her seat, uncomfortable, wondering how she looked, a first in a client meeting.

Stacy had always ruthlessly mocked Kari's appearance. "Wearing your brother's old crap again, Sharpe?" she would say. Kari's family could hardly afford new clothes for any of them. Addiction had made her parents' job record spotty at best. Year after year the three siblings had traded clothes. Each of them wearing ill-fitting rags as they navigated the social pressures of adolescence.

Kari smoothed the lines of her L'Agence pin-striped slacks. The Italian twill suiting fabric felt smooth against her touch. The expensive suit reminded her of the success she'd earned. Her mind flashed to the power she felt as a partner with Barnes & Smith. Walking into court with the backing of prestige and privilege. She jutted her chin forward and bored her eyes into Stacy with intensity. She was no longer a defenseless child, but a successful lawyer representing a woman accused of murdering her husband.

"Okay. I received your file from the attorney who appeared with you at the arraignment. Looks like you pleaded not guilty to the charges. The court then released you from pretrial confinement and ordered electronic monitoring. You want to tell me what happened that night? I only have a vague idea from his notes. If I choose to take the case, I'll request all the evidence from the attorney general's office."

The cuff of Kari's silk blouse poked out from her suit jacket's sleeve, revealing the chunky Tiffany cuff link with the B&S monogrammed logo. A gift from her fellow partners when they asked her to join their ranks. The solid gold links clanked on the table, chiming the song of wealth with each movement of her wrist. Stacy's eyes locked on the cuffs almost immediately.

Typically, Kari left the Jimmy Choo pumps and the cuff links at home. Those items looked amazing in New York, but painfully out of place in Maine. However, for this meeting she wanted to shove her success in Stacy's face.

Stacy leaned back in her chair, crossing her legs. The electronic monitor on her ankle clanked loudly against the table leg. Her cheeks reddened slightly.

"What do you mean? If you take the case? Look, I didn't come down to your grubby little office to beg you to represent me. I thought you agreed," Stacy said.

Kari closed her file, leaned forward on the table, and steepled her hands. "I have *not* agreed. Yet. It depends on several factors," she said.

"Factors? What the hell do you mean by that? I didn't do anything wrong. That's all you need to know."

Kari leaned back in her chair and looked out the window. "For starters, I don't know your side of the events. I also don't know if you can afford my fees." Kari allowed her eyes to trail down Stacy's chest as though assessing Stacy's worth.

"I can afford *you*." Stacy spat the words out like venom.

"Assuming you can afford my services, and that's a big assumption, I will need to know what happened that night. I'm sure you can appreciate why every detail could be important when building a credible defense."

Stacy wrapped her arms around her chest tightly. Chewing on her lip, she said, "Fine. We went to Dry Dock the night he . . . the night he drowned. We went there nearly every weekend during the summer. We'd stay on the boat, then go out for breakfast. I loved those nights." She smiled slightly as she looked down.

Stacy sat silently twisting her hands together. Kari needed to keep the appointment moving. "Did you stay on the boat with him that night?"

Stacy looked up as though seeing Kari for the first time. Her eyes narrowed as she said, "No, you idiot. If I had, he wouldn't have drowned."

Kari made a note on her pad as she tried to remain in control of her emotions. Fantasies of smashing Stacy across the face with her legal pad danced in her mind. Maybe this was a mistake? What the hell would she do in open court if she couldn't control the situation long enough for an interview? She tensed and released her leg muscles, trying to calm herself down as heat and anger rose in her body.

"I know you're upset, but you call me an idiot again or make any other snide remarks and this conversation ends. Immediately. We aren't kids anymore. You need my services, but I don't need you. At all."

Snatching the upper hand, Kari maintained eye contact until Stacy looked away.

"Fine. Whatever," Stacy said. She twirled her hair, looking at Kari. She popped her gum loudly.

"So? Why didn't you stay?" Kari asked.

"Because we had a huge fight. I needed to bolt. That's all. I just needed to bolt," she said. Her eyes glistened as she spoke. Stacy leaned down, grabbing her bag for a tissue. She carefully dotted her eyes, catching the tears before they ruined her perfect makeup. Her fake eyelashes moved up and down in unison like two black caterpillars.

Kari had never seen the invincible, tough Stacy cry. She looked like every other client. Desperate to get out of the trouble, yet unwilling to take ownership of their actions.

"What did you fight about?" Kari asked.

"Look, that's none of your damned business. We just did, okay," huffed Stacy. She clamped her arms tightly across her chest and glared at Kari, willing a fight.

Kari put down her pen. "If you want me to represent you, then you need to tell me everything. Even the things you think aren't necessary for me to know. Sometimes the smallest details pull the case in an unexpected direction. So you either tell me everything or find someone else." Kari stood. "Like I said, you need me. Not the other way around."

Stacy shook her head, recrossed her arms, and said, "Fine. Look, we fought about work stuff. Greg wanted to buy property in Sweetwater to start a housing project. I didn't like the idea. We'd been fighting about it for a while."

"Which property?" asked Kari.

"It doesn't matter. The fight was over work stuff. That's all," Stacy said as she waved her hand.

Kari made a note to return to the real property issue. Maybe it had something to do with Sweetwater Downs? She turned to Stacy and said, "Where did you go when you left Dry Dock?"

"I went home. Where else would I go, you idi—" Stacy stopped herself. Popping her gum instead of insulting Kari.

"Did you stop anywhere on your way home?"

"No. Why would I?"

Kari let it slide and said, "Did anyone see you coming into the neighborhood? Or your house?"

"Like who?" Stacy said.

"How the hell should I know? Maybe a neighbor out walking their dog? A delivery truck? Anything? You need proof you went home because I'm assuming you returned to an empty house. Am I right?"

"Yeah, but. Where else would I go?" she said softly. The tone gone.

"And the police have a video of a woman who looks a lot like you going to your boat, about twenty minutes before Greg returned. The video shows her leaving the pier around the time Greg died."

Stacy softly sobbed, dabbing her eyes. One of her tears escaped her hand. It ran down her cheek, washing the fake bronzer away with it, leaving a light-colored streak in its place.

"It wasn't me."

Kari knew the familiar, flimsy excuse well. Most of her clients started the attorney/client relationship with the same lie. Eventually, the facts of the case would start to shape a defense, despite the client.

"The toxicology report indicated Greg had a substance called bute in his bloodstream. Did he use drugs?"

Stacy shook her head violently from side to side. "No way. Greg would never do that. He drank. We all did. But drugs? No way. That I'm certain of. I don't even know what bute is."

"Bute is short for phenylbutazone. It has been pulled from the market for human use but shows up as an adulterant to street drugs like heroin and fentanyl. That sort of thing. I find it curious that Greg didn't have any illicit drugs in his system, only the bute. Did he have issues with pain?"

"No. Why?"

"Bute is a nonsteroidal anti-inflammatory drug. Veterinarians give it to horses to treat pain and inflammation. Sometimes they take it themselves. Would Greg have done that for pain?"

Stacy placed her elbows on the table and then cradled her face with her hands. She shook her head and said, "Greg was in amazing shape. We worked out together, like always. He didn't have pain issues. If he did, I'd know about it."

"Interesting. So, if he didn't take the bute himself, then somehow he ingested it either unwillingly or unknowingly." Kari flipped through the few pages in her file. She tapped her pen on one of the pages. "Why did he have a bite mark on his abdomen? The coroner opined that the bite would have been made several days before he died. Know anything about that?"

Stacy twisted uncomfortably in her seat. She avoided Kari's eyes, choosing to look away. Finally, she said, "I did that."

"Why?"

"Look—what can I say? We liked to play rough."

The door chimed as Kari's next client walked into the office. She stood to greet the young man. "Have a seat, Jeremy. I'm almost done here."

She closed the conference room door softly, then returned to her seat. "I have another client meeting. We need to pick up later." She made one last note on her legal pad.

"Does that mean you're going to represent me?"

"Yes. But not until you pay my retainer of forty thousand dollars. You will be billed monthly against the retainer."

Kari had prepared a retainer agreement before Stacy arrived for their appointment. She slid the agreement to Stacy and said, "Read the retainer agreement. If you agree to the terms, you can sign it and drop it off along with the forty thousand and I'll start working on your case. If you can't afford my fees, I'll give you recommendations for other lawyers."

"I can afford it," she said with a huff as she slung her LV bag over her shoulder and walked out of the room.

Stacy slammed the exterior door loudly on her way out, making Kari wonder what she had just done. She didn't owe Stacy Marcs Stadt anything. Once engaged, Kari would be stuck with Stacy through the end of the case, for better or worse. She walked to the bank of windows and looked onto the pier where Greg had died, wondering what the future had in store for his wife.

Chapter 18

Ruth's alarm clock chimed again. She had snoozed the alarm three times already but now had to force herself out of the cozy comfort of her bed. She swung her legs around and sat for a minute. Nothing moved in the still house. It had been close to a year since David's death. Despite the passage of time, her home felt empty without him.

The clock blared again, "Okay. Okay. I'm going," she said to the empty room. An hour later she headed for the Old Port. Memories of her life with David followed her to the office. "Come on, Ruthie, let's get a lobster roll at Gilbert's," he'd say to her on a Saturday afternoon. "Maybe have a couple of beers and their fries. Then walk along the waterfront." She loved those days together. The early days before the kids, when they had been free to be together.

Dabbing her eyes with a used tissue, she clicked on the radio for distraction. The sounds of Chopin drifted softly as she turned into a parking spot in front of the office. She slammed her car door shut hard enough to scatter a group of seagulls warming themselves on the pier.

"Kari, I'm here. I'll be right up with your mail," she shouted as she rounded the corner of her workstation. The picture of David sat on the corner of her desk. Despite having the picture with her for years, seeing the two of them smiling on an anniversary cruise stopped her in her tracks. She bit her lip and fidgeted with her scarf, trying to turn away from the memory of the trip. Lightly touching the frame, she picked up the picture and placed it in a drawer.

The depth of her grief took her by surprise because she and David had been estranged for a long time. Living together yet maintaining separate lives. Over the years each had thinly concealed affairs. Her last affair had been with Mack, Kari's private investigator. The two of them had hit it off so well, she had considered leaving David to start a new life with Mack. Then she'd thought of their children. Their reaction would crush her new relationship. Instead of allowing herself to become even more emotionally entangled with Mack, she'd ended things abruptly. Their breakup had sent her into a mild depression for months as her mind repeatedly replayed nights with him. The feel of his rough hands, the sound of his husky breath in her ear as their bodies joined. Every day she thought of him with a mix of wonder, guilt, and longing.

After opening the mail, she walked up to Kari's office. "Good morning, not much to report. The continuance in Martindale has been granted, again. You know, if Johnson keeps requesting continuances, the court will dismiss the case."

"Yes, it might get dismissed, would serve him right. It's been a hassle to keep rescheduling the matter. Oh well, it's his case. He wants to keep punting it, who am I to stop him," said Kari jokingly. "I'm glad you're back, Ruth. Are you doing okay?" she said gently.

Ruth relaxed a bit. She could feel her shoulders drop slightly. "Yes. I'm doing well enough, considering. The first birthday after a death is hard. I appreciate you sending me home. It gave the kids and me time to talk, reminisce, and just be together. It was nice." She forced a slight smile, then looked out the window.

"Okay, if you need more time, please just take it. I can manage," said Kari as she sat back down and turned toward her computer. Ruth glanced at her again as she walked out of the office back to the reception area. Kari's keyboard clacked away loudly as she worked.

A few hours later, the outside door swung open hard, rattling the windows. A well-dressed petite blonde strode in with documents in her hand.

"I'm here to see Kari," the woman said with an entitled air. She leaned into the reception counter and thrummed her French manicure along the wooden surface.

"What's your name?" asked Ruth. She tapped her knees together to distract herself and alleviate her growing annoyance. The last thing she wanted to deal with today was a difficult mess of a client.

"I'm Stacy Marcs Stadt, she knows me."

Ruth glanced away from Stacy's glare, pretending to look at her computer for something. "I don't see you on the schedule. Do you have an appointment?"

"Look, I don't have time for this crap. I have her money."

Ruth pulled her body back away from Stacy as far as she could. "She won't be able to meet with you, but I can take anything you need to give her." Ruth tried to keep her voice steady even though she felt like slamming her keyboard across the woman's face.

"Fine. Just freaking fine. Take it," she scoffed. Stacy threw the papers in Ruth's direction, causing some of them to fly across the counter, swirling to the floor. Ruth glanced at Kari's phone. Her line had been lit up the entire time, indicating she spoke with someone. Good for her. Knowing Kari, she would have intervened, shielding Ruth from the client's nonsense.

Ruth remained rooted in her chair and said, "I'll be sure to give her everything. She'll be in touch." Ruth sat up straighter in her chair while she continued to stare at Stacy. She would never give the rude woman the satisfaction of seeing her scramble for the documents. No way. Learning to stand up for herself had been a hard-won lesson in her life.

Stacy twirled in a whirl of platinum blond, perfume, and cracking gum. She slammed the door hard, shaking the placards.

Ruth exhaled sharply and mumbled to herself, "What a piece of work that one is." She collected the engagement agreement off the floor. Kari had charged Ms. Stadt double her usual retainer and even padded her hourly rate, slightly. Ruth copied and stapled the agreement, smiling the entire time. "Good for you."

"Good for who?" said Kari as she walked down the stairs. "Did I see Stacy Stadt stomping down the pier to the parking lot?" she asked.

"Sure did. Well, you know, it's hard to not see some people," said Ruth with an eye roll. "She's one of the most annoying people we've had in here, but she did drop off a check for forty thousand dollars. That's a lot more than you usually charge." She cocked one eyebrow and winked.

Kari rolled back on her heels and said, "I thought this one needed a little padding, sort of like combat pay. Can you blame me? Besides, defending a murder charge will be complicated."

Ruth handed Kari the new client file. "I can't blame you, at all," she said, shaking her head. "This is gonna be a juicy one. Well, you know, I really don't want to ever deal with her again, but dang, I'm glad you took the case."

"I feel the exact same way. Thanks for opening the matter." She waved the file over her shoulder as she walked up the stairs.

Chapter 19

Kari opened the Stadt file. Seeing Stacy's name on the check made her stomach flip. Quickly endorsing the back of the check, she deposited the funds electronically before allowing herself the time to change her mind. What had she done? "No going back now," she mumbled.

The screeching of seagulls announced the return of a lobster boat to the pier, distracting her from thinking about Stacy's case. She quickly prepared and electronically filed a notice of appearance and several evidentiary requests, formalizing herself as Stacy's attorney. Chewing her lip, she waited for an acknowledgment from the court's electronic system.

Flipping through the few preliminary documents, she noticed that the lead detective from the Portland Police Department had been listed as Clark, Butch. She stopped for a moment to look out the window. Crap. Not him again. "This case can't get worse," she said to herself. She rubbed her tired eyes, willing herself to just pick up the damned phone and deal with this. It won't get easier tomorrow.

She would never forgive Butch Clark for his brutish behavior during the arrest of her brother Doug, even though years had passed. Since returning to Maine, Kari had increasingly wondered if Clark had it out for Jimmy. Somehow he had been on the scene when Jimmy had gotten drunk in the Old Port a year ago, before recommitting to AA meetings. Then he'd popped up again to pull Jimmy over one evening as he drove home. Those things could not be a coincidence.

She scratched her jaw, picked up her pen, and called his number. No matter what Clark had been doing in Jimmy's life, she still had to speak with him about the case.

"Detective Clark," he answered briskly. Horns blared in the background along with a chaotic tangle of shouting voices.

"It's Kari Sharpe. I represent Stacy Marcs Stadt. Do you have a minute to chat about the case?"

She thumbed the phone cord as she waited for his answer. Her hand shook ever so slightly. Letting go of their shared past had remained an elusive goal.

After a long pause, he said, "You want to represent that woman? Good luck. She's a bad combination of feral alley cat and Tasmanian devil. The guys down in intake barely made it through booking her. Hold on." He muffled the phone.

"I'm at a crime scene but have a minute before the lab rolls in. What do you want to know?" he said with a short, impatient tone.

"I'll keep it brief. What's not in the file that I need to know? I already requested everything from the prosecutor, but want to know from you, the lead detective."

"You'll have everything you need. I'm not in the business of helping a defense attorney. Do your own job," he barked.

"I am doing my job. It's standard to speak with the lead detective. You and I both know that." She wanted to add a few choice expletives but chose to refrain. Maybe he would be able to color the information en route to her office. Who knew? In any case, the call would protect her from a claim of ineffective assistance of counsel or malpractice. Showing she'd worked on the file, doing everything as expected, would shield her license and reputation.

"Fine. What's going to arrive on your desk is a thick file of DV calls to the Sweetwater Police Department. Obviously, because the Stadts live in Sweetwater, those guys took the calls."

She tapped her pen, looking up from her legal pad. "Did you say DV as in domestic violence?"

"Yeah, she'd beat the crap out of him. He'd beat the crap out of her. Between the two of them, they kept the Sweetwater boys busy. Just a minute." The line became muffled as he shouted to someone near him. "I'm back."

"So what? They liked to play rough, and it got out of hand at times?" she said, echoing Stacy's words.

Clark scoffed and said, "Is that what they call it nowadays? Okay. Well, you'll also see pictures of the weird crap we found in their house. Like S&M weird."

"Geez," she mumbled under her breath. Kari rubbed her forehead. She had not pegged Stacy and Greg as the S&M type of couple. The case got weirder the deeper she looked.

"It looks like forensics swept the boat but found nothing conclusive. Any theories as to why? Do you think someone wiped the scene?" she asked.

"I have no clue. The evidence guys did what they could, but the foggy marine layer is tough on preserving evidence. It basically chewed through anything usable on the exterior of the boat."

"What about the interior?"

"The boat was locked when the guys fished him out of the drink. The team had to crack the padlock to do the sweep. My theory is that Greg and Stacy locked the interior when they went out for the night; then your client killed him before he had a chance to unlock and go inside. We only found their prints inside and nothing usable outside. Like I said, the marine environment spoiled the exterior for prints."

Before she could ask another question, he said, "Gotta go," and the line went dead.

She jotted down a few notes, then stood up for a stretch. Flipping her wrist over, she looked at the time, nearly three. A good time for coffee.

"I'm getting a coffee, you want anything?" she said to Ruth as she dashed past.

"None for me, thanks," said Ruth absently.

Kari walked behind the building, tracing the water's edge. At low tide the stench of rotting seaweed mingled with the briny ocean breeze. Someone had set up a small memorial near Greg's boat. Probably not Stacy. She stopped to look at his picture. He smiled from ear to ear, looking like a confident young man with the world in front of him. If he only knew what life had in store for him.

Chapter 20

Lori Spec brushed her teeth in a rush. She needed to get to work quickly. Her daughter, Mary, took far longer than she thought possible to get up and ready this morning. The toddler fought her at every turn. "Okay, baby, let's go," she said as she breezed into the small living room.

The shabby gray carpet of the rental looked threadbare and mottled with stains from previous renters, yet she loved it more than she thought possible. Living a life safe from her husband's abuse had been worth staying in the run-down apartment. Mother and daughter shared the only bedroom. Snuggling close to Mary each night comforted Lori as she navigated a life in hiding. Together they had safety and freedom. Freedom to make decisions without Bruce's constant threats. Even Mary seemed more relaxed and joyful. She barely asked about her father. That was telling.

Lori pulled the curtain back from the window to chance a peek of the surrounding area and parking lot. Worry clawed at her every time they left their little nest. Would Bruce be waiting outside for her? The last time she'd left him, he'd found her. She had been staying with a friend for a couple of nights. One morning when she'd left for work, he'd jumped her, smashing her face into the car. The sick sound of her nose breaking had been forever seared into her mind. Carefully scanning the lot like a trained agent, she finally determined that the coast was clear. This time.

"Okay, last few seconds of *Dora*." She stood, waiting for the commercial to start before turning off the television. She had learned the hard way to never interrupt Mary while watching her favorite show. The ensuing tantrum would hardly be worth the few seconds of time saved. A commercial started. "Clap and say goodbye to Dora for the day."

Mary clapped and yelled, "Bye, Dora." Her little mouth catching on *Dora*, making it sound like "Dopa." She blew kisses at the television, then raised her arms for Lori to pick her up. With Mary clenched close to her chest, Lori quickly ran down the stairs to her car. She had become practiced in getting the toddler into the car with minimal time needed. Her mind endlessly replayed scary images of her worst nightmare, causing sheer panic every time they left the apartment.

Long term, they couldn't live like this. The counselor at the women's shelter had suggested giving Bruce time for the anger and shock to lessen before filing for divorce. The car rumbled to life. She jammed the shift into reverse and headed out for the day, looking in her rearview the entire way to the day care. She had told the day care about Bruce and counted on their discretion to keep her daughter safe. She knew that if Bruce demanded to take Mary from the facility, they would have no choice but to allow it.

Lori glanced in the rearview mirror at Mary. The little girl's lips pursed as she attempted to make spit bubbles, unaware of her mother's concern for her safety. She turned into the parking lot of the day care, hoping today would be uneventful for each of them.

Chapter 21

Kari sat at her desk, staring at Stacy Stadt's file. They had not spoken since their dreadful first meeting. Stacy had remained her usual miserable self. Meeting with her had been as bad as Kari had imagined. Soft classical music played on her radio, distracting her momentarily with a combination of cello and piano. She needed to focus. Muster the resolve to call the difficult woman. Her shoulders clenched in tandem with her jaws. Why the hell had she taken the case?

The knot in her stomach twisted over itself, reminding her of the mistake. She wiped her sweaty palms on her slacks, willing herself to remember her successes. They are not the kids they had once been. She silently repeated her favorite mantra: *I am strong, I am capable, I am safe.* The words echoed in her mind, riding the waves of her breath. Inhale. Exhale. Finally, a feeling of confidence nudged the fear aside as she started to believe the words. Feeling somewhat better, she sat up straighter in her chair and dialed Stacy's number.

"Kari. Finally," Stacy answered on the first ring. Without skipping a beat, she launched right in. "Look, when I call you, you *better* answer me."

Kari leaned her head onto the back of the chair and looked at the ceiling. Damn her. Somehow within just a few words, Stacy had made her feel small again. No. Not today. Kari pulled herself upright, squared her shoulders, and took a deep belly breath.

Then she leaned toward her desk, placing her elbows on the surface, and said, "If I'm available, I'll take your calls. Otherwise, you'll wait for me to get back with you, just like my other clients." She tried to sound forceful, yet the words, to her ears, sounded hollow, rehearsed. Maybe because they were?

A phone rang somewhere near Stacy. Without a pause Stacy pounced: "No. You will answer my calls immediately. Look, I paid you a ton of money and deserve respect. And I'll get it. *Got it?*" Stacy mocked Kari's words, as she had done so many times in school. Mimicking almost anything a person said in a weird voice had been Stacy's specialty. Her favorite abuse tactic. Simple. Effective. Cutting. Damn her.

Kari rolled her eyes and looked out the window.

"If you want me to effectively represent you, then get off your damned high horse. All my clients have paid, just like you. If you don't like it, then I'll refund your retainer. I'm not putting up with your crap."

Kari finally felt like herself as she blew the words back at Stacy. This nonsense ended today. Standing with one hand on her hip, she waited for a reply.

After a pause Stacy said, "What's happening with my case?"

Kari shook her head and smiled. Typical Stacy. No apology or acknowledgment of her actions—she just moved on. Kari cleared her throat and said, "I've prepared a slew of motions to be filed this afternoon. You'll receive copies of everything. Also, I'll remind you to keep your mouth shut. Do not talk about anything related to your case with anyone. Nothing at all. You need to stay silent, for your own good."

"Fine." A flurry of voices, then banging accompanied her words.

"I plan to be out to your offices to interview your employees. Is there anyone you would like me to speak with in particular? Someone who knew Greg well?"

"What the hell? Look, you never told me you would be nosing around our business. No way I'll allow it. You're probably just fishing for gossip, knowing *you*," she sneered.

Kari tugged on her ear to distract her from the anger spreading across her body, constricting her chest. Her temperature rose just as she almost launched into an expletive-laced rant at the miserable woman, and then her line blinked. A calendar alert popped up on her screen, reminding her she needed to leave for court in a few minutes.

"That's it. You were warned. I'm finished with you and your case. I'm not dealing with this anymore. You're just not worth it to me. You'll receive a refund, minus the outstanding charges," Kari said firmly.

Her words were met with a long silence. Just before she hung up, she heard Stacy saying, "Okay. Okay. Look, I'm sorry. Is that what you want to hear?" She sounded on the verge of tears. "I need your help and don't want to work with anyone else," said Stacy in a whisper. Her voice was weak, cracking with emotion.

She sounded small, broken, and deeply sad to Kari. After a pause, Kari said, "Interviewing coworkers of the victim and the accused is standard. I do the same thing in all my cases. If I'm going to effectively represent you to the best of my abilities, we'll need to work together. I can't be fighting you and opposing counsel at the same time. It won't work."

"Fine. Interview anyone you want. I won't stop you." The line went dead.

Chapter 22

Stacy disconnected the call with Kari, exhausted. She thrummed her long nails on her desk, looking out the window. Despite the air-conditioning, she felt the flush of heat across her back and face. A sure sign she had been blushing. She needed Kari. She hated Kari. She wanted to be strong but had no way to be strong without help. Or Greg. He had always been her strength. Just Greg. No one else.

Her eyes slowly returned to the office. A picture of Greg on their sailboat sat in the corner of her L-shaped desk. She had snapped the photo when they had taken a fall trip over a long weekend. Maine weather in October had a way of turning quickly. However, that weekend had been glorious. The shoreline had been resplendent in the deep reds, oranges, and mustards of fall in New England. The cloudless days were crisp and the nights chilly enough for their heavy two-person sleeping bag. Every minute had been perfect as they sailed lazily through Maine's coastal archipelago.

Staring at his face, she sought his comfort and guidance. She knew what he would say if he were here: "Drop the mean girl act, it's not going to work." In this situation he would probably add "even to Kari Sharpe." He had been the only person who had seen through Stacy's facade to her vulnerable parts. She loved him deeply for it. Tears streamed down her face, dotting droplets on her silk blouse. Nodding to his image, she blotted the tears from her eyes, careful of her makeup.

Her phone buzzed. "Yes," she said. Her voice cracked slightly.

"Your appointment is here. I set them up in the conference room," said her assistant.

"Thanks. I'll be right there."

She gulped down the rest of her mineral water and stood. Meeting potential clients had been Greg's specialty. He had a knack for making people trust and want to work with him. Her financial future and freedom depended on "dropping the act and being nice," as he would say to her. She smiled at his picture and whispered "I'll try" before walking out of her office to meet the couple.

Chapter 23

Rod Pieters worked as a janitor at the elementary school in Sweetwater. Every day he swept, scrubbed, sprayed, and shined the school, not that anyone noticed or appreciated his hard work. Teachers and students alike simply walked past him like he was invisible. No matter what he did, no one seemed to notice or care. When he took extra time to clean the kitchen in the teachers' lounge or washed every table in the library, not one person thanked him.

He pushed the damp mop around the already-clean hallway floor, trying to pass the time. Summer brought only a few staffers to the building and no students, yet the district decided to keep the janitorial services consistent. They reasoned the reduction in traffic would allow him to do other "important tasks." Like slopping out a plugged crapper wasn't important enough. Damned bureaucrats.

He stopped in front of the glass case in the hallway. It needed a good cleaning to restore it to a high-polish finish. His keys jingled on the ring as he turned the lock, opening its door with a creak. The framed picture sat where he left it the last time he cleaned, right in the center. The most prominent location for viewing. He swelled with pride anew every time he looked at the picture of himself, Greg, and Stacy. They beamed broad smiles from ear to ear, holding trophies for winning the end-of-year fifth-grade kickball game. Other players stood behind them, almost out of the picture.

The casual observer of the photo would likely never notice that his eyes were on Stacy, not looking into the camera as he smiled. She had hugged him tightly after they won. The scent of her lingered on his clothes and skin where she had touched him. The adolescent crush burned intensely for him. He had made the defining goal of the game, causing her to shower him with affection and gratitude. Tales of his athletic ability only grew during the days following the games. He felt certain she wanted to "go out" with him. And he wanted to ask her in the worst way, even if he was not sure what it meant to "go out" with someone.

"Greg, do you think she likes me?" he asked his best friend, Greg Stadt.

"Yeah, man. Why not? You want me to talk to her for you?" Greg asked. A week later the boys planned for Greg to talk to Stacy, asking her if she liked Rod. Once he spoke with her, they'd meet in their secret hideaway in the woods to discuss. Greg never showed up.

The next day he said he barely had a chance to talk to her. Rod thought it was odd that his best friend kept looking away when they spoke. The following week, Greg made excuses when Rod asked him to hang out. One day Rod was riding his bike alone and decided to go to visit Stacy. He worked up the courage to stop in, say hi. Nothing more. When he arrived at her house, he saw Greg's bike near the back gate. Then he heard their voices. Laughing playfully with one another.

His face reddened with anger. Greg had betrayed him by stealing Stacy. That day marked a turning point. Rod maintained the friendship merely to be close to Stacy. Where Greg went, Stacy always seemed to appear. Rod wanted to be near her more than anything. Friendship with a traitor seemed like a small price to pay as he bided his time, waiting for them to break up.

A second turning point in his relationship with Greg happened when he died. Rod had made sure to comfort Stacy while maintaining a respectable distance. Over the weeks following Greg's death, Stacy had become even more beautiful, if that was possible. He turned the picture over in his hand, lightly tracing Stacy's face with the edge of his finger.

"Pieters! There you are. We've been looking all over for you. The sinks in the teachers' kitchen are backing up again. It's a real mess in there," said Joan, the school's administrative assistant.

"I'll get right on it."

He positioned the picture back into its place of prominence and locked the glass door. Someday she would be his, something that should have happened decades ago.

Chapter 24

Kari drove to the Ridge, a Houses by Stadt community. Their website boasted that the development would be a cohesive community of expertly crafted homes. Whatever that meant. The property sat on the edge of Sweetwater, nearly into the next town. Kari had left her office early in the hopes of speaking with Mike Turnel, the construction supervisor. The deep blue of Casco Bay glistened in the sunlight as she left the Old Port on I-95 south toward New Hampshire. I-95 had always been the main road into and out of Maine.

"Where the hell is this place?" Kari griped. She checked her GPS again. It indicated she needed to turn left off the highway, yet no road existed. The left-turn blinker chimed as she drove. Nothing but trees. "That's it. I can't be out here chasing this crap around." She wanted to catch Mike Turnel off guard on a jobsite, away from Stacy. Hopefully distance from the monster would make the guy more willing to share.

Finally, a sign for the development emerged: *The Ridge. Where Memories Are Made.* The gravel-drive entrance crunched and rumbled. Her vehicle bounced on the uneven rutted drive toward a gaggle of trucks. The exterior bones of several houses had been constructed. Although unfinished, the two- and three-story colonials looked stately against the backdrop of thick trees. Various boulders had been arranged along the drive, lining the entrance, a nice touch. The houses ranged in prices from $600,000 to well over a million for the largest corner property.

Five white oversize pickup trucks with enclosed beds clustered near one of the larger homes a short distance from the entrance. Kari pulled up behind one of the trucks and put her vehicle in park. Mud crusted the truck in front of her. Someone had left the tailgate open, exposing the interior mess of tools and building materials. A man walked out of the house and lit a smoke.

Kari grabbed her pen and fresh legal pad. The door slammed behind her, catching the man's attention. He jumped off the plywood front porch, then walked toward her. A plume of smoke followed him as he exhaled his habit.

"Can I help you?"

"Yes, my name is Kari Sharpe, I'm here to speak with Mike Turnel. Can you tell me where to find him?"

The driveway to the house hadn't been graveled. Her feet sunk in mud with every step as she tried unsuccessfully to walk on the scattering of plywood boards.

The man eyed her suspiciously. Taking a drag of his cigarette, he said, "He's our supervisor. Said he'd be here in fifteen, if you want to wait." Smoke leaked out of his mouth as he spoke. "You from OSHA or something?"

Kari laughed, then said, "No. I'm not from OSHA. Last thing I want to be doing is driving around, harassing hardworking people just trying to do their jobs." Waving her notepad in the air, she added, "Promise. It's just a blank notepad." Smiling, she took one more step closer.

The man laughed heartily and rocked from side to side. He shook out another cigarette, lighting the second one with the first. Tossing the butt of the used cigarette into the mud, where others sat discarded.

"Yeah, those guys are always stopping by for spot checks. It annoys the hell out of everyone. Last thing we need is to stop working to deal with a pencil pusher."

They stood silently for a moment. The chattering of several birds competed with the roar of the highway, just beyond the pine trees.

"I'm surprised they'd build these huge houses here so close to the highway," said Kari.

"Well, I'd never pay a million to live near the road. Gotta be better ways to spend gold than listening to that crap all day. But you'll see. They sell these houses to out-of-state people looking for a slice of Maine." He flicked the ashes of his cigarette onto the ground as he spoke. His steel-toed boots were covered in crusted mud.

"There's the man of the hour," he said, jutting his chin toward the entrance. "I better get back inside before he asks me to clock out." He rolled his eyes, flicked his cigarette, and jumped up onto the porch.

A white oversize SUV drove slowly through the property toward the worksite. Kari stood waiting for his arrival, unsure if he would be willing to speak with her. The rumble of the powerful truck stopped as he pulled into the driveway.

"Hello, miss. I wasn't expecting anyone today. Are you here for a tour of the homes?" he said, open and friendly. The short, muscular man exuded husky strength as he moved closer to her. Her eyes trailed down his body, appreciating his physique. The scent of her grandfather's Brut aftershave preceded him.

Tiptoeing along the plywood planks, she closed the gap between them. A bird squawked in the distance. Extending a hand, she said, "I'm attorney Kari Sharpe. I represent Stacy Stadt in her criminal matter involving the death of her husband. I would like to speak with you about the business and the Stadts." She smiled again.

"I know all about you. Stacy mentioned you might contact me. Give me a minute to check on things here, and I'll be right out," he said as he shook her hand.

His warm, thick hand felt calloused and rough under her smooth skin. The plywood boards creaked as he moved, each wiggling a little as he walked. The front door slammed hard behind him.

Kari's shoulders dropped slightly after meeting him. She had worried he would be less than enthusiastic to speak with her, perhaps even hostile. Walking back to her car and the pavement, she pulled out her phone to check for messages.

"Okay, thanks for waiting," boomed Mike's voice.

Kari jumped, startled, oblivious to her surroundings as she read a detailed email from opposing counsel in one of her cases.

"Thanks again for meeting with me. I just have a few questions."

Mike crossed his arms over his chest and nodded. Suddenly the open, friendly man disappeared. He squinted his eyes against the sun as he stood waiting.

"How long have you worked for Stacy and Greg?" She started with the easiest question to get him talking.

"I have been with them since they started the company almost twelve years ago. They hired me as a jack-of-all-trades sort of worker. I can build a house with my own two hands. I do everything from framing to flooring. Not many of us out here who can," he said with a dose of pride. "Eventually, they promoted me to supervisor."

Kari smiled. "Good for you. You must know your stuff."

A slight blush crossed his face. He shrugged his shoulders. "Thought it would never happen. Stacy can be tight with the purse strings, yet here I am. My promotion came with health benefits and a raise. That had to cut into their bottom line."

"Probably right about that. When were you promoted?" She placed her notepad on the hood of her car and jotted notes as they spoke.

"About six years ago. I manage the various jobsites. We typically have several going at the same time."

"Are there several jobsites going right now?"

The Ridge had room for thirty houses. Houses by Stadt offered a "turnkey experience," meaning the new homeowner paid for everything at closing. The arrangement would have required fast turnover to compensate the company for the initial outlay of money during construction.

"No. Just two. This one and a much smaller site on the other end of town."

From their website, Kari knew about the location across town. The website indicated "more opportunities will be announced soon."

"Were Stacy and Greg looking for other property to develop?" she asked.

"Oh yeah, always. Greg wanted to be the premier housebuilder of Sweetwater. Allowing people to move into beautifully designed neighborhoods, not just homes. It made the company different from the builders who merely put up houses. Greg had been really into designing these idyllic micro communities. The problem is that by limiting to Sweetwater, they had to compete with every other builder for properties that came on the market. Getting a jump on those had been part of their success."

"How did he usually find opportunities? Did he work with a commercial Realtor?"

"Not that I'm aware of. He usually heard about opportunities through his work on the town board."

"Sounds like being on the Sweetwater town board really helped him."

"It seemed to."

She rubbed the side of her jaw, trying to relieve the pressure. She had been clenching again. "Did Greg have his eye on any property in particular?"

Mike paused, took his ball cap off, ran his hand over the top of his head, and then replaced the cap. He glanced away and then toward Kari. Finally, he said, "Yeah, he wanted the Sweetwater Downs property. Bad. Like bad."

Kari had heard gossip from Jimmy about the business and its valuable property. She put her pen down on her pad and looked at him. "I didn't realize it was for sale."

Mike looked over his shoulder and then side to side like a child getting ready to spill the beans. "That's just the thing. It's not. The track kept requesting that the town allow casino slot machines, to keep up with what's happening with the other casinos in Maine. They're underwater and need to compete with the slots up in Oxford and Bangor. From what I hear, gamblers really like to drop coin in those." Rubbing his face, he added, "If Greg refused to vote in favor of the slots, the track would have continued to lose money, eventually closing. For good."

Kari bit her lower lip. "That would mean the track would probably have to sell the property in Sweetwater."

"Bingo. It's shitty, but just business. Besides, others in Sweetwater hated the casino proposal. I'm sure you've heard. The fighting is in the news constantly. Angry moms shouted about the debauchery and decline of the town, while businesspeople clamored for the increased traffic slot machines would bring to the local restaurants, bars, and the few hotels in the community. It became a real thorny mess."

"Of course I've heard about the slots issue, just never knew Greg would have withheld his vote for personal interest. The whole thing seems like an abuse of power."

He pulled a red-and-white hard candy from the front pocket of his jeans. He popped it into his mouth. The candy clanked loudly against his teeth. "Of course it is. That's the best part about the Sweetwater town board; they're all openly corrupt. Town snowplowing jobs are given to the cousin of one of the board members, the dredging project near the beach to the family of another board member. The whole thing is rigged. No one seems to care. What can I say." He spread his hands wide apart and smiled. "It's Maine. Everyone knows everyone. For some people it works in their favor. Sure has for Greg and Stacy, until the slot issue."

Kari considered his words for a moment. "One vote was enough to stop the slots?"

"Yep. He held all the cards. Something about the town charter. I'm not sure exactly how it works. I just know he stopped the slot machines from going into the track and waited for the inevitable so he could snatch up the property."

"That's a lot of power for one person," she said.

"Like I said, he wanted the property in the worst way." He looked over her shoulder, his eyes scanning the construction site.

"What's so special about the Downs property?"

"Well, the location is great. The size is what they need for a signature neighborhood. And then there's getting rid of the Downs."

"Getting rid of the Downs? What do you mean?"

Mike leaned toward her, lowering his voice. "Greg hated gambling with a passion. He relished the idea of forcing the sale of the Downs property. Really took pleasure in it."

"Sounds personal, beyond a business interest. Do you know why? Has he struggled with gambling?"

Rays of sunlight bounced off the side of her car, burning Kari's skin as she waited for him to reply.

"I have no idea, but the guys talk, you know how it is. One of the guys said Greg's father blew up their lives by gambling away the family's money," he said. Then added, "At the Downs."

The breeze ruffled the pages of her legal pad. She looked at her notes, wondering how to use the information he provided.

The door to the house slammed. Footsteps on the planks drew her attention away from her notes.

"You heading out for the day?" Mike asked the approaching man.

"Ah, yep. See ya tomorrow."

"I'll let you go too. I know you need to close things here. Just a couple more questions," she said.

"Go for it."

"How close were you to Stacy and Greg personally? As a couple?"

Mike looked toward the highway. "I'm not sure how to answer that. I never socialized with them, in all these years. Never. They also never had any company functions for the employees. It was strictly business with them. Greg obsessed about acquiring properties and building the business. Stacy obsessed about keeping every dime they made. None of us, including me, felt as though they had a shred of loyalty to their employees. Now that Greg's gone, I'm not sure what'll happen to my job." He looked down at his boot. "At least I won't have to be around their fighting anymore. It was bad."

"Fighting? About what?"

"Everything. I'm only in the office first thing in the morning and at the end of the day, but I hear things from the ladies in billing. Those two were constantly at each other's throats. Then they'd be all lovey-dovey. Real odd couple, if you ask me."

Kari tapped her pen on the pad and said, "Married couples fight sometimes. Doesn't seem strange to me. What was unusual about their fighting?"

"It got physical. Fast. A simple disagreement about something stupid would easily blow up into a full-on fight."

"Did he abuse her? Openly, in front of people?" she asked, smoothing her hair behind her ear. A vague pang of empathy for Stacy caught Kari by surprise.

Mike laughed again, then leaned in closer to Kari. "Him abusing her? More like the other way around. She'd punch him, slap him, stomp on his feet, all sorts of things. Occasionally I heard he'd get to a point and then clock her, probably to shut her damned mouth. I'm not condoning violence, but dang. She's a real handful." Mike shook his head.

"Do you think she killed him?" Kari asked. She watched his face carefully as he considered the question.

"She's the first person that came to mind when I heard what happened. Then again, half the town hated Greg because of the slots issue. The other half thought he was a savior. Who knows. I also thought about his friend, Rod. The guy always seems to float into the office to chat with Stacy. Somehow always managing to do it when Greg's gone. The ladies in billing have all sorts of tales about him."

The door slammed again, drawing their attention. Two men walked out. One of them shouted to Mike: "Mike, when you have a sec, I need to show you something."

"Be right in!" he yelled to the man. Turning to Kari, he said, "Anything else?"

"No. You've been very helpful."

After he gave her his contact information, they shook hands again. This time his palms felt clammy.

Kari exhaled softly as she settled into her car. Starting the engine, she glanced at the clock. Maybe she should grab a pizza and hang out with Jimmy? Pinching the corners of her eyes, she tried to ward off a migraine. No. She needed rest more than pizza. After driving out of the Ridge, she made her way back to Portland, thinking about Greg, Stacy, and Rod.

Chapter 25

A few days later, Kari emerged from the courtroom with her opposing counsel, Roselyn Shanahan. Kari held a bundle of documents and folders in one arm, and an umbrella in the other. The weather had taken a turn for the worse the past few days. Everything she owned had been soaked in the downpours. Designer shoes stained from the water; pant legs splashed with mud from the streets. It seemed the bad weather had no end, gobbling up the precious few weeks of Maine's summer.

She glanced at Roselyn as they walked down the center hall of the courthouse. The petite woman had been a force in the courtroom. Every argument Kari proffered, Roselyn opposed quickly. Effectively. Kari cleared her parched throat and said, "You did a great job today."

"I gave it a shot, that's all I can say. I really couldn't get a read on the court's leanings on your motion. Could you?"

"Not really. Justice Pierce is always hard to read."

"This case has been a thorny mess. Nothing is worse than explaining to a client why the court ruled against a motion, while at the same time trying to justify an invoice for services rendered. It's a tough conversation," said Roselyn. She turned in the opposite direction to leave the building. "See ya."

A loud laugh at the end of the courthouse hallway echoed in the enclosed space. A small group of men in suits congregated by the benches outside of a courtroom. The group was most likely waiting for the court to come back into session.

Kari's heart skipped a beat. Her eyes scanned the group, looking for him. She recognized the easy, friendly laugh right away. Finally, her eyes confirmed what her ears and heart had already told her: Bill McGovern stood with the group. The last man she had dated seriously. It had not ended well.

She glanced down at her outfit, suddenly unable to remember how she looked. She wore a slim-fitting, sand-colored linen pants suit and peacock-blue silk blouse. Her long, ivory, belted trench coat draped over her arm, ready to battle the rain. Perfect. She swiped her hair from her eyes and sat on the bench, trying to look nonchalant as she waited for her next matter. Her leg bounced with nerves as she tried to casually switch from one crossed leg to the other. The last thing she wanted would be for him to see her looking at him. Staring at him. Opening a file, she looked down at the documents, unable to read the legal jargon as her mind raced.

One last appearance kept her in the courthouse. Her hands shook, nervous for an unplanned interaction with Bill. Should she say something to him? Sit here and pretend she hadn't seen him? She felt like a nervous adolescent as she weighed her options.

She and Bill had gone to law school together. They'd been placed in the same first-year section and sat near each other in most of their classes. Despite his obvious good looks, Kari never noticed him; instead, she focused on her studies, keeping her head down as she plowed forward. Determined.

One day Bill came up to her after a particularly arduous exchange with their criminal procedure professor. "You did great today, Kari. That was a hard line of questions he asked you," he said.

She smiled, assessing him for the first time and liking what she saw. "Thanks. Would have been nice if he moved on to someone else. Just glad it's over."

He stepped slightly closer to her and asked, "Do you think we could study together sometime? Maybe meet in one of the library study rooms?"

She paused, unsure if he wanted to study or if the question had been a veiled invitation for a date. Tugging on her backpack straps, she said, "Sure. Why not."

Despite her usual rule against studying with another student, Kari agreed to meet Bill at the library.

Kari estimated Bill possessed the very best physical attributes possible for a man: dark, thick, glossy hair; smooth, bright skin; deep eyes; square jaw; and a six-foot athletic frame. His physical qualities allowed Bill to sweet-talk most women. Rumors of his family's vast wealth only enhanced his good looks. Kari rightly assumed he played the field, a typical rich kid with plenty of everything to throw around.

As the semester progressed, they studied together with more frequency. She began to look forward to going to class just to see him. Changing and rechanging her outfit until she felt satisfied with her looks. Distracted, she would walk to class, wondering if he would ask her to lunch or out for a beer.

She also looked forward to the impersonations he did of their professors. Even on the worst, most stressful days, those impersonations would elicit a deep belly laugh from her, busting through her anxiety. One day he strode around a study room, scratching his chin, mimicking a professor. "Mr. James, would you *kindly* explain the rationale in the Esponito case to your fellow classmates? Perhaps you can lift the fog of ignorance veiling this *fine* institution." Bill had even included the professor's Southern accent for effect. She smiled whenever she remembered those days.

Breaking the trace of memory, she brought herself back to the present moment. She chanced a glance in his direction, wondering if he had seen her. He stood talking with several other attorneys. Either he had not seen her or he chose to ignore her as she nervously shifted her frame on the hard bench. Leaning back, she relaxed slightly. She could live with being ignored.

Months after they'd met, they sat in a private study room in the library. The small room contained a six-person conference table and whiteboard. "Let's sit next to each other, Kari. Then we can share the outline," he said with a wink. Sitting close to him distracted her to the point she thought maybe she should leave. With every move he made, a woodsy scent wafted from his body. He smelled clean, outdoorsy, and rich. Very rich. Somehow even in jeans and a T-shirt he exuded the grace of the privileged class.

Bill leaned into her numerous times or brushed knuckles with her as they both attempted to turn a page. Each time a jolt of anticipation shot through her. Then came the anger. Anger at herself for allowing a guy like Bill to distract her. Bill had everything Kari lacked . . . a successful family, generational wealth, and a guaranteed cushy position in the law firm his great-grandfather had started decades prior. Kari's success hinged 100 percent on her own efforts. She knew a romantic distraction could potentially strike a death blow to her ability to concentrate.

The last final of their first of three years in law school had been a long six-hour contracts exam. All law school exams followed an essay format, usually spanning over four hours. However, for contracts, the professor had told the class it would be so difficult that they would be given an extra two hours for the task. As the hours passed, Kari filled one blue book after another with her analysis of the legal problems presented by fictional clients. At the end of the day, her writing hand ached, her shoulders burned, and her mind felt completely drained. Despite everything, she handled the stress better than most students.

The pressure during finals had been so intense the school placed large barrels immediately outside of the testing rooms for those who needed to throw up. Over the hours during testing, fellow students heaving or crying outside of the room unsettled her as she worked through the problems. Final exams struck terror in all the students because their grade depended entirely on the one test. Nothing else. Performing poorly on finals had the potential to torpedo a career before it even began, and everyone knew it.

Kari utilized every second of the six hours allotted to her for the exam. Her fellow students streamed out, some plainly giving up just a short time into the day, choosing to sacrifice the grade rather than continue the torture of the test. Those students never became practicing attorneys.

She finally turned in her stack of blue books, wondering if she could have done more.

Bill sat in the lobby, waiting for her to finish. She had been so absorbed in the exam that she forgot all about him. She had not noticed when he finished.

He flashed his signature "Bill" smile and said, "I thought they'd have to go out and get more blue books for you. Geez, Kari, you must've killed it."

He had a way of always leaning into her, giving her a victory, forgetting about himself.

"I don't know about that. I'm just glad it's over."

"Let's get out of here. Grab beer and pizza on me."

She started to protest, but then he added, "I insist and will not take no for an answer. We deserve to rest. We finished. And never needed a puke barrel."

He pointed to the disgusting open garbage can containing the stomach contents of several of their fellow students. She laughed wholeheartedly to the point of tears. Her oversize response to his simple joke relieved her stress. She felt her shoulders drop.

"You think we can put that on our résumés? It's a real accomplishment," she said.

"I already have it on mine." Bill smiled warmly as he moved closer toward her.

They walked side by side to a local pizza place where many fellow students congregated. When they walked in, several classmates waved them over to join the group, but Bill politely declined and navigated to a quiet back corner. They sat close together at the small, beat-up table, throwing back beers and chatting about everything they had been through to get to the end of their first year.

Later that evening, full of more beer than she thought possible, they walked back to her tiny apartment. He had always done this, insisting that her safety mattered to him. Unlike previous nights, this time a brush of his hand turned into a firm clasp. At her doorstep he pulled her into his warm body, touching her face gently as he looked into her eyes for a moment. He outlined the contours of her lips and then kissed her, mirroring the pent-up passion she felt.

She yielded to him, allowing herself to feel everything offered in the moment. That night marked the beginning of their romantic relationship. Soon they became inseparable. The months and then years of law school floated past. His calm demeanor proved an antidote to her stress.

He left her the night she told him she had accepted the position with the Navy Judge Advocate General's Corps. The Navy JAGC had been her dream job. It offered her a chance to get out of Maine, away from her family's history. A fresh start where she could chart her own destiny.

"That's it? You're just leaving? Just like that, without any warning?" he asked. Stress lined his beautiful face. He ran a shaky hand through his glossy hair. Then stood, kissed her on the top of the head, and walked out. No final words. No further communication with her at all.

Jimmy reassured her that she had made the right decision. He'd said, "Kari, you've been dating the guy for a while and he barely introduced you to his family? An old blue blood clan like his will never bring you in, no way. You and I are trash to them. Grab the job and run." Kari and Jimmy only knew heartbreak at the hands of those they loved. As a result, Kari had a hard time believing anything other than loss might result from her relationship with Bill. The navy had seemed like a much safer bet. A bet on herself and her ability to succeed, rather than a bet on a relationship.

Seeing Bill, even from a distance, brought back a flood of emotion. She felt unsure about facing him. She wondered if he'd heard she'd returned and had simply chosen to ignore her. She also wondered if he'd married in her absence.

As though he felt her eyes on him, Bill turned. They locked eyes, and Bill moved toward her, closing the gap of distance and time in an instant.

"Kari! What are you doing here?" he said as he leaned in to kiss her on the cheek.

"I recently moved back to town."

It looked like he wanted to say more, but then the group of attorneys he'd been with walked past them into the courtroom.

"Sorry, I need to go."

"It's nice to see you," she said.

The beginnings of a smile and a half nod were his only reply. He walked through the heavy door to the courtroom, leaving Kari to wonder if the old spark remained for either of them.

Chapter 26

Kari stood by her office window, looking toward Casco Bay. The rain had finally lifted, bringing warm sunshine to the coast. Everything seemed to teem with life in response to the clouds passing. The seagulls squawked loudly, chattering as they worked. She watched one of them pick up a clamshell, fly into the air, and drop it onto the pavement. After numerous attempts, the shell broke in half, allowing the gull to feast on its briny prize.

Grabbing her phone off the desk, she checked Jimmy's location again. *What the hell are you doing?* she thought as she looked back to the bay. His boat seemed stuck in one position, barely moving. Glancing out the window again, she exhaled, snatched her purse, and walked out.

The dock where Jimmy and many other lobstermen kept their boats was only a short walk from her office. She moved quickly in that direction. They'd had a lunch date scheduled for thirty minutes ago. He never missed an opportunity for a free lunch. He hadn't even called her to say he would be late. She swallowed roughly, forcing the taste of bile out of the back of her throat. Something had happened. Something had happened to *him*.

Determined to get answers, she pressed on toward the marina. Maybe someone had heard from him? She squinted hard and shielded her eyes from the glare of the sun against the water. Finally making it to the docks, she looked around for the harbormaster or another lobsterman.

Seeing a weathered, deeply tanned man, she yelled to him, "Hi, I'm Kari Sharpe. I'm looking for my brother Jimmy Sharpe. Have you seen him? I haven't been able to contact him." She tried to keep the panic at bay. *Keep calm,* she counseled herself. *Everything is fine.*

The man eyed her suspiciously. He glanced her up and down and then finally said, "Yeah, I saw him out there early this morning. Maybe ask Fred, the harbormaster, to reach him on the radio. Knowing Jimmy, he probably dropped his phone in the water. It happens," said the man with a half-sheepish smile. "Fred's shed is over there. Can't miss it." He pointed at a small building toward the back of the marina.

"Thanks," she said over her shoulder as she jogged the short distance to the harbormaster's shed.

A loud alarm sounded in the office, followed by a thump and scrambling. The door burst open as Fred May ran out toward the water. He shouted in his handheld the entire time.

"We need tug assist now! We have a possible man-overboard situation!" he shouted as he ran toward the water. "Right in the middle of the damned bay. Stop the Casco Bay Line. Yes! He's drifting into the ferry route!"

Someone on the other end of the line responded. She strained to hear but couldn't. Sirens blared all around her as everyone jumped into action. Numerous men ran down the pier and leaped onto their boats. Tossing dock lines and speeding into the bay to render assistance.

She glanced at Jimmy's location again. She realized the location had not changed much. But it changed, as though his vessel floated aimlessly. Her eyes clawed the harbor for any sign of his boat.

"What the hell is happening?" she asked a man standing on the dock.

"Not sure, but it sounds like someone might have fallen overboard and their boat's moving into the ferry crossing line. But I don't work out in the bay. I'm a landlubber, just here to paint the bottom of that mess," the man said, pointing to a boat on land. Chipped paint and barnacles covered the hull. "Let's hope they get there in time."

Before she could ask another question, sirens blared behind her. Speeding closer to them. Finally, an ambulance drove into the marina. The driver and his coworker jumped out, ran to the back of the truck, and pulled out a stretcher.

Kari chewed on her lip and clenched her jaw as she scanned the bay, searching for any information about Jimmy. Finally, a small tugboat came into view. Little by little it moved closer to the marina. Fred May barked orders for the paramedics who readied themselves on the wooden dock, waiting for their patient.

The tugboat rose and fell with the swells and tide. As it rose, nothing could be seen behind its wide body. However, when in the water's trough, Jimmy's boat came into view on the crest of the swell. One rose as the other fell. Kari nearly dropped to her knees when she saw that the tugboat had been called for him. She ran to Fred and grabbed him by the shoulder. "That's my brother Jimmy's boat. What happened? Is he okay?"

Fred turned to her, placed a gentle hand on her shoulder, and said, "I don't know yet. He's injured but alive. Once the paramedics look at him, we'll know more." He looked down to his feet, then said, "At least we found him. It could be worse. A lot worse."

She nodded her head slightly. Holding back a tear, she watched the incoming boats. Fred ran toward the end of the dock to grab the line of Jimmy's boat. One of the tugboat operators jumped back to toss their line. As though they had done the same thing a thousand times, one tossed the line to the outstretched hand of the other, not missing a beat. Fred pulled hard on Jimmy's boat, maneuvering its nose close to the dock. Once he announced it had been secured, the paramedics jumped on board.

Fred stood nearby, watching. Kari found herself unable to move. Her legs felt like they had been glued to the ground, rooted in place. Frozen. She shook her head, trying to break the spell.

Moments later the paramedics wheeled Jimmy along the warped wooden dock. His body bounced with the stretcher as they tried to steady him. Blood-soaked bandages covered his left arm. His eyes fluttered between open and closed.

"I'm his sister, Kari Sharpe. Do you know what happened? Is he okay?" she asked as they approached.

"His vitals are weak but holding. He has a very deep gash on his left arm. And constriction injuries on his forearm. If I had to guess, his arm got tangled in the pot line."

Kari glanced down at him. He looked pale and small. Lobstering had always been a very dangerous job. One moment of distraction could mean life or death. He knew the risks and insisted on lobstering alone instead of hiring someone to accompany him into the bay. She cleared her throat, her voice wavering with anxious uncertainty as she said, "Where are you taking him?" Silence hung in the air for a moment, intensifying the tension as she waited for a response.

"Maine Medical. You can ride along or meet us there near the emergency entrance," said one of the paramedics as he loaded Jimmy into the vehicle. "From the looks of the injury, I suspect they'll take him straight to surgery. Might be a while until he gets out."

"I'll grab my car and meet you there," she said.

He nodded and slammed the door. The sirens started, and the ambulance raced away toward Maine Medical Center. She glanced at her watch. An afternoon appointment would need to be canceled.

Fred May caught her off guard, startling her as he spoke. "He'll be okay. I've seen worse over the years. Guys losing a limb or drowning because they get pulled overboard once their arm gets tangled in the line. All in all, he's a pretty lucky guy." He placed a gentle hand on her shoulder. Producing a card, he said, "Here's my contact information. Please let me know how he's doing."

"Thanks. Will do."

She walked quickly back toward her car, thinking about the possibilities that lay ahead for Jimmy. She rubbed her neck, trying to loosen the knots that formed. Her stomach flipped, jetting bile to the back of her throat. What if he had died? She glanced at her favorite spot along the harbor's front walk. Her eyes trailed across the water to the south-east, toward New York. Maybe she should have never left her glittery palace in the sky. Her apartment and office were lofted boxes sitting high above the grime of the city. Safe from everything. Untouchable. Protected.

Her phone buzzed, indicating she had received a text. Pretty Boy. On a whim she had given Bill's contact the nickname when they were in law school and had never changed it. Why would she? It fit him perfectly.

It was nice seeing you yesterday. Sorry I had to run off so quickly. Want to meet for lunch? Maybe next week?

She paused. The ferry line blew its horn, announcing a departure. Cars honked, and several kids skipped past her, laughing. Moms with strollers moved quickly to catch up with them.

Yes. Let me check my schedule and get back with you, she typed, then put her phone back into her pocket. Right now she needed to focus on Jimmy. Get to the hospital. Not worry about her pathetic love life.

A few hours later Jimmy's surgeon came out to speak with her. She and Mack had waited together for news about his surgery. "Ms. Sharpe?" asked the surgeon. She still wore her scrubs and surgical cap.

"Yes. I'm Kari Sharpe. How's my brother?"

"I'm Dr. Standfield. I performed the surgery on his arm. We managed to reconnect the severed nerves and stitched him up. He lost a lot of fluid and is exhausted from the surgery. Right now he's resting and probably will for the rest of the evening. Go home, take a break, and come back for visiting hours in the morning. He'll be more alert by then," she said as she pulled the cap off her head.

"Thanks, Doctor. Will he be able to use his hand again?" she asked, scared of the answer.

"Of course, should be good as new in no time. He's one hell of a lucky guy," she said and walked away with a wave.

"Did he have alcohol in his system?" Kari blurted out before she could stop herself.

"Let me see." The doctor flipped through Jimmy's chart for a moment. "Nope. He was clean."

The loudspeaker interrupted Kari from asking a follow-up question: "Dr. Standfield, you're needed in OR three. Dr. Standfield."

"That's me. I've got to run."

"Thanks again," said Mack to her retreating figure.

Kari and Mack left the hospital together in silence. Once outside she turned to him and said, "I thought he was drunk when he didn't show up for lunch. I just assumed. I feel so small. He's been really trying this time, unlike every other time he tried sober living."

"Hey, kid, don't beat yourself up. After the past year, it was a fair assumption. You're a good sister. He's more than lucky to have you."

"He's lucky to have both of us," Kari said with a smile as she opened her car door to leave.

Chapter 27

The next day Kari went to Maine Medical Center to visit Jimmy after her last court appearance on the morning's docket. The hospital smelled like hand sanitizer and overcooked peas. Not a good combination. She stood in the hallway outside his room. A curtain extended across the glass window, giving Jimmy privacy from passersby. He looked so small and pale. Someone had turned a light on just above his head. The ultra-white light created shadows under his eyes. The only color in his pale face. He was barely recognizable.

His arm had been covered in a thick bandage. Various wires poked out from under his thin cloth gown. She couldn't tell if he was sleeping or just resting.

"Are you visiting?" asked a nurse from the nearby nursing station.

"Yes. I'm his sister. I just didn't want to wake him. He probably needs rest more than to see me."

"Nah—don't worry about that. He'll be drifting in and out all day. He's probably still tired from the surgery. Go right in."

The nurse returned to her computer screen mid-sentence.

Kari went into his room. The soft chime of medical equipment beeped as it monitored his vitals. Jimmy didn't look up. She carefully moved the sole chair in the room closer to his bedside and waited.

"Hey. Was I sleeping?" he asked groggily.

He lifted his bandaged arm to wipe his eye and then thought better of it, switching to the other hand. His hair was matted to his head from the dried ocean water. Sea salt clung to his hairline. A reminder of where his life could have ended.

"You're one lucky guy," she said.

"They keep telling me that. But it's hard to appreciate my good fortune when I feel like crap. My arm is throbbing and burning. But at least it's there, I suppose."

The lunch cart arrived with a squeal and a bang of trays sliding around the moving tower. The woman pushing the cart tapped on the door and said, "Knock, knock. Ready for lunch?"

"I can always eat," said Jimmy with a half smile.

Kari moved the wheeled side tray closer to him. Someone had filled the water container, adding ice and a straw. "Here you go."

The woman placed the unappetizing tray in front of him and said, "Enjoy."

Kari lifted the lid of the main course and said, "Yikes. That's Salisbury steak? I think I'll bring you a sub for dinner. I'm guessing the food won't be much better later."

She unwrapped the plastic utensils and opened the salad for him. Despite its quality, Jimmy dug in. Clearly his appetite had not suffered.

"Hi, I'm Dr. McKinny. I'm the hospitalist here to check on you, Mr. Sharpe. How are you feeling?"

"Like I got yanked from the ocean and had my arm sewed on by a third grader."

The no-nonsense man flipped through the medical records in Jimmy's chart without a look at his patient. "How's your pain level?"

"Bad. Really bad."

"Your chart indicates not to use opioid-based painkillers, so we've given you the strongest next best option. Tylenol."

"Wait. What? Why not? I just had my arm attached. Why aren't I being given real pain medicine?"

The doctor pushed his glasses up the bridge of his nose. "Your medical history indicates alcohol dependence and a family history of drug use. In these situations, it's better to avoid even the chance of addiction to the medications. I'll circle back this evening, and if the pain gets worse, we can increase your dose."

The doctor shoved the chart into the bin at the foot of Jimmy's bed and turned to walk away without glancing back.

"You did this! You! How else would they know about me boozing?" shouted Jimmy. He threw the plastic fork down and jammed his finger toward her.

"Damn right I did. They had to know. The last thing I need is for you to develop an opioid addiction. That'd be just great. And you and I both know you'd do it. As if alcohol isn't bad enough. I'm not taking care of an addict too."

"Taking care of? Is that what you think of our relationship? You taking care of me?"

"Yeah. I do take care of you. Why else would I be here? Living in Maine. Remember?"

"You taking care of me when I go to AA meetings and meet with my sponsor? You don't do anything for me. I'm earning my sobriety. Not you. It's all my efforts."

"I worry about you all the time. Our family doesn't exactly have a long history of being clean. You're no different. Why the hell wouldn't I be worried?"

"Did you think I was drunk when the accident happened? Is that where your judgmental mind went?"

A blush crossed Kari's face. She remained silent.

"Bingo. Damn you. I wasn't drunk. It was an accident. It happens in my profession. A lot. I don't sit in a designer chair behind a fancy desk all day pushing paper, like you do. Some of us work for a living. I was completely sober when my arm got twisted up in the line. And for what it's worth, I've been sober for over a year."

"I know."

His face twisted with anger. "You know? How? Did you have them check me for booze?"

Before she could respond, a short, sturdy-looking nurse walked into the room. She rushed to Jimmy's bedside to turn off the beeping monitor.

"Everything okay in here? Your heart rate is skyrocketing. I need you to settle down." Turning to Kari, she said, "Another five minutes, that's it. He needs his rest. You can come back between four and seven tonight."

Kari stood and waited until she walked out of the room. The mood only slightly changed by the interruption. "I'm leaving. I don't need your nastiness. I'm trying to help you, you jerk. You're all I have. Just you. Remember? We buried the rest of our family. Or did you forget? Why wouldn't I be worried? Give me a break."

He remained silent. Lifting the small plastic container of apple juice, he struggled to open it with one hand.

"Let me get it for you. Knucklehead."

He took a sip of the juice as she opened the dessert. "I'm coming back tonight after work with an Amato's sub. Seeing you eating this crap is just plain sad. And I don't want to hear any more of your nonsense."

"Fine." He took another slurp and added, "And thanks for making sure I didn't get the good painkillers. It stinks, but probably better, even if I'm pissed you did it behind my back."

She smiled and grabbed her bag to leave. "I do all sorts of things behind your back. It's nothing new," she said with a wink as she left the room.

Chapter 28

Mack adjusted himself in his seat as he drove the remaining distance to Portland. His hands sweated on the steering wheel, making him wonder about the condition of his armpits. The last thing he wanted would be to see Ruth looking like a sweaty, hot mess. A year had passed since her husband died, probably not too soon to turn on the good ole Mack charm and ask her out. He knew a woman like Ruth would be scooped up quickly. Timing would be everything. Besides, he had a better chance than most men, given their history.

Glancing in the mirror again, he smoothed back his hair. A blaring honk startled him. The light had turned green while he fussed over himself like a middle schooler. Rolling his eyes, he laughed at his own middle-aged drama. "Some things never change, buddy," he said to himself. He had met Ruth when Kari hired her. They had flirted so much that Mack had begun to wonder if she'd sought an affair. Finally, he'd pressed her ever so gently for a date, hoping to not offend her if he had misread the signals. He hadn't. Their first date had quickly turned into a string of dates, culminating in private Saturday afternoons at his place. He'd wanted her to leave David but never made his intentions or love for her clear. One day she'd ended things abruptly. Something about needing to "do right" by her marriage. Then David had died.

A small smile moved across his lips as he thought about her. Today, after meeting with Kari, he planned to ask her out for lunch. Just lunch. Nothing too pressure filled about lunch. He had been so anxious about asking her out, he'd barely slept last night. He had not wanted to jump the gun and ask her out before she felt ready. However, he also had no intention of missing out to another man.

Easing his Buick into a parking spot, he resisted the urge to check his hair again. He wore a clean shirt and relatively clean pants. He looked down at his sad, frayed shirt and wished he had chosen a different one. *Get a grip on yourself, big guy. You've asked out dozens of women.*

If he started dating Ruth, he would have to decide what to do about his relationship with Debbie. He had met her one night while out at a bar. The night had turned into breakfast. Breakfast had turned into a very interesting morning together. However, he considered Debbie the sort of gal a guy had fun with, bouncing around with to pass the time. She was nowhere close to Ruth's league as far as he was concerned.

Mack exhaled as he yanked the door open. He cleared his throat and said, "Hello, beautiful. How's my favorite paralegal doing today?"

Ruth turned toward him and smiled from ear to ear. The bright blue in her scarf set off her eyes perfectly. Even her hair looked better, full of life. "Oh, Mack, you always say that," she cooed.

"True, but when I say it to you, I actually mean it." Normally he would breeze past to Kari's office. Today he placed his elbows on the counter and leaned toward Ruth. "How have you been? I've been thinking about you."

Ruth shifted in her seat and said, "I'm okay. Better than I would have thought. David and I had been so distant with each other for so long, as you know. I guess I had become accustomed to living without him over the years. I don't know." She smiled ever so slightly.

Is she encouraging me to ask her out? Take a chance.

He stood back and brought his broad shoulders square. "The weather has been so perfect. How about we head over to Gilbert's for a lobster roll and beers? On me, of course," he said with a wink. "Maybe next Tuesday if you're free?"

Mack knew she liked to watch her soap operas during her lunch instead of making plans. Today he hoped she would make an exception.

Just as she was about to say something, Kari ran down the steps toward the reception area. "Sorry, Mack. I forgot we never rescheduled today's meeting. I need to dash out of here to meet with one of the town board members. Is everything I need in there? Did you serve Rachel Ossip?" she said, pointing to the folder he had in his hand.

He extended the folder to her. "Sure did. I managed to nail her as she walked from her car to her office. Damn near missed her too."

Kari flipped through the file quickly, then handed it to Ruth. "Let's get the proof of service filed right away, okay?"

"Sure thing. I'll get it done today."

Kari turned to Mack and said, "Sorry to dash on our meeting. We can talk about Stacy's case later in the week or next week after I get through these interviews."

"Tuesday morning is free on your schedule, Kari. If you want me to add a meeting with Mack."

Ruth glanced at Mack quickly and then down to the computer. A slight blush moved across her face.

"Tuesday works for me too," he said, smiling at Ruth.

He and Kari walked together toward their cars. "Jimmy's fine. Thanks for asking," she said, needling him. A broad smile on her face. "You finally get the courage to ask her out or what?"

"Maybe." He grinned. "Is he home now? Did they release him? I need to check in on him," he asked, stopping near his car.

"Yes. He was released earlier today, after another round of tests. He's home one more day; then tomorrow he plans to head back out, pulling pots. This time he agreed to hire someone to go out with him, the knucklehead," she said, shaking her head.

"I'm glad to hear it," he said. The car door squeaked loudly when he opened it. Yelling to Kari, he said, "Let me know if you need anything else on Ossip. Otherwise I'll issue an invoice."

Kari leaned down to put her bag in the back of her car. He almost repeated himself when she slammed the back door shut and said, "No, that's it. You can give Ruth the invoice next week. Lover boy." She smiled, then got into her car before he could manage to say anything.

Just as well she mocked him for his crush on Ruth at nearly every opportunity. This time, maybe his crush would blossom into a real relationship with the only woman he ever truly loved.

Chapter 29

The Sweetwater town hall was located approximately twenty minutes from Kari's office. Leaving the redbrick buildings and cobblestones of Portland, she navigated to the highway and headed south. Various vehicles passed her as she merged into traffic. Plates from all over the country mingled with those of Mainers as tourist season continued in full swing. Most out-of-state drivers struggled to find their way around. Desperate tourists attempted U-turns in the middle of downtown streets as they circled the old city, trying to find their footing. Although Portland had improved their street signage slightly over the years, small towns in rural Maine never bothered. Most locals simply knew their way around.

Sweetwater's population had grown quickly as out-of-state people moved to Maine for the laid-back lifestyle. Stacy and Greg had profited from the real estate boom as demand for their luxury homes rose with the tide.

Kari planned to meet with every board member on the Sweetwater board to try to understand how the casino issue impacted their work. She had met with Mike Turnel, the construction manager with Houses by Stadt. He'd confirmed what Jimmy had told her regarding the vote for the casino. Greg Stadt had had no intention of ever voting to allow the casino into the town. As a result, many people in the town hated him for it. But hated him enough to drug him and drown him? By declining to vote in favor of the casino-style slots, Greg had practically ensured that eventually the distressed business would close. She wondered how his fellow board members felt about his refusal to vote in favor of the measure.

The Sweetwater town office building sat far back from Route 1, making it hard for Kari to find. Finally, after making a few passes, she saw a small sign indicating she had made it to the location. The red-brick building looked newly constructed. Several visitor parking slots welcomed the occasional person needing the town office. Snagging a close spot, she parked and headed in.

A cold rush of air hit her the moment she entered. Light classical music played through a speaker hanging sideways on the wall. A young woman with heavy black eyeliner sat at the front desk and turned to Kari.

"Help you?" she said. Her tired voice sounded as though she would rather not help but was instructed to give everyone the bland greeting.

Kari handed the woman her card. "I'm Kari Sharpe, here to see Margaret Mitchell."

The young woman half rolled her eyes as she turned back to her computer. "I don't need that. I know who you are. Been seeing a lot of you on TV. You win a lot. I like that."

Caught off guard by the compliment, Kari adjusted the bag on her shoulder and said, "I appreciate that. Am I still on with her for our meeting?"

After an awkward moment of silence, the young woman turned to her and said, "Yeah, she'll be out in a few. It takes her a while to get up here. You'll see." She smirked, then returned to her screen.

Kari stood in the waiting room, viewing the photos on display. The black-and-white pictures showed the town over the years as it morphed and changed into the town of today. People in Victorian-era clothing smiled for the camera in front of a wooden building. She guessed it had been the first town hall. Or whatever they called it back then.

The opposite wall showcased the headshots of each of the town's board members. Kari glanced at the receptionist. The young woman stared at her screen with intensity. Kari snapped a picture of each headshot.

"I'm glad you're looking at our pictures. We have quite a history," said a soft, shaky voice.

A petite woman with gray hair in a bun and glasses stood a couple of feet away from her. The glasses were so thick Kari had a hard time telling if the woman was looking at her or the photos. "Are you Ms. Mitchell?"

The woman laughed and placed her spotted hand on her chest. "Oh my, please call me Margaret."

Kari shook Margaret's hand. Her tiny palm felt cold and fragile. Normally Kari met the world with a firm handshake. This time she barely returned the woman's grip as she shook it, for fear she would snap it in half.

She glanced at the receptionist as she walked past. The Gen Z woman smirked and nodded. The flower tattoo on her neck poked out past her unnaturally jet-black hair.

Kari followed the older woman to the back of the building. Margaret's plain, tan therapeutic shoes squeaked as she slowly walked one careful step after another. Small black bobby pins contrasted sharply against the gray of her carefully constructed bun. Her pace was so deliberate and unhurried that Kari had a difficult time not passing her.

"Here we are. Please have a seat, Ms. Sharpe."

They sat in a small conference room near where the town held its board meetings. The room had no exterior window. Instead, a window opened to the town assembly room. During meetings, the board members sat at the end of the large room behind a raised wooden semicircle facing the audience section. A lectern stood between the board and the audience, enabling concerned citizens to voice their opinions.

A puff of air escaped from the chair as Kari sat down. Glancing at Margaret, she said, "Please call me Kari." She placed a fresh legal pad on the small conference room table and sat back in her chair. "Thank you for meeting with me, Margaret. As you know, I would like to speak with you about the proposed casino project here in Sweetwater and about Greg Stadt."

Kari placed her business card on the table and slid it toward Margaret. The wood of the table warm under her hand.

Margaret smiled as though she just saw an old friend. Then she shook her head and said, "If only Greg would have voted in favor of it. The whole town would be different by now. We all wanted it. The casino-style slot machines would add a tremendous amount of money to our little neck of the woods."

"Yes. I've heard the measure was very popular with many people in town. Yet, despite its popularity, Greg Stadt routinely voted against it. Why do you think that is?" asked Kari.

Margaret leaned back into her chair, crossing her frail arms across her chest, and said with a huff, "How should I know? He said he thought the kids would suffer. Every vote he echoed the words spoken by various moms' groups. Probably his wife Stacy pushing him to do it. She's an odd one. They were odd together."

"Odd together? What do you mean?"

"Stacy and Greg had an unusual relationship, to say the least," said Margaret. She looked through the window to the assembly room and then back to Kari.

"Why do you say that?"

"Everyone knew she would be the death of him. A woman like that, so unhinged. So lacking in self-control. I'm surprised it took this long for her to finish him off." Margaret bobbed her head up and down slightly as she spoke. Her bun danced.

"Did you ever personally see Stacy act erratically?" Kari asked. She leaned in to hear Margaret's soft voice and placed her forearms on the polished conference table.

"We all did. One night she came here and interrupted our meeting. Just started yelling at him, like a disobeying dog. It shocked everyone." A scowl formed across her heavily lined face.

"When did this happen?" Kari asked.

Margaret waved her hand in front of her face. "Oh, I don't know. Probably a year ago. Poor guy. He turned bright red and then excused himself to speak with her."

Kari considered her words. It had been well established that Stacy and Greg's relationship had been turbulent at best. Kari wanted to know if it had impacted Greg's work at the town.

"Was this a public meeting?"

Margaret chuckled, covering her mouth. "Oh gosh, no. It was our weekly session. It's when we go over what's happening, what's coming up. That sort of thing." She smiled and then added, "Greg just got up from the meeting and went into the hall with Stacy. They looked like they were getting into something. Their hands were flying everywhere. Stacy pushed him on the chest hard; then he pushed her back! Can you imagine?"

"What was the fight about?"

"Beats me. Once they finished, he came back in the room like nothing happened. Like nothing at all happened." Margaret leaned into her chair and folded her hands in her tiny lap.

"What can you tell me about the proposed casino project?" asked Kari.

"Humph. I can tell you it'll happen now that Greg's gone. That's for sure."

Kari pretended to take a note as she considered her words. "Why would you say that?"

"Because Greg's alternate will vote in favor of it. Plain and simple. This should be a done deal very soon. Then we can all enjoy the influx of money to the town."

"I assume you were always in favor of the casino being in Sweetwater?"

Margaret pulled her lavender cardigan snuggly against her body. "Oh yes, I loved the idea from the start. Those nice people gave me a free pass to go to the Oxford casino anytime I want." She lifted her head, proud as she spoke. "My sister Gail and I go there nearly every weekend; it's a real hoot. I like the nickel slots, but Gail plays a quarter at a time, like she's rich or something. Even though the casino man gives me money to use when we go up there, I still only play the nickel slots."

"Assuming the measure goes through, will Sweetwater have the same type of slots as Oxford?"

"Oh yes and then some. The nice casino man said they plan to build us a senior center and a community center, right here in Sweetwater. Can you imagine? A real community center. He said he would give Gail and me the same sort of passes for Sweetwater, and he promised to keep giving me 'playing money,' as he calls it." She laughed heartily. "I always love playing with someone else's money. I've worked for Sweetwater since the day I graduated from high school, and this will be without a doubt the best thing for our town."

Kari set her pen down, looked at Margaret, and said, "Sounds like a real advantage for the town to have the casino. I'm still having a hard time understanding Greg's opposition."

Margaret stirred in her chair. She frowned as she became visibly agitated. "That guy is just selfish, that's why." The thin veneer of civility finally vanished. "He would rather make his own money than share in the reward like the rest of us. Just selfish, that one. He won't be missed. Heck, if Stacy hadn't done him in, someone else would have. It was only a matter of time. A selfish guy like that always finds a bad end." Margaret struck the table with her fist a few times for emphasis. Blue veins visible under her paper-thin age-mottled skin covering her bones.

"What do you mean? Share in the reward?" Kari asked.

The Town of Sweetwater had always been known to have a crooked board. Rumors had spread that winter plowing contracts and summer field maintenance work went to the family of one board member. An expensive dredging project had been rumored to go to the company owned by the brother of another board member. The list went on. Yet, despite the very public corruption, the voters of Sweetwater had reelected the same board members.

"The nice casino men had given everyone gifts. 'Playing money,' a deal on a new car, that sort of thing. Those guys were so nice, and stupid Greg had to ruin everything. He refused their gifts and just kept talking about the kids. Like he cares. They don't even have kids." She pounded her fist again. Her face flushed with anger.

"What happens with the vote now that Greg is dead? You mentioned an alternate?"

"Our alternate Rusty Homes will vote in his place. But we must wait for two months until the next vote. That's how it works. We are open for public comment every other month; then the following month we vote, on the record, in front of whoever cares to show up," she said. She glanced into the adjoining assembly room. "We have plenty of chairs for the public, but almost no one shows up for most measures."

"Is that so? Even for this issue? From what I've read in the paper, seems like the entire town has an opinion about the casino issue," asked Kari. She glanced from Margaret to the assembly room. She estimated the room could easily hold fifty people.

"Oh sure, that's the exception. Everyone has an opinion and plenty of people came to the meetings. Many of them spoke in favor of the casino. In fact, we had more people supporting it than not. Yet still Greg wouldn't budge. Maybe everything worked out the way it should. Rusty and the rest of us will take care of it." She gently rubbed the medallion she wore.

Kari jotted down her impressions of Margaret. A minute later, she looked up at Margaret and said, "I'd like to reach out to the other board members to discuss the issue. Would you mind sharing their contact information?"

Margaret stiffened; her eyes scrunched in a puzzled expression. Clearing her throat, she seemed ready to say something when Kari added, "It would save me the legwork of finding them on the internet or having to serve the town a subpoena for the information. Your choice."

Margaret looked away, then down. She twisted in her seat as she considered her options. "Fine. The last thing we need around here is some legal mumbo jumbo. I'll prepare a list of contact information. If there's nothing further?" she trailed off.

"Nope. Nothing at all, you've been very helpful. Would you like me to wait here for the contact information?" She pushed to receive it today.

"No. I'll have Courtney at the front desk print it for you," she said as she rose from the table.

Kari quickly gathered her notepad and pen. They walked back to the reception area in silence. Once there, Kari extended her hand. "Thanks again, Margaret. I appreciate your time today."

Margaret glanced down at her offered hand, nodded, and walked away.

After Margaret had made her way to the back office, Kari turned to Courtney and said with a wide smile, "Was it something I said?"

Courtney laughed, waved her hand around, and said, "No, she's the moodiest old bat on the planet. Runs hot and cold. Never really know what you'll get with that one."

The printer behind Courtney hummed to life and quickly produced the list of board members. Courtney grabbed the paper, glanced at it, and then drew a line across an entry. "Guess he's not on the list anymore," she said without emotion.

Despite herself, Kari smirked at her comment.

"Thanks, see ya," said Kari.

"Yep," said Courtney without looking up from her phone.

Kari shoved the contact list into her satchel. Grabbing her phone, she scrolled emails, responding to a few as she made her way through the new messages. Once she'd answered all the emails, she listened to the voice messages. One caught her attention: Bill. She had neglected to propose dates to meet for lunch.

The air-conditioning blasted in her car, cooling it from the heat of the sun. After a moment, she clicked on his message, placed it on speaker, and listened.

"Hi, Kari, it's me. Sorry again about court the other day. I wish I had seen you sooner, it would have been nice to chat." He paused. *"I'd really*

like to meet up. Maybe for lunch? It would be great to reconnect. Text me when you have a minute. Okay?"

Despite her ghosting him, his voice sounded smooth and confident. Just as it always had. She loved to listen to him speak. Something about his attitude gave her confidence too. At times, during law school, she fed off his energy, allowing it to lift her when she felt buried under all the pressure.

She hesitated to respond to him. Then in a moment of courage she opened a new text message and wrote:

Hi, I got your message. Lunch would be nice. Maybe next week? Wednesday?

A second later he replied.

Perfect. Our place at 12:30?

She gave his message the thumbs-up, then put down her phone, smiling from ear to ear.

Chapter 30

Beth Thornberry sat in her messy office at Sweetwater Downs. The morning had been spent going through invoices, past-due statements, and shut-off notices for the business. She had done everything she could to save the old place, including taking out a business loan, an equity line of credit, and more credit cards than she thought possible. Agreeing to borrow money from Ryker had been the last thing she would have considered doing, until things became desperate.

Once she'd felt the noose of financial debt tightening, he'd swooped in with his casino money to rescue her. The lifeline had kept the business going for a little while. She'd squirreled $10,000 away, then used a substantial portion of the balance to update the restaurant and bar, hoping a more modern look would bring customers back to harness racing. It hadn't.

She rubbed her tired eyes. Looking toward the paddock, she saw Sophie's Luck prancing around. The stubborn adolescent tugged at the reins, refusing to work. Little by little Joe had managed to coax a winner out of her.

Glancing at her wristwatch, she realized Dr. Sweely would arrive any moment. She needed to make a list for the veterinarian of the various physical issues she and Joe had observed over the past month in several of her horses.

The desk drawer creaked as she pulled hard to open it. Rummaging around, she pulled out a small box containing the key to her medicine stash. The metal medicine box had been affixed to the wall in the office years ago after an incident involving one of the staff stealing heavy-duty pain medications used on harness racehorses. The employee had stolen small, undetectable amounts of the drug from the medicine kit, which had been previously located in the tack room. One day she'd looked undeniably wasted, prompting an inventory of the medicines. When Beth had realized much of the pain medications had been stolen, she'd secured the drugs in the metal box inside her office.

The lid of the box squeaked when she opened it. Various glass vials of drugs sat next to bandages, clot-stopping powders, and other necessary items for the care of the horses. In case of an emergency, she could treat an animal on the spot while they waited for Dr. Sweely.

Her eyes went right to the half-empty bottle of phenylbutazone, also known as bute. Dr. Sweely had loaded them up with the anti-inflammatory last month. Only one horse currently needed to take it. She looked out to the paddock. Her eyebrows pulled together as she considered her options. She needed to have more on hand but wanted to avoid a conversation about how much had been used since his last visit. A horse would suffer serious side effects if the drug had been overused. She had no reasonable explanation for using so much bute.

Rubbing the back of her neck, she placed the bottle into the medicine box and locked it.

A tap at the door startled her. "Come in," she said.

"Hey there, sorry to bother you. Dr. Sweely is here, thought you might want to know," said Joe.

"Perfect. Thanks, I'll be right out."

The scent of horse and hay hung heavy in the dark interior of the barn. Beth glanced around to find Dr. Sweely. She couldn't see him but could hear his gentle voice soothing a mare a few stalls down from the office. "Okay, girl. Just a quick check." Even the shyest horses relaxed around him.

Beth held the edge of the stall. The thick wooden door had been smoothed on the top edge from years of hands opening and closing it.

The mare stood staring into the barn. Her large dark eyes rimmed in a perfect fringe of thick lashes. A real beauty.

Beth cleared her throat and said, "Hey, Doc. Thanks for coming in today."

Dr. Sweely pulled one side of his stethoscope out of his ear. "No problem. Anything specific you need me to look at?"

"Just a few minor things. The stable has been pretty free of injury." She knocked on the door of the stall and said, "Hopefully it stays that way." Her hands shook as she spoke. After a pause she added, "I took an inventory of our medicine cabinet, and we could use more bute, if you have any on you."

"Okay, I think I have some in my car. I'll just have to check the records. Which horse do you need it for?" he said. He continued to examine the mare as he spoke.

Instead of responding, she pretended not to hear him and simply drifted away toward the tack room. Closing the door behind her, she leaned against its heft and closed her eyes for a moment. The wooden walled room contained open lockers where each horse's bridles, saddles, and other supplies had been organized. The deep, pleasant smell of leather lingered in the space.

What had she done?

Chapter 31

Kari hustled through the Old Port on her way to meet Bill. They'd agreed to have lunch at a small sandwich shop in the Old Port. She'd asked Bill to pick a place. She had been surprised at his quick suggestion of Brown Bag. It had been their favorite restaurant during law school. At times, they'd gone to the small shop numerous times in the same week. Like many businesses in the Old Port, it had a large interior containing a maze of numerous small side rooms. She and Bill had had a favorite table in one of the small rooms to the back of the establishment. They'd spent long hours with their heads huddled together, studying and flirting as they worked their way through law school.

Upon returning to Maine, she'd lacked the courage to return to "their place." She'd thought the memories and emotions residing in the physical space would be more painful than she needed to take on. Today, meeting Bill at the shop marked her return to the establishment and possibly to him. She had still not worked out whether she wanted to rekindle their relationship. The pain of their breakup obscured her memories of the happy years they'd spent together. Yet the mental images of their intimacy pulled her toward him. Only time could help her to understand the complex emotions she felt toward him and them as a couple.

She arrived at Brown Bag exactly on time. Upon entering, she searched the crowded, large main room for Bill. The noise of numerous people's voices jumbled together. A long line snaked from the counter through the restaurant. The marble mosaic floor echoed the sounds. She scanned the room for him.

Not seeing him in the main room, she worked her way through the crowd to one of the small back rooms as she mumbled, "Excuse me, pardon me." People stepped aside, allowing her to pass. She found him in the smallest room at the very back of the café.

He sat at the same table they had favored, looking at his device. She had to catch her breath as memories of their time together flooded her mind. He had worn a polo shirt in the navy blue she loved on him. She had chosen to wear a deep-emerald silk blouse, the color he favored on her. *Could it be a coincidence?*

He must have felt her eyes on him because he looked up and smiled. Standing, he pulled her into a warm embrace, holding her for a moment. The smell of his woodsy cologne and the warmth of his body against hers were intoxicating.

"I'm glad you came," he whispered as he stepped back from their embrace. He pulled the wooden straight-back chair away from the table for her. "I wasn't sure if you'd be hungry, so I took the liberty of ordering an appetizer for us to share."

The appetizer plate consisted of hummus, crudités, cheese, and crackers. The noise of the lunch crowd rumbled in the background. Banging from a renovation project clattered from the opposite side of the wall. Yet, over the clatter, Billie Eilish's "Birds of a Feather" found her, soothing her nervous energy. She placed her hands in her lap so Bill wouldn't see them tremble.

"Thanks, I can always nibble," she said, knowing it would take her a minute to steady her hands.

"Look, Kari, I'll get right to it. I owe you an apology for how I acted years ago."

"I—"

"Please, I need to say this now or I never will." He paused and began again. "I'm sorry for not talking to you or even trying. My silence was childish, and I've regretted it for years."

She looked away from him, intent to remain composed. Three young men walked into the back room dressed in khakis and button-down shirts, chatting as they grabbed the next table. She squeezed her hand into a fist, then released it.

Turning back to him, she said, "Why did you just walk out on me? I thought we meant more to each other than that. Geez, we had been together for three solid years, during the hardest time of our lives."

Bill leaned into the table closer to her. He ran his fingers through his hair and said, "I know. Our relationship meant everything to me. It still does. I've never forgotten us."

He took her hand, softly holding it in both of his warm, gentle hands. Like he had always done.

She shook her head and said, "You have a funny way of showing it. You never contacted me. Not even once to see if I was okay. You blew off my texts and calls as though I never meant anything to you. It was mean."

She retracted her hand as she struggled to hold back years of tears and frustration. He'd made her feel like rubbish to be tossed aside on a whim. Jimmy had said it showed how he felt about her. Trust had been broken. Kari had a hard enough time trusting people. Regaining her trust after it had been broken may be impossible.

"I know, and that was never my intention. I loved you so much, Kari. I intended to propose. I had been ring shopping with Phil just a week before. I wanted to wait for the right time to pop the question. Formally introduce you to my family, do all the things people do during that exciting time in their lives. Then came your navy news. I felt like you didn't care about us. You never even discussed any of it with me. I assumed our relationship must have meant more to me than you. Otherwise, how could you make that choice? You had to know a navy career would strain us or end us. You didn't seem to care. You just dropped me and went for it. My ego was shattered."

Her foot tapped nervously. Palms sweaty. She hated this sort of stuff. Growing up, no one in her family had discussed their feelings. She twisted in her seat, uncomfortable, as anger rose quickly.

"Nice, so now I'm the villain? Do I need to apologize for your bad behavior? I won't, you know. I have no intention of blaming myself for your horrible, callous actions, so don't even try to make this seem like something I did to us. You chose to cut us off. *You* did that."

"I'm not trying to gaslight you or blame you."

"Sure as hell feels like it," she said, her arms clasped tightly around her chest. "At least I tried to contact you. Tried to talk about things."

"I just mean to say that it took me off guard. I thought we both wanted the same thing. To stay in Maine, get married, build our careers and family. I didn't know how to handle the fact that you would be leaving for an entirely different life without me."

She knew she had made the decision for both. The prospect of marrying and having kids scared her. So much of a woman's role as a wife and mother had been predetermined by societal norms. She never wanted to be placed in the narrow box of domesticity. Forced to put her family's needs ahead of her own at every turn. As their relationship had deepened and grown toward the logical next step of marriage, she'd become increasingly uncomfortable, the way a caged animal must feel.

Even though Bill had been supportive of her career goals, she'd known everything related to home and hearth would eventually fall on her. She'd also known she lacked a role model for being a wife and mother. Her mother's choices had been something Kari had desperately avoided. The decision to take the navy job had made her feel powerful again. It had also allowed her to test his feelings for her. She shifted in her seat, uncomfortable with the realization.

"We could have continued to talk and see each other while I served. You didn't even want to try. You just ended everything with a wall of silence," she said. She wanted to add that she felt like he'd thrown her out like trash, but remained silent.

"I know. It was childish. We could have tried. I don't know if it would have been enough for us. We were inseparable during law school. Distance might have killed us."

"Yes, you are right about that. I saw several colleagues struggling to keep relationships intact as they began their naval careers. It seemed difficult at best. But you never even gave us a chance."

She picked up a few olives and crackers. She needed to calm her racing mind.

"Kari, we could pick up from where we left off. I still love you very much. More than you could imagine. I've always loved you."

Despite her best efforts, tears streamed down her cheeks, the emotion finally gushing out. Bill stood, pulled her close to him, and whispered gently, "I'm so sorry I hurt you, Kari. I'm so sorry I hurt us."

She relaxed into him, placing her head on the side of his chest. They stood so close during the embrace that their hips touched. Her mind traveled to the area of her body unearthing long-buried memories of their intimacy. Remembered images merged with the feel of his body.

"You really hurt me. I'm not sure I can trust you again. What if something else happens and you decide to just walk away from me without a single word? Who even does that?" *Or what if I make choices that suit me, and you once again throw us away?*

"I won't. I promise. If you give me a second chance, I'll be everything you need in a man. Always here for you, steady and kind."

They stood joined for another minute, finally breaking apart as her device chimed an alarm.

"I guess some things never change." He laughed. They sat back down.

Kari had always used the alarms on her device to make sure she left each calendar event on time for the next. Over the course of the day, as many as ten alarms chimed. She found her system to be comforting, as though she had a very competent assistant.

"Crap. I need to head out to interview a potential witness in the Stadt case. I have a ten-minute cushion to get to my car and start the drive or I'll be late."

He turned to her and said, "Stadt? You mean the guy they pulled out of the harbor?"

"Sure is. He volunteered as a board member for the Town of Sweetwater. Apparently everyone hated him because he refused to vote in favor of the casino project. Maybe not everyone, but enough."

"Interesting. You mean the Magellion Group's interest in loading up the old harness-racing place with slot machines?"

She turned to look at him, wondering how he knew the name of the casino people. The Magellion Group's name had stayed out of the public light, something they preferred. The New Jersey company worked in the shadows, as far as Kari could tell.

"How do you know about the Magellion . . . ?"

"Are you guys finished with this table?" the curly-haired brunette asked.

"Yep, it's all yours. Let me just grab these out of the way," said Bill.

He scooped up their food and drink dishes. Kari waited for him to place everything in the bin. "Ready?" she asked, letting the question drop.

"Yep. Let's get out of here," he said. He placed a hand on the middle of her back as she walked past him, her mind fixated on his touch.

Once outside she turned to him. Unsure how to end their meeting. She shifted from foot to foot, needing to bolt, yet wanting to stay.

"I'll tell you about the case later."

"There's going to be a later? I like the sound of that." He smiled and winked. His beautiful, dimpled cheeks looked rosy and healthy, as always.

She smiled, kissed him on the cheek, and dashed away.

Chapter 32

Kari thrummed the steering wheel, trying to focus on the interview she had scheduled with Reed MacIntry, a Sweetwater town board member. Bright sunlight bounced off the dash, nearly blinding her as she merged onto the highway. The grimy front window of her car further obscured her view. "Damn it," she murmured as she struggled to find her sunglasses.

A few minutes later she exited the highway, entering the small town of Sweetwater. The board members lived in the town as required for their position. Visiting each of them on a Saturday seemed like a better idea than interrupting their workday. She had made an appointment with Reed but had not for the others. She wanted to streamline her efforts as she sought to find a plausible alternative to Stacy for Greg's death. Stacy's defense hinged on her crafting a more favorable interpretation of the facts. Maybe someone on the board did him in? Who knew. Her mind returned to her telephone calls with Rod Pieters, Greg's best friend. Something about that man made her skin crawl. She made a mental note to investigate him further after she turned the soil on the board.

Her GPS chimed, announcing a right turn into a new neighborhood. The colonial homes, so typical of Maine, had been placed far apart from one another. Each homeowner enjoyed the comfort of space from their neighbors. The heavily treed lots and set-back homes looked like the postcard of the American dream.

Finding number thirty-six, she pulled in front of the house and turned off the car. A couple of moms pushing strollers walked past her as they chatted. The babies sat upright, alert to their surroundings. The screeching sound of several blue jays caught her attention. One of them sat on a bough of the massive blue spruce at the end of the MacIntry driveway. Its blue feathers contrasted with the deep green of the tree.

As she walked up the driveway, the garage door opened. A tall, athletic-looking man in his mid-thirties pulled out a lawn mower, oblivious to Kari. Before he could pull the cord, she yelled, "Hey! Hi, I'm Kari Sharpe. Are you Reed MacIntry?"

He turned to look in her direction. "Geez, I didn't see you walking up the drive. Sorry about that. Sure am. Call me Reed."

His broad smile and youthful good looks caught Kari off guard for a second. She had expected a more average person from his picture in the town hall. She closed the gap between them, extended her hand, and said, "Please call me Kari. And thanks for meeting with me, especially on a Saturday. I won't keep you long."

He leaned his muscular build against a shiny red BMW X7. The vehicle in the third bay was a newish Honda Odyssey minivan. Nice, but nowhere near the flash of the BMW.

"Nice ride," she said.

He jutted his chin back and said, "A boy needs his toys."

"I just have a few questions."

"Shoot."

"How long have you been a board member in Sweetwater?" she asked.

She hadn't brought a pad of paper for their meeting, preferring to appear casual, even if there was nothing casual about defending someone accused of murder.

"I've been there a little over four years."

"Why did you choose to run for the position?"

"I'm a Realtor, and I thought it would be a good gig for the contacts. You know, keep up with what's happening in the town, maybe get first dibs on properties coming open. Marketing, basically."

"Has it been a good gig?"

He whistled, ran a hand through his hair, and said, "It's been amazing. Better than I could have imagined."

Kari assumed he meant that he had received bribes from people in the town and outside of it to grease the wheels of various projects. Everyone had known this happened in the town, but no one seemed to care enough to stop the corruption. As long as things ran properly, the Sweetwater citizens went on with their lives without putting much thought into local governance.

"Has the board's composition changed much over your years on it?" she asked.

She needed to steer away from the corruption for now.

"No, not at all. It has been the same group since I started. It's a motley bunch, but we get things done."

He sidestepped toward the lawn mower. "You don't mind if I just check on this, do you?" he said, pointing to it.

"Not at all, please go ahead."

The gas cap creaked as he twisted it open. He dunked the gauge in it a few times to check its fuel levels.

"What can you tell me about your fellow board members?" she asked.

He had walked away from her, into the darkened interior of the garage. A moment later he emerged carrying a red gas can.

"Well, let's see . . . Greg is dead, but was a real pain in the ass. Margaret and Archie are the old-timers. They've both been on the board for decades. At this point, Margaret tells Archie how to vote, and he does it. Lori Spec is the newest member. She works at Maine Medical Center. From what I can tell, she is a true concerned citizen, wanting to do what she can for the town. A real gem on the board."

"How so?"

"She was the only one who could manage to get through to Greg. All sorts of initiatives passed because of her. Otherwise, Greg would vote against the board at every turn. At times it became a real annoyance. Especially to Margaret. She always liked to run a tight ship. Get things done, that sort of thing."

"I met with Margaret at the town's offices. She seems very knowledgeable about the town."

He finished filling the tank and put the can down. "Margaret knows everything about the town and everyone in it. Nothing happens around here without her involvement. Believe me. I made sure she's my ally."

"Is the casino initiative one of those things Greg wouldn't budge on?" Kari asked, despite knowing the answer.

The door to the house opened and then slammed shut. An adolescent boy who looked around thirteen walked out. He was the spitting image of his father, in a crisp white baseball uniform.

"You about done, Dad? I have to go to practice."

"Almost, dude. Give me another five minutes and we'll head out. Okay? Go grab a water bottle while you wait," Reed said, ruffling the boy's glossy dark hair.

"Oh yeah. I forgot it." The boy turned and ran back into the house, slamming the door behind him.

Reed smiled at Kari and said, "Sorry about the door slamming. No matter how many times I tell those rug rats not to do it, they do. It drives my wife crazy. To answer your question, yes. The casino project was huge. I wanted the pool that had been promised by the Magellion Group, you know, the casino company. Heck, we all wanted to green-light the project, everyone except Greg. He wanted to watch the Downs fail and grab the real estate for development. We all knew it. The guy would not budge no matter what anyone did or said. Lori said she'd meet with him one last time to try and convince him to vote in favor of the measure. I'm guessing they never met."

Before Kari could ask another question, the door to the house swung open again. This time a little girl emerged with a yellow Lab. The dog lazily wagged its tail as it walked over to greet Kari. The skinny girl wore shorts and a Bluey T-shirt. The corners of her lips were rimmed with red from a sugary drink.

Kari leaned over to pat the dog. His blond fur flew off him as she ran her hand across his broad back. In response, the dog leaned his large, warm body against her leg.

"Take Fenway back in the house and get your shoes on. We need to leave for your brother's practice."

The little girl grabbed Fenway's collar with her tiny hand and pulled him away from Kari. "I don't want to go. It's boring," she protested.

"Just go," he said. Turning back to Kari, he added, "Kids, what are you gonna do?"

"I've kept you for far too long," said Kari. The last thing she wanted would be to burn a bridge with him, especially given how much information he'd shared. She pulled out a business card from the pocket of her capri pants and handed it to him. "If you think of anything else, please contact me."

"Sure thing," he said, looking at the card and nodding. He laughed and added, "Hopefully I'll never need your professional services for myself or either of those knuckleheads." He yanked his thumb in the direction of the house as he spoke.

The driveway sloped downhill toward the street. She walked its length, admiring the perfectly manicured lawns. A few of the homeowners had chosen to install two-foot-high granite walls into the slope of their front yards. An elegant, expensive landscaping feature reserved for the nicest Maine homes. The deep scent of warm pine carried in the air.

Kari drove her vehicle a short distance out of his neighborhood and found a quiet place to pull over. She wanted to make a few notes from their conversation before she forgot the precious details he had shared.

Everyone on the board hated Greg for not voting to approve the casino. But hated him enough to drug him? And then drown him? She shook her head and exhaled sharply. *Maybe the obvious answer is that*

Stacy finally did him in and the cops grabbed the right person. The thought had occurred to her more than once.

Her phone chimed, announcing a text message. She dug it out of her messy Tory Burch top-handle bag and looked at the screen: Bill. She smiled and glanced out the window.

I know this is last minute, but you free for a drink later? Maybe around 8 pm?

She put her phone into the cup holder with a thunk. Nope. Sorry, pal. This won't be that easy. Although she wanted to see him, she intended to play the game. Make him work a little. Delay her responses to his messages. Maybe be unavailable when he asked for a date. Make him wonder whom she spent her time with.

She texted Jimmy instead of responding to Bill. You free for dinner? I could grab a pie and bring it to your place.

He texted back almost immediately. Yep, get extra toppings. Don't be a cheapskate.

She smiled and gave his response the thumbs-up. Jimmy had been doing much better after his accident. His arm had begun to heal beautifully, even without his full participation in physical therapy. He had been steadily working with his Alcoholics Anonymous sponsor and attended online meetings as he recuperated.

Then she texted Bill. Sorry. Busy tonight. How about brunch tomorrow at Becky's?

Sounds great. 11?

She gave him the thumbs-up, placed her phone back in her purse, and pulled out of the parking spot. Less than ten minutes later, she drove into Lori Spec's neighborhood. The beautiful, newly constructed neighborhood made Kari wonder if she should move from her small home in Portland to the suburbs. When she chose the house, the

Realtor had referred to it as "quaint." After moving in, she'd discovered that "quaint" must've been another way of saying decrepit. The endless cost of repairs, not to mention the hassle of scheduling a parade of handymen for the work, depressed her.

She found Lori Spec's home quickly, parking in front of it on the street. Turning off her car, she yawned, tired from her morning run. One last interview, the rest could wait a day or so. She needed to dash back to the office to draft a couple of motions before she would officially feel ready to start the weekend. Thoughts of meeting with Bill tomorrow morning for brunch drifted through her mind.

After slamming the door behind her, she walked up to the stately home. The neighborhood was not as high end as the one she'd just left, but still very nice. The homes were large, but not sprawling like in MacIntry's cul-de-sac. It had no large trees lining the street or entry. Instead, small new trees had been recently planted along the neighborhood's streets.

She rang the bell and waited. Nothing. She rang it again and stood back, waiting. Glancing at her wristwatch, she started to walk away, cursing herself for not making an appointment to meet with Lori Spec.

Suddenly the door flew open. "What is it? I'm trying to watch the game. And if you're trying to sell me something, skip it. I'm not buying."

The angry man held one hand on the doorframe and the other on the door as he spoke. He wore a grungy, loose-fitting T-shirt and basketball shorts. The entire ensemble looked slept in.

Kari took a step toward him and stretched her hands out wide. "No worries here, I'm definitely not selling anything. My name is attorney Kari Sharpe. I represent Stacy Stadt. I'm here to speak with Lori Spec about her work on the town board."

His face reddened under the thick coating of stubble. He took a menacing step toward her. "Is this some sort of damned joke? Why the hell are you really here? To harass me?" His entire body coiled, ready to pounce.

"I assure you I'm not here to harass you, but to merely speak with Ms. Spec. Is she your spouse?" Kari asked, hesitating. From the look on his face, she had no idea if he would slam the door or punch her. Either way, she needed to defuse the situation.

"Yeah, she's my damned wife. She took our daughter and left. Just like that. Not a word from her. She just left. If you find her, tell her I'm looking for her, and when I find her, our daughter is mine. She'll never see Mary again. And if her nosy sister is behind this, you can tell her to go to hell! She'll get what's coming to her."

He slammed the door in her face. Better than the alternative. Kari walked back to her car quickly. She could hardly wait to get away from him.

A teenager lazily rode her bike past Kari, then circled around and headed back toward her. Her eyes darted between Kari and the Spec house. As she approached Kari, she started to slow down, then looked at the house again. She bit her lip and fiddled with her handlebar pads as she slowly stopped.

"Are they gone? Like gone for good?" she asked Kari as she approached. The young woman hunched into her handlebars and popped her gum as she spoke. Greasy hair hung around her face, obscuring her eyes.

"Who?"

"Mrs. Spec and Mary. I babysit for Mary but haven't been asked in a while. And I don't see Mrs. Spec's car anymore."

Kari hadn't anticipated that one of the board members would go missing.

"I really have no idea," she said. The young woman in front of her couldn't have been more than fourteen, yet the dark circles under her eyes, unkempt hair, and slumped shoulders made her look older. Before Kari could say anything, the garage door to the house across the street opened.

The young woman's eyes darted to the home. She popped her gum and said, "I've gotta go. See ya."

"See ya."

Kari got back into her car and started the engine. Before she could take off, a loud tapping on the side window startled her, making her jump slightly. A woman leaned over to meet Kari eye to eye. She smiled and waved at Kari slightly, beckoning her to open the window.

"Hi, I'm Peg Wilter, Kimmy's mom. Can I help you with something? I saw you talking to my daughter." The redheaded woman looked far too young to have a teenager. Unlike her daughter's, Peg's face shone with health, leisure, and youth.

"Maybe. I'm Kari Sharpe. I'm an . . ."

"Yes. I know. I've seen you on TV. You're the lady lawyer who wins. Are Lori and Mary okay? We've been worried about them."

Kari shifted in her seat, turning toward Peg. "Why would you be worried?"

Just like her daughter, Peg glanced up to the Spec house nervously. "Well, you see, they have a history. I hate to be a gossip, but we all think he beats her. She'd have bruises from 'falling' one too many times, if you get my drift." Her eyebrows jutted skyward as she spoke in a low conspiratorial tone.

Peg tapped the edge of Kari's door as she spoke.

"Her husband said she left. Where would she go if she had left? Do you know?" asked Kari.

Peg straightened herself, placed her hands on her hips. "Beats me. Maybe her sister's house?" She leaned in closer. "I'm actually wondering if he killed Lori and Mary," she whispered. "The guy is terrible. He's mean to everyone around here. He even told one of the kids to 'go to hell' when she tried to sell Girl Scout cookies to him. I hate to be a gossip, you know, but he really is a jerk. Poor Lori and, my gosh, Mary. What a sweet child."

Peg glanced back to the house and then to Kari. She added, "I've said way too much. Last thing I need is to get tangled with that guy. My husband warned me not to get involved with them. We wouldn't even let Kimmy sit for Lori unless we knew for sure Bruce would be gone from the house the entire time."

"When was the last time she sat for Lori?"

"That I can answer easily. Kimmy was over there the night before they pulled that guy out of the harbor. Well, you know, he was also a town board member," she said as though revealing a precious jewel of information. "It really makes me wonder about this town. But, you know, I don't want to gossip or anything. I thought something happened because Kimmy was later than I expected. Lori had always been so punctual. I was exhausted from waiting up for Kimmy; well, you know, mothers always worry about their kids."

"Are you sure about the date? Maybe Kimmy sat for Lori another night that same week?" asked Kari.

"I'm positive. I was late meeting with my morning walking group because I was so exhausted from waiting up for Kimmy. Rebecca, the organizer of the group, made a point of making me look bad for being late, right on the group text. Can you imagine? Right on the group text."

"Do you still have the text?" asked Kari.

Peg straightened and pulled her phone out of her back pocket. Her eyes narrowed as she scrutinized the text chain. "Of course. Here it is. Rebecca can be such a rude snob at times," she said in a huff. She extended the phone to Kari.

The date matched the day Greg was pulled from the harbor, just as Peg had said.

Before Kari could ask another question, the door to the Spec home flew open with a loud bang. "Mind your own damned business for a change, Peg!" he shouted from the doorway. "Go home. No one cares what you think, you nosy gossip!"

Peg turned from Bruce to Kari, rolled her eyes, and said, "See what I mean? That guy's a real jerk. Not like I was gossiping or anything." She started to walk away from Kari and then seemed to think better of it. "Can I have your card? My husband will never believe I met you. Neither will my book club. We don't get many famous people on our block."

Kari gave her a card and jotted down Peg's contact information.

"Can I contact you if I have follow-up questions?" asked Kari.

"Sure, why not," said Peg over her shoulder as she jogged back to her house.

Finally, a breakthrough. If Kari could convince a jury that Lori, not Stacy, had been the last person with Greg, maybe she would raise enough reasonable doubt to clear Stacy of the charges. She thought Greg's death had to be related to the casino and his work on the board. She just needed to prove it.

Chapter 33

The next morning Kari walked along Commercial Avenue to meet Bill for brunch at Becky's Diner. Becky's had been a Portland staple for as long as Kari remembered. They were known for their tall stacks of blueberry pancakes, coffee, and scrambled eggs. Perfect for any day of the week, but especially on a lazy Sunday.

Becky's had never taken reservations. On the weekend the line for a table stretched down Commercial Avenue. Everyone knew the wait would be worth the reward.

Kari glanced down the line, searching for Bill. He stood near enough to the front that Kari suspected he had been waiting for at least thirty minutes. Walking up to him, she placed a hand on his arm and said, "Hey there, thanks for doing the heavy lifting in line."

He leaned toward her, kissing her on both cheeks. When they had been a couple, he'd always greeted her with a kiss on the lips. He brushed his hand down the length of her arm. "You look fantastic. It's nice to see you."

They stood awkwardly side by side until Bill broke the silence. "Are you having a good weekend?" he asked.

"Yep, it's been relaxing and productive. I worked yesterday morning, just half a day, then took the rest of the night off."

She left out that she had spent the evening with her brother. Instead, she let her comment hang in the air, leaving him to wonder whom she had spent Saturday night with.

"Working on a Saturday? You aren't in New York anymore, Kari. We don't work on Saturdays in Maine. Heck, most attorneys don't even bother working on Friday afternoons in the summer. I don't. My sailboat calls my name around eleven a.m., and that's when I clock out."

Kari shuffled uncomfortably from one foot to the next. Looking down at her feet and then toward the street. Of course Bill could afford to walk out of the office midday on Fridays. He had a guaranteed income for life. Something she would never have.

Clearing her throat, she stood a little straighter and looked at him. His facial features were relaxed, tanned, completely free of malice.

"Are you still at the Falmouth Yacht Club?" she asked, although she knew the answer.

Bill's great-grandfather had been the first member of their family to be asked to join the prestigious, expensive sailing club. Every member of Bill's family had learned to sail as they'd grown up, living the country club life in Falmouth. During law school, Bill had taken her to the club on a few race nights. She had felt completely out of place, wearing black sneakers, jeans, and a concert T-shirt while the preppy audience of wealthy individuals had sipped champagne and watched the J/Boats racing in Casco Bay. Although Bill had tried to put her at ease, Kari had fumbled. Unsure of how to act in their company.

"Of course. At this point our family has a legacy membership," he said proudly. He placed his hand on her back as they moved forward. The soft feel of her brushed linen blouse kissed her skin under the warmth of his steady touch.

"I'd love to take you to dinner there. See my family, maybe join race night?"

As they had moved into the shade of the building, he took off his Ray-Bans, enabling her to see his beautiful blue eyes.

"I'd like that, but I won't be used as ballast again. I'll sip champagne on the shore with the other spectators." She laughed.

Finally, they made their way to the front of the line. A stout, sturdy-looking woman in her late fifties stood behind the reception lectern. "How many?" she asked them abruptly.

"Two."

"Follow me," she said without a glance in their direction.

The scent of Maine maple syrup mixed with the comforting aroma of coffee and freshly grilled pancakes. Kari's stomach rumbled in response. Every table was full in the simple, no-nonsense establishment. Formica tables were covered with plates, coffee cups, and tumblers of juice. Hungry patrons slathered butter on their stacks of pancakes. A toddler banged the tray of her high chair with a lidded cup.

The waitress ran her less-than-clean rag over the vinyl bench of a booth in the back of the restaurant and placed plastic-covered, smudged menus on the table. "Coffee?" she asked.

"Yes, two, please, and two orange juices," said Bill.

The waitress walked away quickly without a reply.

Bill turned to Kari and said, "Sorry, I know you can order for yourself, but in this place you've gotta strike while the iron is hot."

Kari smiled and tugged a napkin out of the silver holder. "I get it. They're always so jammed on the weekends. I have no idea how they manage." She wiped the table with the napkin, pushing a few crumbs off the side.

"How's your practice going? I think it's amazing that you hung out your own shingle."

Bill had neither had to hang his own shingle nor seek a competitive position with a law firm. After passing the bar exam, he had taken three months off to travel Europe and then joined his father in the law firm his grandfather founded.

"Thanks. It's been going great. It was a little rocky in the beginning, but then things picked up for me."

"Of course they did. Your win last year with the young sailor must've sent your client list into orbit. You were the talk of the town," he said. His face reddened as he spoke. "I followed you from a distance, not sure if I should reach out. I've been—"

The waitress roughly placed their drinks on the table and said, "Ready to order?"

"I'd like the short stack of blueberry pancakes with the potato hash," said Kari.

"Same for me but I'll do the tall stack."

The waitress walked away from them without a word. The line cook rang the bell and shouted an order number for another member of the staff to pick up. Then a family with two small kids walked past. The boy stomped his little light-up shoes as he walked, turning them on with each step.

"Yes. The media really helped me. But you know how it is. Everything we do is piecemeal. For every case that ends, we need a replacement, or our client list will dwindle. It was the same in a big firm, but everyone shared the load, keeping the lights on. Even if one attorney's client list decreased, the other attorneys held everything together."

He sipped his coffee, watching her as she spoke. She shifted in her seat, slightly uncomfortable under his gaze. Bill had a way of watching her with so much intensity that at times she felt overexposed.

"Maybe representing Stacy Stadt will do the same thing for your practice," he said.

"Maybe. We'll see," she said, shrugging her shoulders.

He leaned across the table and asked, "How's it going? You think you have a workable defense?"

She sighed and looked out the window toward the harbor. Locals and tourists strolled in the sunshine, stopping at the various tables along the walkway to view handmade crafts.

"I might have something. One of the Sweetwater town board members left town the day they found the body. It seems too coincidental to not be something. And then there's the Magellion Group. Maybe they played a role in his death? I'm still putting things together."

He leaned back into the bench seat and said, "Magellion Group? You think they would have killed Greg? Seems like a stretch to me."

"Who knows. They're a New Jersey–based casino business. Those guys are used to playing hardball. It wouldn't be hard to convince a jury that the big bad out-of-state casino company did it." She glanced at the food on a nearby table. "You know how criminal defense is. I just need to toss around enough alternate facts to create a shadow of doubt."

The waitress placed their food on the table, then pushed the plates roughly in front of them. "Anything else?"

"Nope. We're good," said Bill.

She scribbled something on her pad, ripped off a sheet of paper, and slapped it on the table. "Pay at the front."

After she walked away, Kari and Bill looked at each other and laughed. Picking up her fork, Kari said, "Normally I prefer a place with better service, but damn, these are the best pancakes. Look at all the blueberries. Yum." She drenched her stack in thick syrup and shoved a forkful into her mouth.

Bill had done the same and said, "Seriously good." His words somehow broke through the pancakes he chewed on. "I had no idea you'd returned to Maine. Then I saw you on the news. You looked so amazing, so intelligent and in control of the world. My heart skipped a beat."

She squeezed ketchup near her hash and said, "Yet you never reached out."

He frowned and looked out the window, then back to her. "I'm a coward. I thought you hated me and didn't want me to contact you. Seeing you in court gave me courage and a casual way to approach you."

She smiled. "I'm glad we're here. Together. Glad we reconnected."

"Me too. More than you know."

They devoured the rest of their brunch and walked back onto Commercial Avenue. His hand brushed her knuckles as they walked. One block later, he clasped her hand in his. She allowed the advance, even encouraged it by turning to him and smiling as she squeezed his hand.

Kari had been so focused on building her career that she had neglected this side of herself. The romantic part of her that yearned for the love, support, and connection of a partner. Online dating had been nothing but a chore she felt obligated to engage in.

She moved her thumb across the smooth skin of his hand. Glancing at him, she had no idea if he would break her heart again. Only time would tell. That afternoon she planned to enjoy everything he offered as the day turned to night, and night turned to morning.

Chapter 34

Ryker sat at his makeshift desk in the back of the casino in Bangor, Maine. The place had been nothing more than a run-down, sad event space. The threadbare rugs, shabby furnishings, and stale air had likely hosted numerous jittery brides over the years. Guests were treated to store-bought nacho chips and greasy meats from a buffet line. The place was pathetic. He lifted his head, rubbing the back of his tired neck. After the Magellion Group had invested in the building, it still looked somewhat tired, but far better than it had. Either way, Ryker hated it. He hated everything about Maine. The locals, food, weather, all of it. The sooner they opened the casino, the better.

His phone buzzed loudly. The annoying ringtone had been selected for only one person. Ignoring his calls would be deadly. Swiping the phone off the desk, he answered, "Yes, sir."

"How far away are we from installing machines at Sweetwater Downs?"

"I've been assured it will be on next . . ."

"You know what. Save it. I've heard all this before. The town-voting nonsense, next month it'll pass. On and on you keep saying the same thing with no results. And now not only do we have an unpredictable municipality, but thanks to you, Kari Sharpe has been nosing around my business interests."

Ryker leaned back into the executive office chair. "I'll take care of it, sir. Right away."

"You better. If it wasn't for your nonsense, this would have been solved. My partners and I are getting impatient. We've sunk a great deal of money into the business and need to see some return on our investment. Now. Or we'll bring in someone who can handle the mess you created."

The man hung up on him. Ryker gasped at the not-so-veiled threat. He had been in the business long enough to know that no one walked away from Magellion with a line on their résumé. "Prick," he muttered as he threw his phone down.

He poured himself a long drink of Clase Azul Reposado to steady his nerves. The crystal glass shook ever so slightly as he brought it to his lips, not bothering to swirl the ice cubes. Rolling the tequila around his mouth, he released its essence, allowing it to burn its way down the back of his throat.

There was no way around it. He needed to silence Kari Sharpe.

Chapter 35

The next morning, instead of heading to her office, Kari decided to take a drive to Sweetwater Downs. Her schedule had been jam-packed the rest of the week with numerous court appearances and client meetings. Today was her only available slot of time to speak with Beth Thornberry, the owner of the Downs.

The day promised to bring hot weather atypical of a Maine summer. She opened her window, allowing the cool morning air to breeze through her car. Yesterday's brunch with Bill had been wonderful. They'd continued the date by walking along the waterfront, eventually stopping at a café for a "real coffee." Becky's Diner had great food but very basic coffee. In many ways it felt like they had merely picked up where they left off so many years ago. She looked at her reflection in the rearview mirror. Smiling, she tucked her hair back behind her ear.

She drove past the whitewashed wooden signs of Sweetwater Downs. The faded green letters had been the same ones that were there when her father took her to the track on Sundays. With nothing to do while he drank, gambled, and smoked, she'd counted the letters in each sign, checking for differences.

After turning into the entrance, she slowed her speed so as not to kick up too much dust on the gravel and dirt road. Everything about the Downs was stuck in time. Even its owners had not changed. Instead, a new generation of Thornberrys had taken the helm. Grabbing her water bottle, she took a long, gulping drink.

Another vehicle pulled up beside her as she parked in front of the main barn, away from the visitors' entrance. A sturdy, self-assured man jumped down from the truck and strode over to her as she stepped out of the car. "Sorry, ma'am, the Downs is closed to the public today. We reopen on Thursday for the big race night."

"Thanks, but I'm not here to watch the races. I would like to speak with Beth Thornberry. Can you help me find her?" said Kari. She walked closer to the man and handed him her card. "I'm attorney Kari Sharpe."

He tipped her card to his ball cap and walked away, leaving Kari unsure if she should follow or wait. She decided to follow. The barn had a sharp, distinct aroma of fresh horse manure on hay. Kari knew the smell well. As a teen she'd supported her pot habit by mucking a neighbor's stalls. The five horses had loaded their stalls with crap every night. Kari had viewed the piles as pure gold. Gross, and the easiest money she'd ever made.

"Can I help you?"

Kari turned toward the voice. A woman in her mid-fifties with a gray pixie haircut stood waiting for Kari to reply. "Hi, are you Beth Thornberry?"

"Sure am. I understand you're a lawyer. Are you here from the bank? I told them I'd have the payment later this week," said Beth with a hint of annoyance.

"Oh gosh no. I represent Stacy Stadt. She's been charged with the murder of her husband, Greg Stadt."

Beth scuffed the heel of her well-worn cowboy boot on the rough wood of the barn floor. "I don't have time for this. All I can say is that Stacy did the world a favor. End of story. If that's all, I need to be getting back to work."

"Why would you say that?" asked Kari.

"All he wanted to do was run my business into the ground. He wouldn't listen to reason; he wouldn't participate in VIP days here or at any of the other casinos. No. All he wanted was to get his hands on my land. Now that he's gone, this place will survive."

"How can you be so sure?" asked Kari.

"Because the public wants slot machines; the town wants a pool and community center. Everyone wants the measure to pass, except one person. He was so stubborn at the board meetings. Even his fellow members rolled their eyes when he objected to the measure."

Kari glanced away from Beth into the barn, then back. "Would you say you're glad he's gone?"

Beth lifted her chin toward Kari, narrowed her eyes, and placed her hands on her hips. A flash of realization crossed her scrubbed face. "Nice try, but you aren't going to pin this on me. Your client killed her husband. End of story. Now leave. I have work to do."

Beth turned to walk away from Kari. A horse brayed and shook as a man walked it out into the paddock.

Kari said, "Would it surprise you to know that the coroner found bute in the victim's blood? Isn't that an anti-inflammatory used in veterinary medicine? On horses?"

Beth spun around. "How dare you suggest I had anything to do with it? Get out or I call the police," she yelled, jamming her finger in the air.

Kari smiled and held her hands up. "No problem. Just thought you'd find it as interesting as I do. That's all."

Once back in her car, Kari glanced at her watch; then she gulped down the rest of the water in her bottle. The cool beverage ran down her chin, dripping onto her lap. Something about the dust and horses in the barn really challenged her system. She coughed loudly and pulled out a mint.

The meeting had ended so quickly, she still had time to stop for a coffee and muffin before hitting the office. Good thing. She needed a little more caffeine to get her day rolling. Before she could pull out, a black Cadillac Escalade drove into the Downs and parked near the public entrance. A large cloud of dust from the fast-moving vehicle washed over the vast greens.

Beth had followed Kari to the parking lot. Beth then turned to greet the Escalade. As she approached, the driver got out, nodded toward her, and opened the back door. A man in slim-fitting black jeans stepped down and walked toward Beth. Kari had no idea what was said between them, but the conversation looked tense. The man pointed his finger in Beth's face, while Beth looked away, shaking her head like a scolded child. Then they stopped and turned toward Kari in unison.

"Time to go," she muttered to herself.

Pulling out of the parking spot, she drove slowly past them, noticing the New Jersey plate on his vehicle. She repeated the numbers out loud, committing them to memory. After driving the length of the entrance and exiting the property, she pulled over to scribble the letters and numbers on a scrap of paper.

Mack had said he would come into the office later that day. She planned to ask him to identify the driver of the Escalade. Glancing at the clock one more time, she decided to go to Maine Medical Center before getting her coffee and going to the office. With any luck Lori Spec's supervisor would know how to contact her.

Kari drove the short distance to Maine Medical Center. The sprawling campus had been the largest medical facility in southern Maine for years. Finding the last visitor parking spot, she pulled in, grabbed a notepad, and made her way to the entrance.

An ambulance's sirens roared as it screeched toward the emergency entrance. Its lights bounced off the tan exterior of the building as the noise of its siren echoed in the narrow area. The paramedics jumped out of the vehicle as it stopped, quickly rushing their patient into the emergency room. A team of nurses and doctors hurried to take over.

The automatic double doors opened with a whoosh as Kari approached. Once she entered the facility, an elderly man greeted her. "Welcome to Maine Medical Center. Can I help you with directions?"

"I would love that. I need to speak with someone in human resources."

She started to feel antsy as he went on and on describing every detail of the short walk to the human resources department. She cursed herself for engaging him. Should have looked at the damned directory instead.

The hospital smelled strongly of antiseptic and sickness. Soft music played throughout the building. Patients and their families congregated in the various waiting rooms she passed.

The human resource offices were at the back of the facility in a separate area, far removed from the business of healing.

"Hello, I'm attorney Kari Sharpe. I would like to speak with Lori Spec's supervisor," she said politely. She only knew Lori worked at Maine Medical. Nothing more.

"Sure thing, I'll call her down. Do you have an appointment?" asked the receptionist.

"No. I was hoping she'd be free for a quick chat."

The receptionist spoke on the phone in a chirpy tone. She hung up and said, "Please have a seat. She'll be right down."

Kari sat on one of three seats in the small waiting area. The usual collection of motivational posters favored by workplaces hung on the walls, right next to the required work-related signage about safety.

"Hi, I'm Lisa Jertz. Are you Attorney Sharpe?"

Kari turned to greet the friendly, tall woman. "Yes, I am. Thanks for coming down to meet with me. I represent Stacy Stadt in connection with the death of her husband, Greg Stadt. I understand Lori Spec and the victim worked together as board members in the town of Sweetwater. I haven't been able to find her and hoped you might be able to help me."

Lisa's eyes darted to the receptionist. She tugged at her ear. "Come on. Let's grab a room."

They walked quickly to a nearby small conference room. Lisa turned to Kari and said, "She didn't show up for work one day. She had been here for almost eleven years and then nothing. Not a call, nothing. Just never showed. I'm worried about her, as her friend."

"That's odd. I assume you've tried calling her?"

Lisa nodded. She placed her hands on the table and then clasped them tightly. "Of course, my calls go right to her voicemail. It's not like her. We've all worried about her safety so many times over the years."

Kari sat back in her chair and clicked her pen top. "Why?"

"She was a victim of domestic violence; we all knew it. She'd come in with bruising on her face, neck, arms. You name it. Poor thing. We all tried to help her, but she would insist everything was fine. Then she just disappeared." Lisa looked down at her lap, then back to Kari. She swiped a tear from her eye. "We're all hoping she left him for good this time."

"It had to be hard to see her pain and not be able to help. Hopefully she's safe. Uh . . . where would she go if she left? Any thoughts?"

Lisa dotted the corner of her eyes with a crumpled tissue. "Hold on. I brought her personnel record. Of course, for privacy reasons I can't disclose any information about her. However, as her friend, not supervisor, I can tell you she has a sister in New Hampshire," she said, trailing off. She flipped through the documents, closed the file, and said, "I've said far more than I should."

Kari peered at the personnel folder and said, "Was that her photo? In her file?"

"Sure is. She's just a wisp of a person. Very blond hair, petite, cute. Poor kid." Lisa shook her head as she opened the folder and looked at the photo.

Lori's picture on the wall in the Sweetwater town office had been taken in a different light than the one in front of her. Lori's hair looked like a deep dirty blond or soft brown in the town photo, yet in this picture her hair appeared several shades lighter, almost a platinum blond.

"You mind if I snap a picture of her photo? It could help our investigator to find her."

Lisa hesitated and looked toward the door. "Anything to help her. I can't imagine her caring about keeping the photo private. All of us have our HR pictures on our badges." She lifted her badge to show Kari.

Lisa's hand trembled slightly as she turned the picture to Kari. "We're all praying she's safe. It's all we can do for her now."

Lisa grabbed a tissue from the box and pressed the corner of her eyes, careful not to allow tears to run down her cheeks.

"I appreciate your help and will be in touch if I have anything to share about her whereabouts."

After she said her goodbyes, Kari quickly returned to her car. Sitting for a moment, she pulled out her phone and looked at the photo of Lori Spec. Lori and Stacy looked remarkably similar. The police had relied on eyewitness testimony identifying Stacy as fighting with Greg the night he died. They'd also placed Stacy on the boat with Greg using footage from a nearby business. Kari needed to scrutinize the security footage the prosecutors provided with their evidence. Maybe hire an expert to break down the footage. She also needed to find Lori. Immediately.

Chapter 36

Mack lingered in his small apartment most of the morning. Kari had asked him to find Lori Spec's sister. Lori Spec's maiden name had been Morse. Once he found her birth certificate, he used the names of her parents to search for a sibling. Bingo. Brenda Morse. A few clicks through the New Hampshire motor vehicle records resulted in a home address for Brenda in Derry, New Hampshire. She lived in the same home for over twenty years.

Lori had been a different story. His skip trace only managed to find her current address in Sweetwater, Maine. Not helpful. Based on Kari's interaction with Bruce Spec, he knew going to the address to speak with Bruce would prove to be a waste of time. Although it might be fun to rough the guy up a bit. The schmuck.

Instead, Mack decided to take the drive to New Hampshire to visit with Brenda. Maybe she would shed light on what had happened to Lori. But first he needed to call a buddy in the Maine State Troopers Office.

Mack had worked with Jason Klink for years before Jason left the Portland Police Department for the Maine State Troopers. Everyone had felt the loss when he'd left, particularly Mack.

Mack hit Jason's number on his favorites list and waited. Finally, he answered, "Hey, old-timer. You ready to come out of retirement? Do a real job?"

"Not a chance. I'm still in my pajamas, doing my job without a lick of government paperwork to fill out."

Jason laughed and said, "I get the feeling you aren't calling on a personal matter. What's up?"

"I work for the attorney who represents Stacy Stadt in the murder charges."

"Oh, right, Kari Sharpe. I saw an interview with her about the case in the paper. What can I do for you?"

"Would you mind running a name through the system? I need to know if a potential witness owns a car."

Mack gave Jason Lori Spec's name and waited. He scratched the stubble on the side of his face, making a rough sound. "Nice. Is that your face?"

"Sure is. I told you, I'm still in my pajamas."

A few minutes later Jason said, "Well, what do you know. We found her vehicle, a Toyota Camry, in the Kennebunk rest stop approximately seven weeks ago. We responded to a call from the toll operator, who thought someone needed help. Apparently the woman had been staring at the abandoned car for about a week before she called us. A true Good Samaritan."

"Did you guys have it towed?"

Mack heard multiple clicks.

"Looks like we contacted Bruce Spec about it. He was listed on the insurance card. He refused to come out. The field notes indicate Bruce had various colorful words to say about the vehicle and his wife, Lori. They towed it to the lot off Commercial."

"Interesting. Attorney Sharpe needs to speak with Lori Spec, the registered owner and possible victim of domestic violence. But it sounds like she ditched the vehicle and fled," said Mack.

"That's a good bet if you ask me. The system shows she had tried to get help from the Sweetwater guys, but none of them would assist. They marked it as 'domestic' and closed the inquiry, despite noting her obvious bruising. Looks like they handled it with real professionalism."

"Yikes. Sadly, I'm not surprised. Thanks, man. I appreciate your help."

"Anytime my friend, anytime."

After a quick shower and shave, Mack jumped in his Buick and drove west, to Derry, New Hampshire. He took small two-lane roads for most of the trip, enjoying the beautiful scenery. The temperature rose as he drove away from the cool, moist coastal breezes, into the interior of Maine and New Hampshire. Thick walls of massive trees lined the road. Pines, oaks, and maples mingled with beech trees, shielding the areas beyond the road from sight. In the fall, the drive had been a favorite of tourists looking for the ideal spot to see the fall colors.

Mack tapped his fingers against the steering wheel and sang along to Jimmy Buffett's "Margaritaville," thinking about his last date with Ruth. They had gone bowling together, spending the night eating fries and pizza while making fools of themselves as they tossed balls down the lanes. After several games they extended the date to ice cream on the boardwalk in Old Orchard Beach. The night had been perfect.

Nearly a year ago, after his divorce, they had had an affair. She'd wanted to get away from David, while Mack just wanted her. Ruth's company had soothed his postdivorce broken heart and loneliness. Maybe being with him had made her appreciate what she had at home, because she had broken things off just when he'd started to need her.

She had said she wanted to work on her marriage. Not make things worse. Now neither of them had a home front. Neither were married. The chemistry had been unmistakable from the first time they'd met in Kari's reception area. He'd felt drawn to her, like the invisible tug the ocean must feel from the moon. After she'd broken it off, the pull had become stronger. It had gotten so bad that at times he'd dreaded going to see Kari for fear he would make a fool of himself. Then David had died. Mack had waited cautiously on the sidelines for her grief to pass, but wanting all the while to start up with her again.

He'd wanted to make her his before anyone else swooped in. Yet he'd played it cool. Flirting without too heavy of a sexual undertone.

Complimenting without coming off as creepy. Then, finally, she'd given him a signal that she would entertain a date. He could not recall a time he had been more excited about anything. They'd planned to have lobster rolls at DiMillo's, a pierside restaurant close to Kari's office. He'd even bought a new shirt for the occasion. Since that afternoon, they had spoken on the phone numerous times per day and had gone out on more than one occasion.

He passed Pawtuckaway State Park. The drive was almost over. Thankfully. Although he enjoyed the scenery and alone time, he needed to get back and clean his apartment. Ruth had planned to come over this evening. The place looked like it had been ransacked by a squirrel or curious, untrained canine. If she saw the mess, Ruth might conclude, as his ex-wife had, that he was too much work.

The GPS chimed, alerting him to make a few more turns. Finally, pulling up in front of the navy-blue Cape Cod–style home, he surveyed his surroundings. Brenda looked like she lived a comfortable life. The yard had been well maintained. The front stoop was adorned with yellow pots full of colorful flowers. Two red Adirondack chairs sat near the deep-purplish-blue hydrangeas in the beds. An American flag fluttered in the breeze.

He knocked on the front door and waited, hoping Brenda would be home and willing to engage. A rustling from inside and then the curtain pulled back. He waved slightly and smiled. A brunette woman stood looking at him. "Hi, can I help you?" she asked as she opened the door.

"Yes. I'm Mack Bowen. I'm a private investigator hired by attorney Kari Sharpe. Are you Brenda Morse?"

The woman stiffened when he announced his occupation. She stepped slightly back into the house and closed the door a few inches, holding the edge of it like a shield. "Who sent you? I don't have anything to say to an investigator."

"Sorry, ma'am. I don't mean to alarm you. Are you Brenda Morse?"

The woman looked like she would either cry, scream, or slam the door in his face. Mack wanted to put her at ease.

"I am. Why?" she said flatly.

"We're searching for Lori Spec, your sister. Her vehicle has been found at the Kennebunk rest stop in Maine. Do you happen to know where I can find her?"

Brenda's grip tightened on the edge of the door. Her face turned into a scowl. "You can tell Bruce to go to hell. He'll never see her again. She's long gone," she shouted and slammed the door shut.

"That went well. On to plan B," Mack muttered as he walked back to his car.

A car rolled slowly past the house and pulled into the next driveway. The young female driver looked at him as she stepped out of her vehicle.

Plan B involved a hopefully short stakeout of Brenda's home. Either she would lead Mack to Lori or Lori would visit her sister. If Lori had fled her husband, going to her only relative in New England made the most sense. She'd show up eventually.

A few hours later, Mack had acquired enough snacks, drinks, and reading material to keep him going throughout the stakeout. The evening would be boring as hell. Cracking open his first bag of chips, he reclined his seat slightly, glad for the cushy, old-school-style seats of his LeSabre.

Time passed at an astonishingly slow pace as he waited for something, anything, to change. Just as he planned to call it a night, a car pulled into the driveway. He snatched up his binoculars and watched as a petite blonde got out of the driver's side and pulled a child out of the back seat. They walked together to the front door, where the woman tapped, then walked inside.

"Gotcha."

Roughly twenty minutes later, the woman he suspected to be Lori Spec drove out of the development to a condo building nearby. He took numerous pictures of her vehicle and the development before setting a pin to be sure he nailed the location. Lori and her child walked a short flight of stairs to her unit and then disappeared inside.

Kari had asked him not to approach her. She feared Lori would flee if she thought her husband had found her. "Let's hope her sister doesn't spook her into running," said Mack to the empty car. He rubbed his tired eyes, thinking about his next move.

He glanced at his watch. Seven o'clock, plenty of time to make it back to his place for the night. He dialed Ruth and waited for her to answer. With any luck they'd chat away his ride back to Old Orchard Beach.

Chapter 37

Kari pushed herself the last quarter mile of her run. Her legs burned in protest. Anxiety drained from her body as her heart pumped, the faster, the better. On the last few hundred feet of the run, she slowed her pace to walk the rest of the distance to her home. A cooldown, long stretch, and a hot shower were her rewards for the effort. That and Thai food.

The bag of food sat waiting for her after she finished showering. Perfect. She grabbed it, not bothering to take it to the kitchen. Instead, she sat on the couch in front of the TV and dug in, pouring the rich panang curry directly into the rice container. The delicately spiced curry ran down the sides of her cheeks as she devoured it.

Her watch buzzed with an incoming call. She glanced at it: Bill. Although she wanted to speak with him, she had not eaten all day. He would have to wait.

Finally, after finishing, she called him back. "Hey, what's up? I saw you called?"

Light classical played in the background, Bill's favorite. "Hold on. Let me lower it down." A few seconds later he said, "Not much. Just calling to say hi. Did you go out for a run?"

She stacked the nearly empty containers of food and walked into the kitchen, "Of course I did. It's my nightly ritual. Keeps me sane. Sometimes I think it's the only thing that does."

"It always has, even in law school. I never knew how you did it. All that running, I mean. It seems exhausting to me. How's work going?"

She shoved the bag and empty rice container in the trash, then grabbed a large glass of water. "Pretty good. I think I might have the beginning of a workable defense for Stacy Stadt. I just need to nail down a few things."

"Sounds fascinating. Do tell."

His chair creaked as he waited for her to speak. Bill preferred the Stressless line of furniture for lounging. At those prices, the thing should not make a peep, she thought.

"Well, turns out Lori Spec, one of the Sweetwater board members, left town the day Greg was pulled out of the harbor. It's just too much of a coincidence, if you ask me. I think there's something there."

"Maybe. Did they know each other well? Other than their work on the board?"

Kari leaned against the ancient Formica countertop in her kitchen. "I'm not sure. I do know that the board used Lori to make Greg vote along with the group on various issues. Apparently she had met with him to talk about his vote on the casino issue the night he died."

"Geez. You think *she* did it?"

"Beats me, but I don't have to prove that. I just need to give a jury enough reasonable doubt to acquit Stacy or convince the prosecutor to dismiss the case. Offer an alternative to convicting my client. You know the drill."

She walked back to her small family room. The television had been muted, but the images continued to play the drama she watched.

"Didn't you mention Greg had been poisoned with some horse tranquilizer?"

"Yeah, it's called bute. Why?"

"Does Lori have access to it? Is she into horses or a veterinarian?"

His attention to the details of her case struck her as odd. Attorneys spoke with each other about their cases, but usually, at least for her, the details never really stayed. Instead, they'd act like soundboards for each other and then quickly forget the matter until the next conversation. Yet he remembered.

"I'm not sure. But Beth Thornberry does. She's the owner of Sweetwater Downs. I think she's in thick with the casino people."

"You mean the Magellion Group? Why so?"

Something about his questioning felt forced, strained. As though he had an agenda for asking the questions. She looked out the front windows, considering what to say.

"I just have a hunch," she said, leaving the details behind. She stretched her legs out onto the sofa and asked, "Enough about Stacy's case. How's your work? Is your dad retiring anytime soon?"

Bill sighed, then said, "Nothing will ever get George to retire. Especially knowing his lazy son would be taking over the reins. No way. He'll stay until the day he dies and then float around just to watch what I'm doing."

"I'd probably haunt you, too, if you took over my firm." She stifled a yawn. "I'd better get going. I think the day and my run are catching up with me."

"Okay. You sound beat. When will I see you again? I'd like to take you to the White Barn in Kennebunk."

She had never been to the expensive restaurant, but knew Bill's family often used it for events. Yawning again, she rubbed her eyes and said, "Sounds nice. Let's chat later in the week to pick a date."

"Sounds like a plan," he said cheerily, then disconnected.

As Kari got ready for bed, she thought about their conversation. Every time they had been together either in person or on the phone, Bill had managed to ask about the case against Stacy. His interest struck her as odd, even troubling. She made a mental note to ask him why he cared so much about it. The bed creaked as she pulled the covers up, nestling into the cozy warmth of her down comforter. She yawned again, thinking about his questions. Too tired to focus on his words, her mind drifted, thinking about the last time he'd lain in bed with her. She smiled at the recent memory as she snuggled in for the night.

Chapter 38

Kari spent the morning walking the waterfront looking up at the red-brick buildings. She searched for cameras. The file sent over from the prosecutors at the attorney general's office included still shots from grainy video footage they'd recovered from the fish market's camera. The black-and-white images merely showed a petite, very blond woman walking in the direction of the boat around the time of the murder. Then, according to the video's time stamp, the woman exited the area, or at least it appeared to be the same woman.

The photos were not great but would provide yet another nail in Stacy's coffin. Alone, the video failed to prove she killed her husband, but combined with their turbulent marital history, the fight at Dry Dock, and his injuries, including her bite mark on his abdomen, it added up to a potential conviction.

Most establishments in the Old Port had no cameras either inside or out. The crime rates in Maine hardly warranted the effort. Despite the swell of tourists over the last few years, Maine remained very safe. She hoped she would find at least one more security camera to help her create an alternate theory to explain Greg's murder.

Finally, after walking the distance from Dry Dock to the scene of the crime, she gave up and decided to make her way along Commercial Avenue. Maybe she'd get lucky. Sure enough, one of the local bars, the Irish pub Rí Rá, had a lone security camera. She made note of the time they opened and went to her office.

After a few hours, she called Rí Rá, hoping they'd have footage from the night of Greg's death. "This is attorney Kari Sharpe, may I please speak with the manager?"

She heard muffled speech and then the man who answered said, "Yeah, this is Jordan."

"Hi, Jordan. I'm attorney Kari Sharpe. I'm calling because I noticed that Rí Rá has a security camera outside of the front door."

Music in the background flared up. Jordan said, "Hold on." The sound became muffled. "Marcie. Turn it down. We aren't even open yet." After a few seconds, he came back. "Okay. Now what do you want? Something about our cameras?"

"Yes. I'm wondering if Rí Rá's uses the camera out front, and if so, how long do you save footage for?"

"Oh yeah, we use the camera, and we keep the footage for at least six months. It's a real pain. The owner insists we do it after being sued by the family of a guy killed in a drunk driving accident. We need to be able to show our patrons walking out of the bar, not stumbling out. He thinks it'll save the day if we're sued again. I think it's just another pain-in-the-ass thing I need to get done around here."

She leaned back in her chair and looked out the window. "Do you think I could review the tapes for the days I need?"

He coughed a loud smoker's hack and said, "Why do you need them?"

"I represent Stacy Stadt in connection with the death of her husband, Greg Stadt."

"Hmm . . . you mean the guy they pulled out of the harbor?"

"Yes, would you mind if I look at the footage? It has nothing to do with Rí Rá. None of the people involved were at Rí Rá the night of the death. I just need to nail down a few things and hope the footage from out front will do it for me. I'd really appreciate it."

She held her breath and waited. He had no reason to allow her to look at their video feed. If he refused, she would subpoena the records, something she wanted to avoid. If Stacy appeared on the footage, Kari would never turn it over to the prosecution. A subpoena would ensure she had to share whatever their video contained. Good or bad.

After a few seconds he said, "Sure. Be my guest, but you'll need to pack your patience. It takes forever to go through that stuff. The camera captures hours of boring footage. I'm guessing you won't need all of it."

She had glanced at her calendar for a slot of time to propose when he added, "Just drop by anytime and find me. I'm always here." Then he disconnected the call.

Midmorning, Kari walked the short distance to the Irish bar. The barstools and chairs were still on top of the various tables. The dark interior smelled like a combination of cleaning supplies and stale beer.

A young, tired-looking waitress approached Kari. "We aren't open yet," she said. "Come back at eleven thirty."

"I'm not here for a drink or food. I'm Attorney Sharpe, here to see Jordan. He said I could just stop by."

The server's eyes scrunched together as she assessed Kari. "Yeah, you're the lady looking for the cameras. Follow me." Then she turned and quickly walked away.

She led Kari through the service door into the dark interior of the establishment. "Here's the video room in all its glory," she said with an eye roll.

A dark-haired, bearded man sat at the messy desk in the cramped room. The glare from the computer screen and the overhead lights bounced off his filthy glasses, obscuring his eyes. He barely looked up from his computer screen when she walked in. "Are you Jordan?" she asked.

"No. I'm Larry, but he told me you might drop by. You're the attorney, right?" he said, glancing up in her direction.

"Yes. I'm Kari. Thanks for meeting with me."

"No worries." He got up, moved a box of loose papers off a nearby chair. "Have a seat and tell me what you're looking for. Jordan said I could just give you the tape, but I'm guessing you don't have one of those," he said, pointing to the dusty black VHS box. "Without one, good luck. We can just check the reel together. Save you some time."

"Thanks. I appreciate it."

"What do you need?" he said as he turned the monitor so she could watch as he navigated through the reels.

"I need anything you have from the night of July twelfth until approximately three in the morning."

The room stank like dust, mold, cigarettes, and alcohol. She started to feel slightly panicky about being in the space. Between the mess, cramped quarters, and stale air, she fidgeted in her seat, trying to keep from bolting.

He jammed one of the tapes into the machine and said, "Let's see what we have on that day. It'll just take a minute to get to the right night."

The player squealed as its wheels rotated the tape through the footage. He clicked the mouse a few more times, stopping and rewinding until he landed on the right time parameters.

"Bingo. Okay. What are we looking for, exactly?" he asked, turning to Kari.

Kari pulled her phone out of her pocket and showed him the picture she'd snapped of Lori Spec at the Sweetwater town offices, as well as the one from Maine Medical. She also showed him the picture she had of Stacy Stadt. "I'm trying to find either one or both women. I'm assuming neither one of them came into Rí Rá that night, so if you focus on the exterior camera only, that'll speed things up."

He glanced at the pictures as he continued to view the footage. After a few minutes, he fast-forwarded it, then played it again. "What do we have here?" he said.

Kari sat closer to him as she leaned in for a better look. Her nostrils stung as she inhaled his strong body odor. She had to stifle a cough as she desperately tried to breathe through her mouth only.

"You see something? I can hardly tell what I'm looking at."

"Yeah, give me a minute." He fast-forwarded, reversed, and then played the video. "Here she is."

The grainy image showed Lori Spec walking quickly from somewhere off camera, looking at her phone. She waited near the curb. A few minutes later, a small vehicle pulled up to her. She got in and they drove away.

"Looks like your friend grabbed an Uber that night," he said as he scratched his nose. "I don't see the other one. You need anything else?"

"No. This has been amazing. How can I get a copy of the tape?" she asked.

"Just give me your card. I can send you stills and the parts you need to your email."

Kari stood and then turned to him, shocked. "You can do that from that ancient system?"

"Normally no, but I managed to convince the boss to get a converter. We digitize our footage all the time for various reasons, usually involving a drunk driving accident or fight. We have way more cameras inside. The interior ones usually pick up all sorts of interesting things. It'll only take me a few minutes to send everything to you. Even stills, with time stamps."

"Thanks very much. This is far more than I was even hoping to get from our meeting," she said. She stood, scooped up her bag, and then did her best not to wipe off the back of her pants in front of him, unsure if she'd sat in something.

Once back at her office, she eagerly checked her email. Sure enough, he had sent the recording along with a couple of still shots. One of the Uber, including the plate, and the other of Lori's face. Both shots included the time stamp. Perfect.

She sent the file to Mack and asked him to get the name of the Uber driver. She needed to nail down that he'd dropped Lori off at her home in Sweetwater sometime after the murder occurred. Once she did that, then she would speak with Nell Braider, the prosecutor, about searching Lori Spec's financial records for any large transactions involving the track.

She needed to tie Lori together with Beth Thornberry, the owner of Sweetwater Downs. Or she needed a connection between Lori and the Magellion Group. Somehow she still had to explain how the bute had gotten into Greg's system.

She stood and stretched. Glancing at her watch, she realized that she had only about fifteen minutes until her next client meeting. She decided to text Jimmy.

Remember when you told me about the guy you and Chet spoke with at Dry Dock? The one from the racetrack? Do you remember his name?

Three dots popped up almost immediately, indicating he was writing something. Finally, the name appeared.

Seth Moyer. Why?

After his text he sent a contact card for Seth Moyer. She hadn't expected that from Jimmy. Maybe they hung out?

Thanks. Just working a hunch. Talk later.

She tapped on the number in the contact card and waited as the phone rang.

"Hello?" said a man.

"Hi, I'm calling for Seth Moyer. Is this him?" she asked, hoping he wouldn't mistake her for a scam caller.

"Why? I'm not buying anything or giving you a credit card number, so just take my damned name off your call list, lady. I don't have time."

"No, sorry. I should have identified myself. I'm Kari Sharpe, Jimmy's sister. He said you worked at Sweetwater Downs. I just need to ask you a few questions about the place. I'm not trying to sell you anything. I promise."

"Geez, sorry about that. I made the mistake of opting into text alerts for something, and now all I get are these stupid calls and loads of text messages. I'm thinking about changing my number."

She picked up her pen, flipped the page on her legal pad, and then said, "Yeah, that's annoying. It happens to me too. I won't keep you long. Jimmy said you were laid off from the track. What happened? If you don't mind me asking."

"I don't care at all. Beth, the owner, has been having trouble keeping the place running. The crowds have died down to just a trickle, and it's putting a lot of financial pressure on her. She claimed I'm just the latest cost-cutting measure."

"I'm sorry to hear that. I know how jarring being laid off can be. What sort of work did you do for her?"

"Pretty much everything from helping groom the horses to general barn maintenance. You know, electrical, plumbing, whatever was needed. I poured my heart into the place for years, and then she just laid me off. Said it hurt her to do it. I'm sure it didn't."

Kari looked up from her pad. "What do you mean?"

"She had been hanging out with the fat cats from the New Jersey casinos, flying high, riding in a big fancy Cadillac and everything. Then suddenly she needs to lay off people. I don't buy it. Something stinks over there after those guys showed up. I don't know what, but it just stinks."

Kari considered his words. She hadn't expected him to be so angry. "Do you know anything about bute? They use it to treat inflammation in horses."

She heard a door opening and slamming shut in the background. Then a faucet turned on. "Sure, I do. Beth used it at the track all the time when a horse needed it."

"Did a vet administer it to the animals? Or was that something done by the staff at the track?"

"Both. When Dr. Sweely came by, he might give a horse some or just restock Beth's stash for later use. Either way."

Kari jotted down the name of the vet. "You said 'stash.' Did Beth keep the drugs hidden somewhere?"

He laughed heartily. "After some time she had to because too many of us dipped into the supplies for our own *medicinal purposes*, if you get my drift."

"Sure, I can see that happening. But isn't it something that has to be injected? I assume that's how it's administered to horses."

"That's only because we can't get the horses to take a nip or two of the stuff like the rest of us do."

Kari chuckled and said, "Good point." She stood to turn her blinds to a different angle to block out the hot sunlight. "Do you know where Beth keeps the supply of bute?"

"Oh yeah, she locks it up in her office. She has a metal box on the wall where the drugs are kept. She also locked her office door. If you ask me, she probably was just trying to keep the drugs for herself and her Cadillac friends. Wouldn't surprise me."

"Does anyone else have access to her office or the medications?"

"Not that I know of. She keeps a pretty tight lid on things."

"You mentioned a Dr. Sweely? Do I have the name correct?"

"Yeah, he's an old-timer out of Standish. Comes to the track once per month unless there's an issue with one of the horses. I might have his number here somewhere. You want it?"

"Yes, that would be amazing."

Loud ruffling of papers, the creaking of drawers, and then she heard him muttering under his breath: "Where the hell is that card?" After a few more minutes, he returned with the number.

"Thanks a lot. You mentioned that Ms. Thornberry hung out with people from the casinos in New Jersey. What do you think that was about?"

"They've been adding their machines to our casinos in Maine for a while now. Making a mess of the whole damned place. If you ask me, those stupid slots will ruin Maine, one broke jerk at a time. Slot gambling, heck, any gambling can take people down quickly. The only one who seemed to get it was Greg Stadt. That guy would never approve slots into the racetrack."

"Yes, that's what I heard. Do you have any idea why not?"

"I don't know him personally, but one of the guys at the track said someone in Greg's family spent every waking minute there, gambling and drinking away their family's fortune. My hunch is that he had a personal vendetta against the racetrack that went far deeper than going after a business opportunity ever could. It's the only thing that explains his flat-out refusal to allow the measure."

"I didn't realize Greg had a connection to the Downs," she said. The lie was smooth on her lips.

"Oh sure, he did, just like many people in southern Maine. Until the casinos opened up north, the track was the only place in Maine to gamble."

Kari put her pen down and rubbed her eye with the back of her knuckle. "Yes. Now it seems people have more choices. And maybe the Downs will get slot machines."

"Yeah, might happen." A door slammed and someone yelled something. "Anything else?" he asked, distracted.

"No. Not at all. You've been very helpful. I appreciate it. Feel free to reach out if you think of anything else I need to know."

He laughed. "I've had my run-ins with the law, so who knows. I might just need your help." Then he disconnected the call.

Seth had given her valuable information. She might be able to use him on the stand if the case went to trial. She made a note of his comment about "run-ins" with the law. The last thing she needed would be to hinge an entire defense on the word of a felon. She would need to vet his criminal history before using him on the stand, at the very least bring up his history for the jury to hear from his side, before the prosecution could use it to undermine his credibility.

She dialed the number for Dr. Sweely. As she waited for an answer, she looked him up. He had nearly no online presence, only a very basic Google page that had probably been autogenerated for the business.

"Dr. Sweely's office, how may I help you?" asked a pleasant-sounding woman.

"Hi, my name is attorney Kari Sharpe. I'd like to speak with Dr. Sweely about a case I'm working on. Is he available?"

"Hold one moment, please." The phone clicked to classical music as she waited for him to answer.

"This is Dr. Sweely." His voice was gruff with the wear of age on his vocal cords.

"Good afternoon. I'm attorney Kari Sharpe, I'm wondering if you wouldn't mind answering a few questions related to veterinary medicine?" A few seconds passed. Nothing. "Uh, I heard you're an expert at the treatment of horses. I won't keep you long. I could make an appointment if you prefer?"

"Fine. I only have a few minutes, so shoot."

"Thank you. Have you ever heard of phenylbutazone?"

"Of course, we use it for horses all the time."

"Did you treat the horses at Sweetwater Downs with it?"

A door shut loudly. "What's this about? You know I can't answer anything about my patients," he said angrily.

"Do you remember the man pulled from the harbor a month ago?"

"Sure, why?"

"The coroner found bute, the street name for phenylbutazone, in his bloodstream. I need to figure out how it got there."

"I won't answer anything related to the treatment of specific animals. You know that I can't."

"Fine. Did you ever experience a loss of your supply of the drug?"

"A loss? You mean like theft?"

"Yes."

"No, but I keep all the pharmacological supplies locked up. I'm the only one with the key to the secured area in the office. I know other veterinarians have had break-ins, so I had the safe installed years ago."

"Have you heard of any recent break-ins involving the theft of bute in other veterinarian offices?"

"No. None in the past year or so. The Maine veterinary group is relatively small. We're all on a LISTSERV. If it happened, someone would have said something to warn the rest of us."

"Thanks. That's good to know." She paused. "How often do you go to Sweetwater Downs?" She teased the edges of confidentiality, wondering how far he would allow her to go.

"I visit all my patients at least once per month and more if necessary. I can't answer anything about specific patients, as I said."

"Have you noticed that you've prescribed more than usual for the Downs?"

He huffed loudly and said, "That's enough. I've nothing further to say to you." The phone disconnected.

She had clearly hit a nerve when she asked about the Downs. Did he know something had been off over there? Maybe she'd stumbled on the source of the bute. She stood and stretched, then bent slightly to jot down her impressions of the good doctor. Guarded. Defensive. Not forthcoming.

"Kari? You there? Your client is here," said Ruth over the loudspeaker on the telephone system.

"Thanks, I'll be down in a few," she said.

Kari closed Stacy's file and picked up the one for the incoming client. After taking a long drink from her now-cold tea, she checked herself in the mirror, making sure she had no food in her teeth. She glanced down at her navy pantsuit, smoothed the lightweight wool sweater vest over the belt, and walked downstairs to face a different set of problems.

Chapter 39

Dr. Sweely hung up the phone and stared at it momentarily. *What has Beth gotten herself into?* He ran his veterinary practice out of his residence in Standish. The small white Cape Cod–style home had come with an in-law suite attached to the back of the house through a small hallway. Over the years, he had used the extra space as an office, eventually adding on to the small suite to accommodate the x-ray machines.

He thought about Beth Thornberry. He had known her since she was just a kid helping clean stalls for her parents. Now she owned the track. She also owned every problem that came with running the business. Lately, a lack of customers had hurt her bottom line to the point that she had cut back on his visits to an unmanageable amount. For the good of the animals, he had insisted on seeing any injured horses, offering to delay receiving payment for his services. The animals came first. The money could wait.

Now she had done something to bring the attention of an attorney to him. That could not be good. He crossed his small office and pulled her file from the large mahogany filing cabinet. The wide plank pine floorboards creaked slightly as he walked. Sitting back in his leather executive chair, he spread the file across his large glass-covered desk. How much bute had he prescribed?

He glanced at the framed pictures of his smiling family that adorned his desk. Each week his wife, Chrissy, cleaned the office, dusting the photos with care. They had built a nice life together. The last thing he needed was legal trouble involving the misuse of drugs. The records indicated that Sweetwater had received roughly the same amount of bute until July. During their last visit he had given Beth more than usual, and his notes indicated that she had needed it to treat one of the mares. She'd claimed that she had run out and wanted a restock for her cabinet. Yet the amount she'd requested exceeded what he'd expect, considering the health of her stable. *How did I miss it?* He picked up the phone to call her.

She answered almost immediately. "Hi, Dr. Sweely."

"Hi, Beth. Hey, I just took a call from an attorney . . ." He glanced at the scribble pad on his desk. "Attorney Sharpe from Portland. She said she was interested in knowing how much phenylbutazone I had dispensed to the track. Do you know why she needed to know this?"

Silence. Finally, Beth cleared her throat and said, "I . . . I'm not sure. She didn't say why?"

She sounded like a kid caught breaking the rules. He looked at the pictures of his family as he listened to her. His face reddened as anger rose from the pit of his stomach. He balled his fists and said, "You listen here, Beth, I've been practicing veterinary medicine for over forty years. I've never had a complaint against me. Ever. And I don't intend to be involved in whatever nonsense you've created for yourself. I won't be giving you any more medicine to dispense without me. From now on, if one of your horses needs something, you pay me for a visit. You understand?"

What had she done?

A tractor roared to life in the field next to Dr. Sweely's office. The sound traveled quicker than the aroma of fresh-cut grass. His small windup clock ticked time as he waited for her to reply.

"You still there?"

She cleared her throat and said, "Yes. I'm sorry. I'm sorry. Nothing happened; you won't have any trouble." She sobbed quietly and said, "Things have been very hard around here financially. I had been counting on the slot machine measure to pass so I could get the investment from the casino company. Now I don't know if that'll happen."

He leaned forward, placing his elbows on the desk, thinking about what to say to her as he listened to her sob story. "I'm very sorry to hear about your troubles, but like I said, I absolutely will not have my reputation tarnished because of your actions. Do I make myself clear?"

She hiccuped a reply. "Yes."

"Okay, then. Make an appointment through the office if you need anything." He ended the call.

The direction to call the office had been a not-so-subtle distancing from her. Normally she would call his cell phone to make an appointment, as many of his patients had done. He made copious notes of the conversation, including his impressions of her reactions. If law enforcement questioned him, he planned to tell them everything he knew.

Phenylbutazone had not been a controlled substance, but as a powerful anti-inflammatory, it had been used as an additive in illicit drugs, mainly heroin and fentanyl. Maine had a serious and growing drug problem. The last thing he needed was to be tangled in a mess, especially on the cusp of retirement.

Beth Thornberry can go to hell, he thought as he slammed her file closed.

Chapter 40

Beth Thornberry threw her phone onto the desk. She placed her head in her hands and sobbed openly for the first time in years. Her shoulders heaved with every tear that tumbled from her watery eyes. What had she done?

A quick knock on the door startled her. The door flew open.

"What the hell's wrong with you?" asked Ryker as he walked into the room.

Normally he never came into her office. Instead, she met him near his Escalade, or they stood outside near the paddock. He said horse manure made him queasy. She expected him today, just not so soon.

"Everything. That's what's wrong. Everything," she sobbed. She had passed the point of no return into the "oversharing" category. "I just got a call from Dr. Sweely. Apparently that nosy lawyer, Kari Sharpe, has been poking around his office, asking all sorts of questions about the care of my horses. My horses. How dare she."

Ryker stood staring at her with his cold, dead eyes. "Looks like you now have a second problem."

She looked up at him, wiped her tears with the back of her hand. "Second problem?"

"You owe me either some space for my slot machines in your fine establishment or the repayment of the loan I generously gave you. What's it going to be?"

She stood and rounded the desk to close the door. The last thing she wanted was for anyone to overhear their conversation.

"You know I can't repay you right now, nor can I allow the slots in here. I'm waiting for the town to vote. It'll happen. The only person who opposed the vote is now gone. It'll all work out now."

Ryker rubbed his chin and smirked at her. "Oh. You don't know?"

"Know what?"

"Two of the Sweetwater town board members are now missing. Your mousy little friend Lori Spec has flown the coop. She won't be voting for anything anytime soon."

Beth felt like someone had just punched her in the gut. Her knees wobbled as the room spun. She fell back into her chair. Looked at the floor. Spent.

"Don't get too comfortable, sweetheart. This place is going to be mine soon enough," he said with a smirk as he knocked on the desk.

He opened the door and walked out. Surrounded by the pictures of deceased family members, she knew they would be disappointed in her if she lost the business. She wanted to cry but had nothing left to give.

Chapter 41

Lori and her daughter, Mary, snuggled on their tiny couch together. The thin blanket stretched across Mary's shoulders and legs, but barely covered Lori. She stroked Mary's baby-fine blond hair to put the toddler to sleep. Yawning deeply, she thought maybe she needed the nap more than Mary.

Working at a variety store in rural New Hampshire for what barely passed as minimum wage had been difficult but necessary. Her back and feet ached from the hours of standing, carrying boxes of inventory, and dragging the large, heavy mop over floors that would never look clean. Mary's little arm fell to the side, slack. Lori listened closely to her breathing. It had become deep and rhythmic. Finally, she'd drifted off. She waited another minute to be sure she didn't startle Mary as she slid off the couch to stand.

She carefully tucked the edges of the light-blue blanket under Mary's feet and left the room. Sitting at the kitchen table, she faced the mountain of bills that had accumulated since their move. Everything had a price. Even freedom. She exhaled loudly as she navigated to the bank app on her phone. Her breath hitched as she nervously waited to see the dwindling balance.

The account contained $4,000. She had gone through $6,000 since they'd fled their life in Maine. Her leg bounced as she considered the implications of their financial situation. In a short time, their basic living expenses had drained the account, even with her job. The costs of day care, gas, rent, and groceries were high. It all added up.

She stood to stretch as she considered possibilities. Find a new job? A cheaper apartment? Stop eating? No. None of those were workable options for her, and she knew it. She needed a divorce and access to the money she and Bruce had saved. She also needed to work in human resources, as she had always done. Her income would triple quickly if she felt safe enough to return to her profession.

A small sound from the living room drew her attention. She peeked around the kitchen corner to check on Mary, who kicked her little legs and murmured in her sleep as her body acted out a dream. The poor child had been through so much turmoil because of Bruce. Seeing her mother beaten, crying, broken had to have taken its toll. What would she do if Bruce found the two of them? The thought had been more than she could manage. For now, she needed to take one day at a time. The counselor at the women's shelter told her that with each passing day, she became safer. She just needed to hold on a little longer before filing for divorce.

"Mommy?" asked Mary from the couch. Her voice breaking Lori free of her daily worry grind. She scooped Mary up into her arms and held her tight, breathing in her smell. Lori's shoulders dropped as she began to relax.

"Let's snuggle a little longer, okay?" she said to Mary.

Mary clapped her dimpled hands and did her best to spread the blanket over them. Lori leaned into the pillows and allowed herself to feel the love and warmth shared between them. The bond of mother and child strong.

Chapter 42

Mack sat in Kari's conference room, waiting for her. He needed to update her on the things he had learned. Although he could have handled the update over the phone, he took the opportunity to come into the office to see Ruth. They had been steadily dating, becoming closer every day. They spoke on the phone nearly every night and saw each other most days, either for lunch or to spend time together in the evening. He could not have been happier.

Ruth leaned against the doorframe and said, "I'm thinking about making Italian food tonight. How do you feel about a nice pasta dinner at my place?" She smiled, looking relaxed. She wore a navy-blue collared polo shirt over white cigarette pants. She looked fantastic, as always.

He glanced out the window, ran his hand over his head, and said, "How about if I grab everything you need and we can have it at my place? Maybe go for a sunset walk on the beach when we're done eating?" He smiled at her, trying not to come on too strong.

She had invited him to her house numerous times, but he always maneuvered the date either to his place or to a public location. The thought of being at her marital home bothered him. It was a dead man's house. A dead man's life and wife. It felt wrong.

Ruth smiled gently and walked over to him. She placed a hand on his shoulder and said, "You have to come over sometime. I get it, you probably feel uncomfortable there, because of David, but I need you to be okay with visiting me." She rubbed his shoulder softly as she spoke.

"I've cleaned a lot of his things from the house. The place feels like mine now, not ours. Please come over. It would mean a lot to me," she said and squeezed his shoulder.

He felt the tension drain from him as he nodded his head. He took her hand. "You win. What time should I be over?"

She pinched his cheek. "Dinner's on at six thirty."

"Great. What are we having?" asked Kari as she walked into the room.

"Sorry, kid. Two's company, three's . . . well, you know," said Mack with a wink.

Ruth walked away. "I'll leave you guys to it," she said as she shut the door behind her.

Kari looked at Mack. He could feel his cheeks burning with embarrassment. Kari had been like a daughter to him. It felt strange to have her seeing him flirting with his new girlfriend. Strange and creepy, but he needed to get over it.

"Thanks for coming in today. So, what happened in New Hampshire? Did you find our friend Lori Spec?"

Mack opened the file he had brought and handed Kari a sheet of paper. "Sure did. Brenda wouldn't tell me anything, but eventually Lori showed up. I tailed her to this location. I also learned that she left her vehicle in the Kennebunk rest area. The state troopers found it abandoned."

Kari chewed on the end of her pencil. She looked out the window and back at Mack. "Lori needed a babysitter the night Greg went into the harbor. The footage from Rí Rá's shows her getting into an Uber. Were you able to speak with the Uber driver?"

Mack rubbed his jaw. He flipped through pages until turning to his notes on the Uber driver. "Sure did. He confirms that he dropped Lori off at her residence in Sweetwater at roughly two o'clock in the morning."

"Does he have a record of the drop-off location? It's been a little while since then. Is he sure?" she asked.

"Sure as I've ever seen. Yes. I asked him the same thing. He said he remembers because he wondered why someone from that neighborhood found herself out in the Old Port at two in the morning. He also said he was more than a little angry to be taken away from the traffic in the Old Port. Apparently drunks are excellent tippers," said Mack with a smirk and wink. "He remembered every detail about it. Even that he picked her up in front of Rí Rá's."

Kari leaned onto the table, placing her forearms on the wood. "I can place Lori at the scene of the crime, at the approximate time of the crime. Now I just need to connect her to the bute. I still have no idea how Lori would have gotten it. But this at least solves one issue for me. Thanks, Mack, you've been very helpful. Do you have anything else for me?" she said as she flipped through her investigative file.

"Yep. You had asked me to figure out who owns the black Escalade you saw at Sweetwater Downs."

"That's right. I totally forgot."

Mack grabbed the yellow Post-it Note pad on the conference room table and scribbled a name for Kari. He looked up at her. "The truck belongs to Ryker Jones. He works for the Magellion Group and is in every way bad news."

"Bad news? How so?" she asked.

Mack shifted and clasped his hands. "I crossed paths with him on a job I had in New Jersey a few years back. A man hired me to find his ex-girlfriend. Apparently she had acquired the man's credit cards and racked up a substantial enough debt to make him think his spouse might notice. Anyway, I hung out in various casinos in the Jersey Shore area. That's when he noticed me—Ryker, I mean. One night as I walked back to my vehicle from the casino, Ryker followed me out. I won't get into the details, but suffice it to say, it got physical. Fast."

Kari watched him intently. "I had no idea. I mean, I knew the Magellion Group had invested in the Maine casinos. I just didn't realize they sent their attack dog up here."

He looked out the window toward the harbor. A fishing boat returned from the day's work. It pulled up pierside with the fish market, ready to hand over the precious catch of the day.

"Let's put it this way, if Beth Thornberry is talking to Ryker Jones, something went very wrong in her life. She's in deep. That's all I can say. You need to find a different way to approach the case. The last thing you need is that animal coming anywhere near you. After he threatened me, I ran his information through the system. He has an extensive criminal record. All violent offenses. Stay away from him, Kari. I mean it. This case isn't worth it. Stacy Stadt isn't worth it."

Kari pinched the bridge of her nose, trying to ease the growing pressure she felt. "All right, I'll try to steer clear of him, but I can't make promises. I have a duty to represent my client, no matter where the case takes us. I'm on the cusp of crafting a very solid defense for Stacy. I can feel it. I just need to make a few more connections."

"Fine. All I can say to you is that once Ryker gets involved, he won't leave things alone until you're neutralized as a threat."

Kari grimaced and looked down. "If he does come sniffing around me, it'll only confirm that I'm on the right track."

"Stubborn as always," he said as he shook his head and stood. "Stubborn as always."

"I'll be fine. You don't have to worry, but I do really appreciate your concern and help. Frankly, I'm surprised you have time," she said, smiling. Kari raised her eyebrows and yanked her thumb toward the door.

Mack's face reddened again, and he looked down. Embarrassed to be called out. "Yeah, I like her a lot. Maybe more than I want to admit. What's your next step with Stacy's case?"

"I plan to subpoena the financial records of Sweetwater Downs and Beth Thornberry. And if needed, I'll hit the Magellion Group as well. Making a connection between Lori and Beth is essential to explain how Lori acquired the bute. Based on what you said, I'm hoping I don't need the Magellion Group's financials, but I'll see where this thing takes me."

Mack held the door open for her. He glanced at Ruth. She sat upright at her desk, typing on her computer. He could watch her all day.

"Do you have a trial date yet?" he asked.

"Yes. It's in two months, so I need to get cracking on this. Time seems to fly by quicker when I need it to go the slowest."

"I get that. Call if you need anything else. I'm around."

Mack waited for Kari to dash up the stairs to her office. Once she was gone, he rounded Ruth's desk, kissed her on the top of the head, and said, "See you tonight, beautiful."

"Oh, Mack." She laughed and waved him away.

Mack smiled and whistled the whole way to his car as he thought about seeing Ruth this evening. Then his mind drifted back to Ryker Jones. He became angry thinking about Ryker coming near Kari. Hopefully she'd navigate around involving the Magellion Group. Her safety depended on it.

Chapter 43

Ryker Jones stretched his legs next to the linen-covered table at the Falmouth Country Club. The club offered a respite from the normal shabby surroundings he had suffered while in Maine. Glancing at his dinner companion, he felt satisfied that his time in the state would soon end, one way or another. He could hardly wait to get back to the Jersey Shore.

A waiter came to their table to tidy up after their lavish surf-and-turf dinner. The food had been spectacular. "We'll take two whiskeys on the patio," said his companion. "Please pour from my collection, if you don't mind, Marshall."

"Yes, sir. I'll bring it right out. Would you also like a box of cigars?"

The man smoothed his tie, stood, straightened his dinner jacket, and said, "Of course."

He glanced at Ryker for confirmation, as if he needed one. The men had eaten at the club numerous times over the past few months, and each evening they'd spent together had been capped off by a cigar and a smooth tumbler of Macallan. Ryker had to admit, the man knew how to live, despite residing in the backwater of Maine.

Ryker followed him through the restaurant. The understated elegance of the club perfectly matched the quiet luxury adorning its patrons. Even though none of the diners wore labels on their clothing, they exuded class, generational wealth, and luxury. Everything Ryker aspired to, but somehow never had. A cute brunette with a sleek bob smiled at him as he passed. He returned her smile with a wink, noticing the three-carat Tiffany-set stone on her hand. The perfect companion to her one-carat earrings-and-necklace set.

The heat of jealousy rose from the pit of his stomach as his eyes bored into the back of his companion's head. The man's life irritated him. The wealth irritated him. The fact that he worked for the man irritated him. *All I need is one swing at the guy. Just knock the smug look off his face.*

Marshall had beat them to the patio. He had pulled two Adirondack chairs to a cozy, quiet corner. A small wooden table covered with white linen sat between the chairs. Marshall placed monogrammed cloths on the arm of each chair and then set out the whiskey. He offered the men a cigar with a bow and nod of formality. Ryker puffed a few times to make sure the flame took to the Arturo Fuente Opus X. The premium aged tobacco tasted of earth and leather. After a few minutes, he enjoyed the notes of espresso and cocoa the Dominican brand was so famous for.

The man turned to him and flicked his cigar ash. "How's our little project moving along?"

Ryker swirled his whiskey, moving the sole ice cube against the heavy crystal tumbler. "I'd say we're moving right along as planned. With any luck, we'll have a vote in Sweetwater next month."

The man puffed his cigar. He watched several people walk across the patio to the restaurant. The sun had started its colorful descent over the club's main golf course.

"And this time you're sure Sweetwater will approve the casino measure?"

"Yes, sir. I don't anticipate any issues," said Ryker. A pang of uncertainty clenched his stomach.

The man crossed his legs with the elegance reserved for the ultra-wealthy. The pang of jealousy returned.

"You've said that before. And now Kari Sharpe is meddling. Make sure the measure passes. I'm not a patient man."

Before Ryker could reply, the man placed his drink on the small table between their chairs and stood. "I trust you know your way out?" he said over his shoulder.

The man walked toward a small group of people gathering near the bar. He slapped another member on the back and said, "I hope you played better tonight than you did last week. That was just embarrassing."

Ryker hated them. All of them. Damned rich people had no clue what the rest of the world went through. He relived the fantasy of blasting the man across the jaw. Maybe knock out a few teeth. It would be satisfying, to say the least.

He threw back the last of his whiskey, took one more pull on the cigar, and then stood to leave. He had done everything he could to move the needle in Sweetwater; now he had to hope that the two alternate board members would reward his efforts by voting in favor of the casino measure. But first he intended to visit Kari Sharpe.

Chapter 44

Kari yawned and tried to focus on the motion she'd drafted in a real property case. Two neighbors were fighting over a narrow strip of land on their joint border. She couldn't be less interested. Exhaustion from an overnight with Bill made her even less interested. They had started the night in the Old Port for dinner at their favorite seafood restaurant. Before living in New York City, the upscale establishment would have felt intimidating to her. Growing up, eating fast food had been a treat. She never would have imagined dining in such an expensive establishment.

Her phone chimed with a text message. She glanced at it: Bill.

Thanks for a great night, even if I can barely keep my eyes open today.

Same. Just glad I'm not in court or meeting with clients.

How about we go on a sunset cruise this weekend? I can grab the tickets and a basket.

Kari looked out the window and smiled. Sunset cruises on an old clipper ship were one of her favorite things to do. The ship had been lovingly restored by a team of volunteers. Now its handmade wooden decks, rails, and brass shined with care. During the cruise, the staff took its patrons into the harbor, circling various islands and old military fortifications. Cozy blankets were provided if the ocean breezes felt too cold. A local market offered picnic baskets of cheeses, wine, and various snacks for the occasion.

Would love that, but I'll grab the basket, she wrote with the addition of a heart.

Everything with him had fallen into place effortlessly. They fit together; the bond was undeniable. Smiling, she returned to her work.

A few moments later Ruth came into her office and said in a low whisper, "Kari, there's a man here to see you. He doesn't have an appointment but says you know him. What should I do?"

"What's his name?" she asked.

"Ryker Jones. He said it's related to your representation of Stacy Stadt. Do you want me to make him go away? He gives me the creeps."

Ruth looked over her shoulder as she spoke as though she expected the man to magically appear behind her.

"No, it's fine. Tell him I'll be down in a minute."

Kari pulled the small mirror out of her desk drawer and checked herself. She looked tired. Nothing she could do about that. Standing, she stretched for a minute and yawned. Why would Ryker Jones want to meet with her? she wondered, then muttered, "Only one way to find out."

She took the final step down the office stairs and saw him standing in the reception area. His hands on his hips, glaring at Ruth with an edge of impatience.

"Mr. Jones?" she said as she approached.

He turned to face her and said, "Finally."

She pretended not to hear his rude comment but never offered to shake his hand. Mack had warned her that Ryker Jones was a dangerous man. Someone she should try to avoid. She wanted this meeting to be over. Fast.

"Please come in and have a seat." She motioned to the conference room.

Ryker walked into the large room and placed himself at the head of the table. The power position. He looked at her with cold, hard eyes as she sat a few seats away from him.

Her stomach clenched in his presence. She shook her head slightly, trying to shake off the queasy feeling. Folding her legs, she placed her hands in her lap, not wanting him to see that they trembled slightly.

"How can I help you?"

Ryker's eyes slowly trailed over Kari's chest and abdomen. He took his time assessing her, like a piece of meat. Her palms sweated as she waited. She maintained her composure, not flinching or looking away, despite wanting to run.

"I'll get right to the point, Ms. Sharpe. I'm sure, like me, you are very busy." He paused and looked out the window and then back to her. "You have been making my boss very uncomfortable by poking around Sweetwater Downs. There's a lot riding on the passage of the measure to allow the slot machines in the fine establishment. I suggest you back off. Immediately. Find a different approach to representing the Stadt woman." He placed his elbows on the table, steepling his hands.

She could feel the warmth of his breath on her face as he spoke. The stench of it clung in her nose. She wanted to recoil but refused to allow him to bully her.

"How dare you come into my office and threaten me. I'll represent Ms. Stadt and every other client of mine in the manner I see fit. I could not care less who your bosses are or what they want," she said as she started to stand. "I suggest you leave."

He made no move to stand. Instead, he reached into his sport coat and produced folded documents. "I thought you might react like this, so I brought you a little gift."

He opened the documents and slid them across the table to face her. She barely had to glance to know what they were. A bar complaint to the New York State overseers. Her knees buckled slightly as she tried to maintain her composure.

He smirked at her and said, "You have a nice little practice going for yourself. I'd hate to have anything happen to it. People don't like to know that their lawyer was accused of mishandling client funds. We both know that. You would never work again in this little hick town if this were to get out. I'm sure the *Portland Press Herald* would be eager to run a full article on the scandal. Hiding from something like this worked in New York, but would never fly in Maine. We both know I'm right."

"How did you get this? The complaint was dismissed for lack of evidence. Then the file was sealed."

She sat and looked at him. Who the hell was this guy?

"That's the great thing about working for powerful people." He smiled. "They can make anything happen." He clapped his hands softly and stood. "I'll let you consider your options. Just know that I'm not the sort of person who makes idle threats. I have better things to do with my time."

She squared off at him. "Go to hell."

He chuckled, placed his hand on her shoulder, and said, "Sweetheart, I'm already there." He walked out of the conference room without another word.

Her cheeks burned with anger. She barely could see the documents as her mind reeled, spinning out of control. She clasped her arms around her abdomen, then looked around the room and counted things in her presence. One table. Three pens. Six chairs. Window. *Breathe, Kari.* She exhaled again, feeling slightly better as the panic attack passed.

Her hands shook as she picked up the papers. The documents laid out the accusations made by a former client. She had represented the young man in a wrongful-termination suit he'd filed against his employer. During her engagement, he had made sexual remarks and asked her out more times than she could count. His behavior had veered from friendly to highly inappropriate the longer she worked with him. With every rebuke, he had become increasingly nasty. She had considered asking the firm to remove her from the case, but as a young associate, she'd needed to put her head down and work. Not complain. Besides, she'd known the male partners would never understand, so she'd handled it.

His behavior had gotten so bad that she'd asked her assistant to sit in on their meetings. She had also taken copious notes of their encounters to protect herself.

The case had resolved with her negotiating a very favorable settlement on his behalf. Both she and her paralegal had been thrilled to finally put the case behind them and move on. A few months later, the office had received the bar complaint. He had accused Kari of mishandling his settlement funds. The large law firm had had an attorney, Bob Juda, who worked to defend the lawyers in the firm against bar complaints or to advise them on ethical issues. She would never forget his calm demeanor as he explained that the firm would represent her, free of charge. "We protect our attorneys," he said.

As a young associate, Kari had had no access to the client funds, held in a trust account. Every lawyer had understood the complaint for what it was, just a jilted, mean man trying to hurt her reputation. Even the bar overseers had seen through the specious complaint. They had dismissed it and sealed the records to ensure her reputation remained untarnished. She had no idea how Ryker had gotten ahold of the information.

A woman walked out onto the pier behind their offices. She was dressed in the rubber knee-high boots and white rubber apron all the employees at the fish market wore. Lighting a cigarette, she pulled the hairnet off her head, hunching on the rail as she smoked, looking down into the water.

"The hell with it," said Kari. Swiping the papers off the conference table, she went into the reception area and shoved them into the shredder.

"Are you okay, Kari? That guy was so creepy. I wanted to hide under my desk when he was in here. He just stood there, staring at me. It was so bad. What did he want?"

"He thought he could intimidate me into failing to give Stacy Stadt the best legal defense possible, but I don't scare that easily," she said with determination.

"I wouldn't think anything could scare a high-ranking naval officer and kick-ass attorney. Good for you. Let me know what I can do to help," said Ruth, smiling.

Ruth's consistent support touched a void in Kari. She had never experienced maternal love and protection as a child. Growing up without the unconditional love of her mother had made Kari fiercely independent, yet painfully vulnerable. Ruth's quick, unconditional loyalty made her tear up. "Thanks, Ruth" was all she managed to mumble as she turned away, not wanting Ruth to see her damaged parts.

The steps creaked as she dashed up to her office. She sat down on the edge of her seat and navigated to the State of New Jersey's database of businesses, searching for the Magellion Group. *Who the hell are these people?* They had filed the expected annual disclosures, using a registered agent for their contact information. She also conducted a real property search, discovering that the company owned several buildings in New Jersey. No surprise. They owned casinos in Jersey City. Nothing jumped out at her during her search.

She tapped her pen on the keyboard, thinking *Who the hell are you people?* as she looked at her diplomas. Turning back to the screen, she googled "The Magellion Group." Her screen filled with articles about their various casinos. One piece caught her attention. It was about their investment into the casino business in Maine. The cover story contained a picture of Ryker Jones standing with George, Bill's father.

"Bill's family is involved with Magellion? Are you kidding me?" she muttered.

Her face burned with anger. She bit her lip as her fists balled in tension. No wonder he had asked so many questions about the case. Bill had used her to feed information to his father. Mistrust burned in her red cheeks. The rich asshole had provided the seed money for the slot machines in Maine. Bill's family had profited from the casinos and had a vested financial interest in the Sweetwater Downs measure passing.

Damn him. Her legs shook from a mix of anxiety and anger. She grabbed her phone and hastily texted Bill.

The sunset cruise is off and so are we. You can tell your dad to go to hell. I won't be intimidated by him or any of his goons. And nice try using me for information about the Stadt case.

A few seconds later she added, Don't bother contacting me. I never want to hear from you again.

She then blocked his number and threw the phone across the room so hard that Ruth yelled up, "Are you okay?"

She inhaled a ragged breath, swallowed. "Yep. Sorry, just dropped my phone."

How could Bill be so heartless? She had had a hard enough time trusting him after their past breakup, and now this? He had seemed so genuine when they'd spent time together. How had she not seen this coming? She needed to get out of the office, away from everything for the rest of the day. Packing up her things, she dashed out with barely a word to Ruth. She needed time to consider her next move.

She drove directly home, intent on going for a long run. As she rounded the corner, she saw Bill's car outside her place. He stood near her back door, waiting for her.

Crap. I'm not ready for this right now. And how the heck did he get here so fast?

He waved at her as she pulled into the driveway. His handsome face twisted with distress.

"Why are you here? I told you I never want to see you again. Leave me alone," she said. She slammed the door to her car and walked up her driveway.

He stood looking at her. Finally, he said, "Please, Kari, let's talk this out. Just give me a few minutes. If you don't want to see me again, then I'll respect your choice. Please."

She looked beyond him toward her unkept backyard. "You should respect my choice. Just leave me alone. I don't want to hear anything you have to say."

He stood blocking her access to her house, angering her even further. "Get out of my way or I'll call the cops. You have no business being here." The intensity of her glare met his saddened eyes.

He stepped to the side. "Kari, please, just a few minutes. I can explain. Just give me a chance." He spread his hands out to the sides. "Please, Kari."

Despite herself, curiosity burned. "You've got exactly two minutes. And don't even try to gaslight me. I read all about George's involvement in the casino industry. Nice family. Real upstanding citizens. And I thought mine was bad," she said with an eye roll. Anger flashed in her again as she thought about the weight of shame she carried because of her family, especially around Bill. Perfect Bill, with the perfect family. She remembered a quote from somewhere, "Even the prettiest packages can contain rot."

The dead bolt on the door opened with a thud. They walked into the side breezeway of the house, which she used as a mudroom. She kicked off her shoes hard enough to send them flying through the small space. Maine had three seasons—summer, winter, and the mud season. Every house in Maine had a mudroom to keep the mess at bay.

They walked into the kitchen. She leaned against the counter. "Okay, this should be good. I can hardly wait to hear your explanation for asking so many questions about the Stadt case. I'm guessing that's the only reason we reconnected. What a jerk. You used me. Physically. I should've seen this coming."

He ran a hand through his hair as he looked at her. When he placed one hand on the kitchen island, she could see it shake slightly. "Where do I start?"

"Why didn't you tell me your family invested in the casino industry in Maine?" she demanded. Her chin jutted out as she spoke. Anger laced her words.

"My family, especially my father, has a hand in nearly everything that happens in Maine. He invests in all sorts of industries, big and small. If it brings money into the family coffers, he'll buy into it."

Kari had met George only a few times. He'd struck her as intense and opportunistic. The sort of guy who always looked beyond the person he spoke with, searching the crowd for someone more important. Once he had even walked away from her while she was speaking, mid-sentence. Other times he relentlessly had name-dropped, as if Kari cared who he knew. To her, their interactions had been nothing but a chore. A chore that had consistently left her carrying more shame than she thought possible. She had wondered if he treated her disrespectfully because of her family's history. The Sharpe name came with a lot of baggage. Maybe if she came from a blue-blooded New England family with a long and prosperous line he'd act differently toward her. Or maybe he was just an opportunistic jerk?

"You know my dad, Kari. Making money is his entire reason for living. What can I say?" Bill's gentle face looked open and sincere. Kari knew him well enough to know when he was lying to her. She knew his "tells," and he had not done any of them. No looking away as he spoke or closing his eyes when he lied. Nothing.

She turned from him, grabbed a glass of water, and downed it. A cardinal sat on the fence line outside the kitchen window.

He moved across the kitchen to her. Placing his hands on her shoulders, he stood close enough for her to feel his warmth. He leaned his forehead against the back of her head and pulled her slightly closer. Her body responded before her brain had a chance to protest. Images of their intimacy flooded her mind uncontrollably. She closed her eyes, allowing the feel of him to surround her. She inhaled his woodsy scent and took hold of one of his hands, moving it to the side to break the embrace.

"Did you tell your father or Ryker Jones anything about Stacy Stadt's case?" she demanded. She stepped away from him, moving back to the door. A hint for him to wrap it up and leave.

"No. Nothing at all. I swear I kept the few things you mentioned in complete confidence. I swear it."

She studied him for signs of deceit but saw none. Maybe he was telling her the truth?

He brushed his hand across her forehead and then cheek, saying, "Who's Ryker Jones? I've never heard the name."

"Give me a damned break. I don't need this. Just leave. I'm going for a run."

"Really. I don't know him." He stepped back from her to lean against the island. The stove's clock ticked in the still room. A half pot of cold coffee sat on the counter, left over from the morning. She had also left the crumbly remains of her bagel on the counter, not expecting company.

"He's the goon Magellion sent to my office to threaten me. That's who."

"Wait, what? Threaten you? What are you talking about?" Bill stood tall, his jaw clenched.

"Yes. He came in demanding that I stop poking around the casino issue and just let Stacy Stadt go to jail for a crime she never committed. Stacy's a real jerk, but she isn't a murderer. Yet he threatened me with exposing the bar complaint against me. Remember the issue I told you about?"

He rubbed his chin, his eyebrows knitted together. "You mean the one with the former client accusing you of mishandling funds? I thought it was dismissed and the records sealed?"

"It was. No one should have been able to acquire the complaint, yet Ryker Jones showed up at my office with everything. He threatened to ruin my reputation if I didn't stop investigating her case. Your father's money-grubbing hands were all over it. I can feel it."

Bill stomped away from her, looking down. He paced the small kitchen, considering her words. "What sort of case is this, Kari?"

She shrugged her shoulders and said, "I thought it was a straightforward homicide case, but the more I dig, the more I'm learning that everyone involved had their own agenda, and no one cared that Greg died. It's a little sick, if you ask me. Mack told me Ryker's a dangerous man. He ran across Ryker on a few matters in New Jersey. He said the guy's capable of anything."

Bill placed both hands on the island, leaning his body back. He hung his head low. "What did my father get himself involved in? This is nuts. What did you say to him?" he said, looking up at her.

"I told him to go to hell. I won't be intimidated by him or anyone else. Screw it."

Suddenly Bill burst out laughing. "Only you would have the guts to say that to a guy like him. Geez. I probably would've said something like 'I'll take it under advisement' or something stupid like that."

"Yeah, I have to say, it felt good to stand up to him. But that doesn't change the fact that it freaked me out. And poor Ruth. You should've seen her. The guy was leering at her. He's a creepy man. Not to mention that I feel like you used me for information and other things. What's wrong with you? You're no better than your father," she said loudly, shoving him on the shoulder for effect.

"I never used you for information or anything else, but I think my father used me. He asked about the case on numerous occasions. I assumed he was trying to show interest in my girlfriend. I had no idea what he was up to. I'm so sorry, Kari." Bill shook his head and looked away. The corners of his lips curved downward as his eyes teared. "I love you more than I thought possible. Getting back together with you has been the best thing to happen to me. I don't want to lose you over this. Not again."

Kari carefully considered Bill's words and demeanor. The anger had drained from her, and she slumped against the counter. "I don't want to lose you, either, but I feel betrayed."

"I'm so sorry. I swear I never shared anything," he said as he pulled her into a hug and held her for a moment. Her shoulders relaxed as she nestled into him.

"You can't stay here alone. I'm worried about your safety," he spoke softly.

"I know. I'll go stay with Jimmy for a few days. He'll just love it," she said with an eye roll.

He stepped back. "Okay. You stay with him, and I'm going to have a few choice words with my father. This is ridiculous. I don't know how involved he is in the day-to-day drama surrounding the casino issue, but this has crossed a line. I'm going to demand that he make sure you're safe."

Kari's eyes filled with tears. She had been so accustomed to protecting herself, she barely knew how to react. They stood for a moment looking into each other's eyes. He brushed a tear away with the back of his hand. "Kari, I'll never let anything happen to you. Not now. Not ever."

Her body stiffened when he offered protection. "I can protect myself. I don't need you or anyone to rescue me."

He pulled her close to him again, hugging her without saying another word. She placed her hands on his back, noticing how his body rose and fell as he breathed.

Her mind swirled around whether she should trust anything he had said. Yet right now, in the moment, she let go and allowed herself to be held.

Chapter 45

Kari tossed and turned on Jimmy's worn-out plaid couch. It smelled of food and old musty yuck. Her back and side ached from trying to sleep on the lumpy mess. Glancing at her watch, she realized she only had roughly thirty more minutes to rest until she needed to start her day. Yanking the threadbare blanket above her shoulders, she closed her eyes.

The hall toilet flushed, and the floorboards creaked as Jimmy walked into the kitchen. The pleasant aroma of fresh coffee wafted into the living room. A few minutes later he walked in carrying two steaming mugs.

"How'd you sleep?" he said, handing her one of the mugs.

She sat up, pulling the tattered blanket over her legs. "Like crap. You need a new couch. This thing is ancient. There's no softness left, only springs, stains, and stink." She took a sip of her coffee. "This hits the spot, thanks."

"You want toaster pancakes? I have blueberry."

She loved blueberry toaster pancakes, and he knew it. "Sure, why not just finish me off with gluten and sugar." She winked at him, then stood. "I'll help you with them."

They walked out of his small living room into the adjoining kitchen. He had never updated the aging house, and it showed. Every room could have used a refresh of paint, but none more than the kitchen. Most of the cabinet doors hung slightly sideways, their tired hinges barely able to handle the task. The Formica countertop had numerous burns and stains covering its once-smooth surface.

The toaster popped up with the first round of pancakes. They smelled incredible, even if they were just freezer pancakes.

He handed her the first batch. "Ladies first."

She scooped a thick glob of margarine from the tub, smeared it on the stack, and then poured on the syrup.

Once they had their food, they padded back to the living room to eat in front of the TV.

Jimmy took a noisy sip of his coffee and said, "Why don't you stay with lover boy? I'm sure he won't have you crashing on an old couch." He raised his eyebrows a few times for effect.

"Nice. I'd rather be here, with my favorite person." She smiled. Shoving an impossibly large amount of food in her mouth, she said between bites, "You look well, like you have been taking care of yourself better. How is it going?"

He looked at her, flicked his eyebrows up, and said, "If you're asking if I'm sober, the answer is yes. One day at a time. I'm seeing my sponsor today and going to several meetings a week. It's helping, but still, I think about drinking nearly all the time." He sighed and looked down as though he had lost his best friend. "I probably always will," he said softly as he shook his head.

"Yep. Just like I'll probably always wonder if you're still sober. Comes with the territory."

"Accusing me of being drunk on the day of my accident was low. Even for you."

"Hey, that's not fair. We've been through a lot. You've been through a lot. And lobstering is dangerous. I'm always worried about you during the day. Your alcohol use just adds to my worry. How's your arm feeling?"

Jimmy stretched his arm out and clasped his fingers open and shut. "Attached. It aches a lot during the day, but at least they managed to get it on without too much loss of mobility. It could've been worse.

All things considered." He shoved a forkful of pancakes in his mouth, dripping syrup down his sweatshirt.

"I'm proud of you. It can't be easy, but you're doing it. Maybe your accident was a real blessing?" she said.

"Yeah, probably was. It really shook me up. Things like that tend to cut through the usual nonsense in our heads."

She moved her last bite of the pancakes across her plate, sopping up every bit of the syrup.

"Yeah, we're lucky. I don't know what I'd do without you."

She put her fork down, sipped the remains of her coffee. "Do you have a to-go cup? I could use some of this for the ride to Dover," she said, holding up her mug.

He heaved himself out of his La-Z-Boy and said, "I have all sorts of tumblers. The trick is finding a lid."

She followed him into the kitchen, where he rummaged through the tumbler drawer.

She loaded the dishwasher while she waited. "Thanks, Jimmy. I appreciate you letting me hide out here. It shouldn't be too much longer. With any luck, I'll have the case wrapped up in short order."

"You going to feed Stacy to the wolves? Be great to see her locked up. She deserves it."

Kari laughed and said, "Not exactly. Even if it would be satisfying to see her suffer. I have a plan that just might work."

"As in you think you might be able to get her off?"

"Yep. I have a hunch that a fellow board member killed Greg. I just can't figure out how she got ahold of the bute. I'm hoping that if I bluff well enough, she'll tell me everything."

"I've seen you bluff in poker. Trust me, she'll tell you everything," he said with a quick laugh.

She stood on her tiptoes and kissed his cheek. "Dibs on the bathroom."

Chapter 46

After leaving Jimmy's house, Kari settled into her car for the drive to New Hampshire to meet with Lori Spec. Sleeping on Jimmy's couch had to be short-lived. The quicker the case resolved, the better. She yawned for the third time in a row, sat up straighter, and opened her window, hoping the cool morning air would revive her. Even one night of tossing and turning had a way of splitting open cracks in her concentration, leaving her feeling somewhat out of control as she navigated toward a possible solution to the case against Stacy Stadt.

She fiddled with the radio station, finding nothing she cared to listen to. She glanced down at the car's clock once again: almost 9:00 a.m. Mack had watched Lori Spec's actions over the past week. He determined that Wednesdays were Lori's day off with her daughter, Mary.

Kari's navigational app chimed, alerting her to make the next right turn. The thick wall of forest blocked her view of the upcoming street sign. She slowed down to a crawl, hoping to catch the turn on the first pass. She drove by a small gas station, a couple of greasy spoon restaurants, and one lone grocery store. Not bad for rural New Hampshire. Many areas simply had a combined gas station and mini-mart for most needs.

Lori Spec lived in a shabby beige complex of roughly twenty freestanding eight-unit condo buildings surrounded by a thick forest. A sign indicated a trailhead leading to a state-run park located in the back of the complex. Kari passed a small pool as she drove through the complex. A few faded plastic lounge chairs were scattered on the worn pool deck. Warped picnic tables sat near several grills. Neatly cut grass, trimmed bushes, and several pots of flowers had been thoughtfully placed throughout, in sharp contrast to the otherwise abysmal lack of upkeep.

Lori lived in a unit near the back of the complex. Kari double-checked the address when she parked. She had no idea how Lori would react to her proposal. Anything could happen, including nothing that would move the case against Stacy closer toward closure. Ryker's visit had rattled her enough that she knew her career and possibly her life depended on resolving the case. *Would a man like that ever stop?*

Kari walked up the exterior wooden staircase to the second story of the building, then knocked on number eleven. A TV played loud enough inside to make her wonder if anyone would hear the knock. She waited and then knocked again, harder. After a few seconds she heard the muffled sound of a woman's voice.

Finally, the door opened. "Hi," said Lori hesitantly.

She wore navy yoga pants and a simple white T-shirt. Her medium-length platinum blond hair matched Stacy's hair color exactly. They were roughly the same height and build, confirming Kari's assumption that the police had misidentified Stacy as the woman on the boat the night Greg died. Their work had been sloppy at best, considering the seriousness of the charges.

"Hi, my name is Kari Sharpe. I'm an attorney in Portland, Maine."

Lori took a step back and closed the door slightly, shielding her body. "Okay," she said with a questioning lilt. Lori's eyes darted from Kari to the exterior staircase as though she was watching for a monster. Strain laced her delicate features as her eyes searched for danger.

Kari tried to reassure her. "I'm so sorry to come here unannounced. I'm not here because of your husband, Bruce, or anything related to him or your marriage. Your location is safe and so are you. I'm very sorry if I alarmed you."

Kari spoke as softly as she could manage, trying to soothe Lori's nerves. She needed Lori to cooperate. Not flee. Kari knew that if Lori ran a second time, the likelihood of finding her would be slim.

"Then why are you here?" asked Lori. She continued to look over Kari's shoulder. She stood very still, with one hand tightly gripping the door and the other draped across her abdomen.

"I represent Stacy Stadt in connection with her husband's death. I need to speak with you about the night you met with Greg. That's all."

Before Kari could continue, Lori stiffened. "I have nothing to say about Greg. He was a nice guy and drowned. It was tragic, but not my concern. Sorry I can't help you. I need to get my daughter ready to leave." Lori stood back and had started to close the door when Kari interjected, pressing forward.

"My client is accused of murdering her husband, but you and I both know it was you on the boat the night he died, not Stacy. I have an idea that I think will work for both of you," said Kari. She tilted her head, smiled gently, and persisted. "If you would let me in, I can explain further." Kari then shifted tones radically from compassionate to firm. She placed her hands on her hips and said, "My other option is that I file a motion to dismiss this afternoon. In it I will lay out the evidence I have against you." Kari paused for a second to let the impact of her words sink in. "I don't represent you, but trust me, you need to get ahead of this."

Anger flashed across Lori's face. "I don't know who the hell you are or why you think you can just come here and threaten me. Get out or I'll call the cops!" She stood back and moved to slam the door in Kari's face. Kari took a step forward and jammed herself into the doorframe, preventing it from closing. Undeterred, Lori repeatedly smashed the door onto Kari's shoulder. "Get out! Get out! I have nothing to say to you."

"Mommy!" The shriek of a child's voice sounded from behind Lori.

Lori turned her head to look over her shoulder, giving Kari a reprieve from the assault. "Not now, Mary. Go back into the family room," she shouted.

The girl burst into tears, making both women pause. Kari had been that child on numerous occasions. She had watched both her father and brother fight with the cops, resisting arrest.

Kari pushed the door hard into Lori's leg, toppling her backward, then stepped inside. She closed the door with a bang and turned to Lori. "Geez. You didn't have to nail me so hard in the shoulder. What the heck? I just want to talk to you."

The blank face of Lori's daughter peered at her around the corner of the small living room wall.

Lori regained her footing and stood motionless. Stunned. She looked back and forth between her daughter and Kari, weighing her options. The dark circles under her eyes were prominent in the morning light. She rubbed her cheek and frowned. Her stubby fingers had been bitten down to the quick. Each one confirmation that Lori had nibbled away moments of terror by ingesting her own skin.

"Just a few minutes. That's all," said Kari. "What happens from here is your call."

Kari looked over Lori's shoulder into the dark interior of the apartment. She shuffled slightly from one foot to the other, waiting. After a moment Lori said, "Fine. But I don't have long."

Kari followed her into the small kitchen.

The sparse apartment had only the basics—an ancient couch, a TV, a kitchen table with four mismatched chairs, and a four-cup coffee maker. Kari wondered if a women's shelter had helped her to relocate, because the apartment looked as sterile as a hotel room. The light scent of an air freshener lingered, mixing with the aromas of coffee and cleaning detergents.

"Can I get you anything?" offered Lori mechanically. She pointed to one of the wooden chairs at the table and motioned for Kari to take a seat.

"No, thanks. I'll get right to the point."

Kari clasped her hands in her lap, turning them over as she paused. She needed to take a cautious approach with Lori. She had been through a lot to get to safety. Kari looked over Lori's fresh, clean face, searching for visible signs of abuse. The simple wooden table wobbled slightly as Kari placed her hands on it. Several crayon-colored pictures had been affixed to the refrigerator with magnets from the apartment complex. Glancing at Lori, Kari swore to herself that she would take the class on trauma-informed communication.

"As I mentioned, I represent Stacy Stadt in the case against her by the State of Maine. However, through the course of investigating the case, I discovered that you were the woman on the boat with Greg the night he died, not Stacy."

Lori twisted in her chair and turned her mug in her hands, fidgeting. She started to say something, but Kari held up her hand.

"Please, let me continue. I have surveillance video of you getting into an Uber around the time Greg died. I also have a statement from the Uber driver confirming where he dropped you off. Finally, I have a statement from your babysitter, Kimmy, and her mother, Peg, confirming the time you arrived home. Everything points to you having been with Greg when he died."

Kari leaned into the table. She unfolded and refolded her hands, watching Lori's reaction. She could feel a crumb under the side of her palm but resisted the urge to swipe it away.

Lori looked away and started to cry softly. "I can't go back. He'll kill me. I can't go back," she said softly, shaking her head. "What'll happen to our daughter? She can't possibly live with him alone." Her mug shook as she lifted it to her lips for a sip.

"I know. But you need to tell the prosecutor and the police what happened that night. Otherwise Stacy Stadt might be convicted for a crime she never committed. You seem like a nice lady, door slamming aside," she said as she waved her hand in the direction of the door. "I'd imagine you'd never want that to happen." Kari paused, then added, "I'm guessing you were used by Beth Thornberry."

Lori's head jerked up, and tears streamed down her face. Her mouth opened, then closed without a sound. "How do you know about her?" she stammered.

"Beth is desperate for the casino measure to pass. You were, by all accounts, the last hope to get Greg to change his mind and vote in favor of the measure. Your fellow board members told me that you were the only person who could convince him to vote with the group. She used you to get to him. And you were the last person to see him alive. You must've delivered the drug that gave him the heart attack."

Lori shook her head hard from side to side as though she was trying to erase a memory. She suddenly stopped, locked eyes with Kari. The dead look in her eyes made Kari shift in her seat, wondering if she had made the right call to barge into the apartment.

Lori broke their gaze, walked to the kitchen sink, and leaned against it. She pulled a tissue out of her pocket, swiped her eyes and nose. Her hand trembled as she lifted the glass to her mouth. Gulping hard, she barely took a breath as she drained the entire glass, wiping her lips with the soiled tissue.

"Heart attack? Geez. Really? I thought he drowned. What do I do? I can't go back there. Bruce will know and will take Mary away. I can't allow that to happen." She loosened her ponytail. Wisps of platinum blond hair fell, framing her face.

Cartoons played in the other room. Every so often Mary cheered and clapped loudly, oblivious to the life-changing conversation happening in the kitchen. Turning back to Kari, Lori said, "You need to leave right now. If you know where I am, so does he. And there's no way I'll allow myself to be taken away from my daughter, not by you or anyone else. Now leave."

Lori looked like she had every intention of fleeing. Stacy's defense turned on throwing Lori into the mix. At the very least, she could proffer the alternate theory of the case to the jury. Although a jury trial came with significant risks for the defendant.

Kari leaned on the table toward Lori, like a friend might do. Then she said, "I know. This is a tricky situation. I respect your need to keep your location concealed. I don't blame you at all for that. However, my next stop is to call the prosecutor to tell her what I know. Not only can I connect you to Greg on the night of the murder, but I can connect Beth to the phenylbutazone that gave Greg a major heart attack. And then there are the wounds on his hands and face, as though you attacked him. As far as I can tell, either Beth used you or she merely helped you to do something you had already planned to do. Either way, it doesn't look good for you." Kari stopped herself from saying more. She needed to give Lori a chance to absorb her words.

Lori's face and body tensed. Anger flashed across her sad eyes as her face reddened. She raised her hand and shouted at Kari, "Get out! I never attacked him or anyone. I tried to help! You've said enough. This ends now." Her screaming words echoed off the walls in the tight space.

Undeterred, Kari pressed forward. "I've already alerted the New Hampshire authorities that I might need assistance. It'll take minutes for them to arrive and haul you back to Maine. In handcuffs. There's nowhere you'll be safe from this. It's not something you can run from. Besides, unless you beat Beth to the punch, she'll pin everything on you. It's what I'd do if I represented her." Kari had lied about alerting the authorities. She had no intention of doing so until necessary.

Lori swayed, then grabbed the side of the countertop to steady herself. Her shoulders hunched as the fake bravado drained from her. Mary walked into the tiny eat-in kitchen. The pink princess pajamas hung on her frame. "Momma, scary." The little girl clung to her mother's leg. Her hair jumbled and knotted from sleep. One tiny pale hand clutched a stuffed bunny.

Lori leaned over and scooped up her baby girl. She pulled her close and inhaled audibly, closing her eyes momentarily. After a few seconds she said, "How about more cereal? Okay? Everything is fine." Mary nodded and patted her mother's cheek with her small hand.

"Go back to the family room, and I'll bring you a nice bowl," she said as she placed the little girl down. Mary stood staring at Kari. "Go on," said Lori, nudging her shoulder out of the room.

After Mary walked out of the kitchen, Lori blew her nose loudly. "What a mess. I just wanted to get away from Bruce. He controlled everything we did. He watched every penny I made; I couldn't even buy toothpaste and pantyhose at the drugstore without him accusing me of stealing his money or having an affair. And the abuse, it had gotten so bad I worried about Mary's safety. I couldn't handle the thought of him hurting her. Then the casino issue came along. Bruce knew I had the chance to receive gifts from the casino company, Magellion, so he watched me even closer. I could barely breathe under his constant scrutiny."

She pulled out a napkin from the stand on the table and wiped her runny nose again. In a huff she added, "Everyone else received all sorts of gifts from Magellion. Yet, when it came to me, they conditioned those gifts on Greg's vote. As though I could control him. I couldn't make him do anything. Then one day Beth showed up at my work. She said she wanted me to try one more time with Greg. She gave me the Tito's as a gift for him."

Kari held up her hand. "Please stop. I can't have you telling me anything else about that night. It'll impact my ability to represent Stacy Stadt."

Lori nodded slightly. She picked at her cuticles and then nibbled on the side of her thumb, drawing a tiny droplet of blood. She tugged at her ear, then twirled a loose strand of hair, lost in thought. After a few seconds she said, "What do I do?" Her eyes pleaded with Kari for help.

Kari leaned toward her and said, "I spoke with a friend of mine before coming here today. If you want, he can represent you when you go to the police and tell them what happened."

Kari twisted in her seat to get something out of her bag. She handed Lori a piece of paper with the name Jeb Gleason on it, along with his phone number.

"He's an excellent attorney who will do everything he can to ensure the best possible outcome for you."

"What? No. I want you to represent me. I can't go with some guy I don't know," she said, shaking her head. She cracked her knuckles numerous times as she pleaded with Kari for help. Lori's eyes darted around the kitchen. Her leg bounced with anxiety, nearly toppling the wobbly table. Glancing at her fingers, she chose her next sacrifice, bringing her middle finger to her mouth to bite the cuticle. "You need to leave. That's it. I'm done. Just get out. I listened, but can't help. Sorry."

"I understand how you feel, but unfortunately, I am unable to represent you because I represent Stacy. In fact, I shouldn't even be here because of the conflict. However, considering everything you've been through with Bruce and that your safety needs to be ensured, I took the chance to speak with you before going to the prosecutor's office."

Lori placed her head in her hands and sobbed, not bothering to stop her tears as they dotted the table beneath her. Her chest heaved as her body curled from the effort of releasing years of fear, shame, and grief.

Kari bit her lip, trying not to become upset. She knew firsthand what it felt like to sob so hard her body curled onto itself. Emotion started to take root, threatening to yank her back into the darkness of her memories.

"What will happen to me? To us?" asked Lori through her tears. The question returned Kari to the present. To herself as an attorney, rather than a frightened child. She sat up straighter.

"I can't say for certain, but I do know one thing. You need an attorney."

Lori sat back against her chair. It creaked as she changed positions. She pulled the scrunchie out of her ponytail, allowing her hair to fall. Turning back to Kari, she nodded and said, "Okay. I'll speak with him."

Kari nodded back and said, "I called him on my way here. He said he can meet you at his office this afternoon, and then the two of you can go together to give the statement. It'd be best if he's with you from start to finish. He's expecting you today at two."

Lori looked away and then back to Kari. "Today? This is happening so fast. I can't just . . ." She hesitated, then said, "I can't pay for this. I can barely afford this place." She waved her hand toward the family room as she spoke, then stood and walked to the cabinet. She pulled out a small pink plastic bowl for Mary's cereal.

Once Lori had left the room, Kari pinched her tired eyes. She rubbed her forehead and waited for Lori.

"I know this is moving fast and understand how stressful this is for you. However, I have a duty to my client and intend to file my motion to dismiss this afternoon, with or without your statement to the police. Once I do that, your location will no longer be concealed. I can't say what will happen to your daughter. You need to manage this as best as you can. I'm giving you that chance out of kindness. I grew up in a rough home and feel for your situation. If it were anyone else, I would've handled things differently. Much differently."

Lori swiped the sheet of paper with Jeb Gleason's contact information on it. She looked at it for a long moment.

Kari knew their time together had ended. She grabbed her bag, turned to Lori, and said, "Thanks for meeting with me. I know I didn't bring the easiest of news, but you're in good hands with Jeb."

After saying goodbye to Lori, Kari sat in her car for a moment; then she set an alarm on her watch. If Lori failed to contact Jeb within the next thirty minutes, Kari planned to get the police involved. "Let's hope I don't need to," she mumbled.

The emotionally charged conversation and the bruising from the door had taken a toll on her. She searched her bag for the hard candies she kept, just in case she needed a sugar rush. Finally, she laid her hands on the thick roll of "very berry" candies and took two. She crunched as she pulled out of the complex.

Nearly everything had been set in motion; a few more phone calls and the trap would be set for Beth. Her mind returned to Ryker's visit. A chill ran up her spine as she thought about his cold, dead eyes. Maybe she would be spending more time on Jimmy's couch than she had anticipated, just in case.

Only a few vehicles passed her on the rural road back to Maine. A few miles later, she stopped at a local variety store for a drink and to top off her tank. She made a mental note to charge Stacy for the gas, the drive time, and a large bag of chips. Why not? Stacy could afford it. As she waited for the tank to fill, she scrolled through her phone. Three minutes left on the timer. The phone chimed with a new text from Jeb Gleason.

Hi Kari, I just spoke with Lori Spec. She's on her way to my office. She wants you to be at the station with her when she makes her statement. Are you able to meet us at two?

Kari quickly typed back: Yes. Thanks for the update. When I left her, I wasn't sure if she planned to call you or bolt. I gave either option fifty percent chance of happening.

Jeb replied: She seemed terrified, but ready to get this done.

Kari replied: Perfect. I'll contact Nell Braider to let her know what's happening.

Jeb: OK, see you soon.

Chapter 47

Lori closed the door on the attorney and leaned against it. She needed a minute to absorb everything and to think about her options. Kari Sharpe had told her to either call the other attorney or she would contact the police immediately. Attorney Sharpe's tone and candor drove the point home. Lori needed to act. Fast.

She swiped her phone off the kitchen table and dialed the number for Jeb Gleason. They agreed she would meet him at the station at two. She also asked that Kari Sharpe meet them. By her estimation, the request added a touch of authenticity. She had worked too damned hard to get away from Bruce. She would never risk her safety or Mary's by going back to Maine. Never. She just needed to buy some time.

After grabbing the only suitcase she and Mary owned, she jammed their meager belongings inside. Nothing fit properly as she pushed and flattened their clothing. Finally, she swiped their toiletries off the bathroom counter into a shopping bag. She needed to leave. Fast.

Mary protested only slightly about the change of their normal routine. Lori promised an ice-cream cone as a reward for compliance. Not the worst thing to promise. After buckling Mary into the car seat, she closed the back door. A loud bang in the parking lot caused her to jump as she opened her door.

A black Cadillac Escalade had rolled up behind her, blocking her exit. A slim man walked toward her.

"Hello, Ms. Spec. Where could you be going in such a hurry?" he said as he approached. The man looked mean. She had seen the same glimmer in Bruce's eyes when he had been very out of control. Recoiling, she glanced at Mary.

"Who are you? How do you know my name?" she demanded. Her voice cracked, exposing her stress.

"Well, let's just say I know a lot of things about you. I suspect you've decided to make a run for it because Attorney Sharpe exposed some hard truths. Am I right?"

Lori didn't know what to say. Her eyes darted back to her daughter. Mary softly kicked her little shoes back and forth, lighting them up, oblivious to their predicament. Two young women walked past with their dogs, chatting and laughing.

He held up a hand to stop her from saying anything. "Relax. I came here with a proposal for you. I think you might like what I have to say."

She slowly closed her door and listened to the man.

Chapter 48

A few hours later, Kari and Nell Braider, the assistant deputy attorney general assigned to prosecute Stacy, stood behind the two-way mirror in the Portland Police Station, listening to Lori give a full account of the night Greg Stadt died. She said she had given Greg the Tito's without knowing Beth had spiked it. Once he'd fallen into the water, she had tried to rescue him, but couldn't before he sank.

"Poor woman. The wounds on his hands and face certainly fit with her account of what happened," said Nell, shaking her head.

"Yeah, she's terrified and desperate to keep herself and her daughter safe," said Kari.

"We've taken all necessary precautions to keep her name and current address out of the public record. No amount of digging around on his behalf will unearth her."

"Thank you," said Kari softly. "The worst part of this for me is how Lori was used. Beth probably saw Lori's bruises and knew she must've been desperate to leave Bruce. Beth used Lori's desperation to set the entire thing in motion by giving her the spiked vodka and sending her to meet with Greg. It's sickening."

Nell shook her head and pursed her lips. "I want the people responsible for this. All of them."

"Me too. After the charges against my client have been dropped. I assume that'll happen now that you've taken Lori's statement."

"Yes, of course. I'll work on it today."

Nell had been known in school as a hard worker who could be trusted to provide reliably good answers when called upon by a professor. Kari had never heard anything negative about the attorney. She told Nell everything she'd learned about the casino issue in Sweetwater and how Beth Thornberry had worked with the Magellion Group to influence each of the board members.

"As you heard, Magellion conditioned Lori's receipt of money on Greg Stadt's vote in favor of the slot machines. Beth Thornberry had access to bute. I'll provide you with the name of the veterinarian Beth uses for her horses. I spoke with him. He became instantly defensive when I mentioned the bute. His response to my questions confirmed my suspicions that Beth gave Lori the drug. As she stated, she had no idea that night would turn fatal."

"Interesting. I'll take his name and will follow up today," she said. She turned back to the interrogation room.

After a few minutes, Nell added, "I'd love to nail Beth Thornberry through the financial records. Math never lies. If we can show a transfer of funds, that along with the bottle of Tito's might just give this office a way to grab her and possibly the Magellion Group, if they provided the funding to Beth knowing how she'd use it."

"Yep. That's exactly what I had been thinking."

"I plan to prepare a warrant to search Sweetwater Downs, including all their financial records. I'm also going to send the boys out to speak with Beth. Maybe she'll break and tell us something. While I'm at it, I'll send them to speak with the veterinarian as well." Nell thought for a moment, then continued, "Lori consented to a search of her house. We'll go there today to recover the bottle containing the bute."

Kari smiled slightly to herself. Lori had confessed that she had hid the bottle in the garage near the compost bags because her husband hated composting. The one small space provided Lori the only measure of control in her chaotic life. As a child, Kari had hid a small wooden box of her treasures in the crook of a tree on their property. Just the mere act of turning the small box in her hands had allowed her to reclaim a measure of her power.

"Yeah, sometimes it's the small victories that get us through," said Kari.

"I'm sure Beth Thornberry's prints are all over the bottle. We'll get her."

Kari nodded, then looked over her shoulder through the glass door. Loud shouts caught her attention. Several uniformed officers walked past, holding a cuffed man. The man shouted obscenities at the unfazed officers.

Nell closed her file and said, "Thanks, Kari. You did an amazing job pulling this together. I'm still considering filing charges against Lori. I haven't decided yet. It bothers me that she just went home. Never called for rescue. Just went home. It's cold and might also be criminal. Or it's like she said, she was desperate to get away. I'm on the fence."

Nell rolled back on her heels as she concentrated. Lori's fate hung on the prosecutor's decision.

Kari considered Lori's traumatized child. She glanced at Nell and said, "I'll let you work it out with Lori and her attorney. This is where I leave the case. Stacy Stadt is my only concern."

"Fair enough."

◆ ◆ ◆

After the interrogation ended, Kari walked the short distance from the police station to her office on the waterfront.

She sat at her desk and dialed Stacy's number. She needed to advise her of the developments in the case. Every interaction with Stacy had been hostile, yet Kari held her own. She sat up straighter at her desk, waiting for Stacy to answer.

"Well, it's about time you called me, Kari," said Stacy in her usual angry, self-important manner.

"I need to update you on a few developments. You'll be happy to know that I believe your case will be dismissed."

Without skipping a beat, Stacy said, "Really? How? Why? I thought we had to go to trial?"

Kari quickly updated her about the evidence she had discovered through her investigation. Then said, "I wanted to avoid trial because of the inherent risk of placing your fate in the hands of jurors. It's a dicey prospect, to say the least." Stacy had not said anything. Kari heard the soft murmurs of her crying. She pressed on: "I'll let you know if anything changes. For now, don't say anything to anyone. The case isn't dismissed yet. Anything can still happen."

"Thank you, Kari. Thank you," Stacy said softly. She sniffled loudly, then added in a whisper, "You did good. Thank you." The phone disconnected.

Tears pooled in Kari's eyes as she struggled to push aside her emotions. Stacy's simple acknowledgment of her work carried so much weight. Until that moment she thought she didn't need Stacy's approval. Yet an unmistakable feeling of belonging filled the void created by Stacy's bullying. She finally saw Stacy as she probably always had been. Deeply insecure, attacking the world like a cornered animal. The bullying had nothing to do with Kari, and she finally knew it.

She opened the window. The sweetly scented air washed over her.

Chapter 49

Beth Thornberry rushed home to grab a few things, including the small amount of cash and passport she had secured in her closet safe. She hastily shoved clothing into bags, hoping to make it to the Canadian border before the police connected the dots and came for her.

Ryker had called her earlier in the day to warn her that attorney Kari Sharpe had found Lori Spec, who had connected Beth to the spiked vodka. He'd said she would best be leaving town, if she knew what was good for her. He'd assured her that he would run the place, with the help of Joe Spencer, her trainer and friend. Once things cooled down, and she had a chance to obtain legal representation, she could come back, he said.

Ryker's tone scared her to the point that she considered turning herself in just to get the protection of being incarcerated. Yet he seemed to know everything. He had spies everywhere. No place was safe for her now. She owed the Magellion Group over $300,000. They would get their pound of flesh, one way or another.

"Come on, Max," she called to her little dog. She put him outside for one more patrol of his backyard before they left their home, perhaps forever.

She ran her hands over the kitchen counters, stood for a moment surveying the space. She had lived there for so long, she barely knew if she would be able to exist without the comfort of knowing these walls always stood to protect her. She tried to remain strong. It was the end of the line for her. Nothing and no one would save her.

She closed the door behind her and Max one last time. Engaging the lock with care, she patted the doorframe, then leaned her head against its painted flank with a heavy sigh.

"Okay, Max. That's enough mushy stuff, let's go." She snapped her fingers for the dog. He ran behind her and jumped into the front seat of the truck.

She heaved two heavy bags into the back seat, slammed the rusty door shut, and settled in behind the wheel. They flew out of the driveway with far more speed than normal. Gripping the steering wheel, she ground her teeth as she hunched forward toward the windshield.

Finally, they made it to the interstate. Once on the main road, she eased up a little. Maybe, just maybe, she would get away from Maine before her life blew up. Maybe. Leaning back into her seat, she tried to relax.

A few minutes later, in her rearview mirror she saw a car speeding toward her. As it came closer, her mind accepted what her eyes already knew. The police had found her. Their lights flashed the urgency she felt.

"Damn it. Now what?"

The patrol car flashed and beeped at her to pull over. Her mind reeled, unsure of what to do. Finally, she turned to Max and said, "I'm sorry, Max." Patting his sweet, innocent face. He looked at her, turning his head from side to side, trying to understand her words.

She pulled over and waited with her hands on the steering wheel in the ten-and-two position, not moving a muscle until the officer arrived.

"Beth Thornberry?"

"Yes, Officer, was I speeding?" She tried to play innocent.

A second officer approached the passenger side of the car. Max barked loudly and scratched the window at him. Then turned to bark at the officer near Beth.

"Step out of the car, please," said the officer on the driver's side. He stood back, adjusted his sunglasses, and watched her as she unbuckled and opened her door. As soon as her feet touched the ground, he spun her around, pinning her to the side of the truck, and said, "Beth Thornberry, you're under arrest for the murder of Greg Stadt. You have the right to . . ." He went on and on. All Beth could do was think about Max. What would happen to him?

"My dog! Max? You can't take me now. He's alone. I can't leave him here," she shrieked. Tears flowed down her face as she desperately tried to ensure Max's safety. She dragged her feet and turned back to the truck, trying to stay with Max. The officer nudged her forcefully.

"We'll call animal control. They'll deliver him to the Cumberland County Animal Shelter. You can ask someone to pick him up on your behalf."

Her knees crumbled under the weight of abandoning her little dog. She loved him more than she thought possible. Looking over her shoulder, she saw his little face pushed up against the rear window of her truck, smearing the glass with his wet nose. He clawed and barked at it, trying to get to her. Even in this moment he tried to protect her. A steady stream of tears flowed down her face, moistening her shirt. The handcuffs pulled painfully on her wrists.

The officer walked her the rest of the short distance to the waiting patrol car. With one practiced move, he shoved her in the back seat and slammed the door. Both officers climbed in and buckled their seat belts. They chatted about their weekend plans, the weather, and their kids as though nothing had happened. As though her life had not fallen apart.

They drove her to Portland, where she faced an uncertain future. She turned one more time to her truck. Max's warm breath fogged the windows as he desperately barked and clawed his way toward her.

Chapter 50

Stacy Stadt pulled up to the small branch of the Sweetwater Bank. Their redbrick office sat on one side of the supermarket parking lot. Dark-purple hydrangeas flanked the nondescript entrance. A large welcome sign adorned the glass door.

She had just finished in court. Finally, she could put the entire mess with Greg behind her and never see Kari Sharpe again. As she'd sat in court, she kept hearing Greg's words telling her to be nice. "Just be nice, for a change," he'd told her so many times.

Kari stood tall and firm next to her. She spoke to the judge with such authority it astonished Stacy that she had been the same person they'd picked on so many times. The scared, skinny kid was gone. Instead, a confident woman stood before her.

The judge had barely looked at her as he'd spoken with the lawyers about how the case would be dismissed. The only time he'd even addressed her was when he explained that the case would be dismissed with prejudice. He had gone on and on about how that meant they could never charge her again, like she was an idiot. It had taken all her strength not to shout at the annoying man to shut up already.

As they'd walked out of the courthouse, she'd turned to Kari and said, "Thank you. So much." The words had been all she could manage. The realization that she had been officially cleared of the charges and the shame she felt for hurting Kari so many times had finally sunk in.

She could barely face Kari. Instead, she'd bolted for the parking garage without looking back.

Once she'd left the courthouse, she'd headed straight to the bank. The short drive had given her the time she needed to compose herself.

She grabbed her Louis Vuitton handbag and slammed her car door. Her heels clicked on the pavement as she stomped toward her meeting with the loan officer. Glancing at her watch, she realized that she had been delayed enough in court to make her twenty minutes late. She hated being late. "Damn it," she muttered.

Quickly walking past the window tellers, she navigated directly to Brad Keller's semiprivate cubicle. Brad had worked with Greg over the years to secure funding for the business as they grew from an idea to a successful, large-scale land developer.

"Hi, Brad," she said as she sat in front of him.

"Stacy, it's nice to see you. What brings you in today?" he said.

She hated the tone Brad had always had when she and Greg went into the bank. Initially he had been reserved, noncommittal, and at times a little snobby. Then, as they became more and more successful, his tone had changed to a fake accommodating deference. He made her sick.

"I'm here to talk about Sweetwater Downs and the money Beth Thornberry owes the bank," she said. She picked a thread off her black dress slacks, then smoothed the fabric as she crossed her toned legs.

"Well, of course, but as you know, I can't possibly discuss another customer's finances with you," he said. He fiddled with his pen as he spoke, then added, "Maybe if Greg were still with us, we could work on something else? A loan for the business or creative financing for one of your buyers, that sort of thing." He frowned and then added, "How are things at Houses by Stadt after his unfortunate accident?"

Stacy ground her teeth, trying to control herself. She envisioned leaning over the desk and slamming his face down onto his keyboard. Instead, she plowed forward. "Look, cut the crap. We both know that Beth Thornberry owes the bank a boatload of money, and you guys are going to be exercising your power of sale soon. I want to get ahead of it and make an offer for the property right now. No Realtors needed."

Over the years Greg and Stacy had learned how to spot gold in the newspaper. Banks always placed a notice in the paper announcing the sale of distressed property. Greg had always said, "One person's debt albatross is another person's lottery ticket." They'd spent their time combing through the paper to spot opportunities, then they would approach the bank before it had a chance to place the property on the market. The banks had relished the opportunity to sell the property quickly, get paid for the outstanding loan owed by the property owner, all while avoiding a Realtor's fee. It had worked out for everyone involved.

"Interesting. Let me check on the property," he said. He moved his mouse around and scrunched his eyes as he looked at the monitor. Mumbling "hmm" a few times, he finally turned to Stacy. "Looks like the notices are prepared and ready to be published in the paper starting tomorrow. Ten days from now, assuming Ms. Thornberry does not pay off the debt, the bank will be able to sell it." He crossed his arms across his chest and said, "And you want to buy the entire parcel? We'd anticipate selling it for well north of two hundred thousand."

"Yes. My offer is two hundred and ten thousand dollars, cash sale, closing in thirty days or sooner if the lawyers can get their heads out of their asses and get their paperwork done quickly."

He rubbed his chin, clicked a few more times on his mouse, and then turned to her. "I'll need approval for this, but I think we can make something happen here."

"Fine, I'll get things ready on my end. You know who we use for our real property transactions. You can call him to arrange everything," she said as she stood up. She leaned over to grab her bag, then turned to him.

He stood, extended his hand. "Thanks for coming in today, Stacy. I assume I'll be seeing the newest development from Houses by Stadt on the former Sweetwater Downs property soon?"

She took his hand to shake it. It felt limp and clammy, matching his pitiful personality. "You and everyone else will be seeing changes soon enough."

Once back in her car, she pumped hand sanitizer on her palms and rubbed them together. The guy made her feel sick. The faster she washed him off her hands, the better. Glancing at her watch, she calculated that she had roughly forty minutes until her nail appointment, just enough time to grab an iced latte. Perfect.

Chapter 51

Joe Spencer patted Max's head and allowed him to nuzzle into his side as they drove to Sweetwater Downs. After Beth's arrest, she had asked him to take care of Max. It had been a request he could hardly refuse. He loved the little dog and Beth. His fingers tightened on the steering wheel as images of Beth in prison tortured him. He yawned loudly, distracting Max from his slumber. The strain of thinking about Beth had made sleep nearly impossible.

The truck bounced slightly as they turned into the parking lot of the Downs. The early-morning sunrise lit the sky with the colorful hues of pinks, reds, and purples. He sat in his truck in awe of the beauty. After a few moments he patted Max and said, "Okay, boy, let's get our day started."

The large wooden barn door rolled smoothly on its tracks. In response, one horse after another poked their heads out of their stalls to see who approached. Each horse stirred, kicking hooves and braying in anticipation of being let out into the paddock.

"Good morning, beautiful," he said to a young mare as he patted her head. After pushing back the iron pin on her stable door, he clicked the lead on her harness and walked her toward the paddock. She shook her head a few times, pulling to go faster. The arthritis in his knuckles ached from straining to hold her lead. "Okay, girl. Give an old-timer a break. You'll get there," he said to her. The thick of her mane brushed his gnarled knuckles as they walked side by side.

After he put the horses into the paddock, he stood grasping the smooth wooden rail of the enclosure. The horses lazily ate grass, unaware of the issues that troubled him. Without Beth running the place, he had no idea what would happen to the business. The casino people and a few others he had never seen before had come and gone since her arrest, but nothing had been mentioned about the future. The only thing he knew was that his paycheck had kept coming, so he'd kept working.

Back in the barn, he found Max sniffing the large pile of fresh manure in one of the stalls. "Come on, boy, get out of there," said Joe to him. The obedient little dog inspected the pile for another second, then ran to Joe's side for scratches. "Good boy," he said to Max's wiggling body.

The rest of the day flew by as he worked to keep everything running as though nothing had happened. Although everyone had heard about Beth's arrest for murder, they had tried to maintain the facade of normalcy. The few waitresses, barkeeps, cooks, and groundskeepers he had spoken with said their paychecks had kept coming, at least for now. He took off his ball cap, smoothed his thinning hair, and grabbed a grooming kit from the shelf. Only time would tell what would happen to the place he had given his life to.

Chapter 52

Kari worked through her afternoon invoices, checking each one for accuracy before Ruth sent them to clients. The next in the pile was Stacy Stadt's final invoice. Smiling, she looked out the window, savoring the moment. Reviewing the statement would be her final connection to Stacy. She initialed the corner with finality and a touch of relief.

She took another few sips of her glass of water, parched from the Italian food she and Bill had had at lunch. The popular establishment had been at the same location for over fifty years, never changing either its ownership or its menu. Her relationship with Bill felt cozy. Almost safe. Although she had no idea where it would lead, it felt good for the moment, and that was good enough for now. A picture of them sat on the corner of her desk. A perfect sunset blazed behind them as they stood on the shore of his yacht club.

The door downstairs slammed, causing her to jump. As far as she knew, Ruth had not returned from lunch. She glanced at her watch—a long lunch. Rolling her eyes, she stood to greet whoever came into the office. Mack's and Ruth's voices and footfalls sounded in the stairwell as they came toward her office.

"What are you two lovebirds up to?" she asked as they came in, holding hands.

They made a cute couple, giggling like teenagers when they were together. Their bodies always seemed to be touching. Shoulders and hands melted together as though an invisible magnet drew them close.

As far as she knew, they had been dating steadily for months. Ruth had transformed from a downtrodden, glum person to a vibrant, glowing, almost bubbly, happy woman right before her eyes.

They stood in the threshold of her office, smiling at one another. Finally, Mack said, "Do you want to tell her, or do you want me to?" He bumped her shoulder as he spoke. Ruth looked up at him with such fondness it made Kari melt. *Does anyone look at me like that?*

Ruth looked down; a blush crossed her cheeks. She placed her free hand on his chest and said, "You do it, dear." They communicated with one another as though they were the only two people in the room.

Mack turned back to Kari, smiling wide. "I've asked Ruth to marry me, and she said yes. I don't know what she sees in me, but somehow she has agreed to be my wife," he said. Then he leaned down and kissed Ruth on the lips.

"What! Wow, I'm so happy for you two," said Kari as she rounded her desk. She hugged Ruth and then turned to Mack. She slapped his shoulder and then said, "I didn't know you had it in you." Then she hugged him tight. His clothing smelled like Ruth's perfume.

"Let me see the ring," she said with a soft clap.

Ruth extended her hand toward Kari. The simple but elegant engagement ring sparkled as she turned her hand left to right.

"You did good, Mack," said Kari approvingly.

"He did. I just love it." Ruth swooned. Then she added, "Ask her."

"Right. I almost forgot. We're planning a simple wedding with just a few close friends, and we want you to officiate it for us. Would you?" said Mack.

Kari stood motionless momentarily. Her eyes teared. No one had ever asked her to be part of their wedding, especially in such a special way. She hardly knew how to respond as she grappled with her emotions.

"It would mean so much to both of us if you married us, Kari. I know this isn't the sort of thing you do, but would you please consider it?" asked Ruth as she filled the void.

Ruth's eyes shone with tears. Mack cleared his throat and shuffled slightly. Then he said, "I plan to ask Jimmy to be my best man. You two are closer to me than anyone else, besides Ruth. I can't imagine our wedding without you guys."

Kari pulled a tissue out of the box on her desk and wiped her eyes. She smiled through her tears of joy and said, "Of course I'll do it. It would mean everything to me. When do you plan to get married?"

"We aren't sure yet but are thinking about planning for October. I've always wanted a fall wedding," said Ruth.

"It sounds wonderful," said Kari. "I'll be there whatever the date."

Kari rounded her desk to sit back down and added, "Thank you for asking me to be a part of your special day. It means a lot to me." Despite herself, she teared up again. She dabbed her eyes and took another sip of water.

"We'll get out of your hair; let you get back to work. I plan to ask Jimmy tonight, so keep a lid on it for now. Okay?" asked Mack, as he turned to leave.

"Absolutely. I won't say a word." She smiled. Then she added, "Ruth, take the rest of the day off. You two should celebrate."

Mack answered for her: "We appreciate the gesture, but I need to scoot. I have a few things I need to do before the end of the week. Thanks, though."

"Of course."

They left her office for the reception area below. The happy sound of their words followed them, lightening Kari's mood. After a few minutes the outside door opened and closed for a second time as Mack left.

Kari sat for a moment, unsure where she had left off. The invoices were finished. Glancing at her desk, she grabbed the file containing the rough draft of the estate-planning documents Ruth had prepared for her. She grabbed a red pen to mark up the testamentary trust. Then she glanced at her clock and decided to leave the office for the rest of the day instead.

On the final step of the staircase, she said to Ruth, "I'm going to take a couple of hours off this afternoon. I'm attending the Sweetwater town board meeting this evening for the Peterson matter. I thought I'd rest a little before it starts at seven."

"Good thinking. It'll be a late night for you. See you tomorrow."

Kari walked outside into the sunshine of the day. Lifting her face to the sky, she appreciated the feel of the sun's warm rays on her skin. She breathed in the salty, briny air and glanced at her watch again. She had several hours until the meeting. Perfect. Plenty of time for a long run, shower, and dinner before the board meeting.

A few hours later, she listened to the radio as she drove to the Sweetwater town board meeting. The song ended, and the host of the show said they were turning to local news. She started to reach for the dial when he announced:

"The man found dead in Sebago Lake has been identified as Bruce Spec, a Sweetwater resident. No foul play is suspected. Turning to the weather, we have a . . ."

What? Bruce Spec, Lori's husband, is dead? As far as Kari knew, Lori had returned to New Hampshire after meeting with Jeb in the Portland Police Station. She had given a full account of what had happened the night Greg Stadt died. Nell Braider had wasted no time in dismissing the charges against Stacy. Then the police had arrested Beth Thornberry, apparently attempting to flee Maine. Now Bruce Spec was dead? *It can't be a coincidence.*

Her blinker ticked as she turned into the Sweetwater municipal offices. Plenty of spots remained open despite the board meeting starting in less than fifteen minutes. Maybe nothing on the agenda garnered public interest, she thought as she pulled into a parking spot close to the entrance.

A few people mixed and mingled on their way into the public hearing room. Kari sat toward the back of the large space, pulled out her Peterson file, and waited. She planned to speak on behalf of the developer she represented in favor of a zoning change. The revision would allow the owner of a Laundromat to offer dry cleaning services. Not the biggest case, but the client had provided her a steady supply of work over the past year, so she would not complain. She glanced at her watch. Just a few more minutes and it would start. With any luck, her matter would be one of the first addressed, so she could leave early.

She crossed and uncrossed her legs, impatient for the meeting to start.

Chapter 53

Margaret Mitchell, the chair of the Sweetwater town board, smoothed the edges of her hairline, then adjusted her tight bun. She and her fellow board members had been in their conference room for the better part of an hour discussing various issues for tonight's meeting.

She had worked with numerous boards over the years. Each had its own challenges. Now that Greg Stadt no longer sat on the board, they had a chance to get a lot of things done for the town. Something she looked forward to.

"We have to get going; it's a few minutes past seven, and I need to get to my kid's game tonight," said Reed MacIntry.

"Not to mention the Sox are playing tonight. I need to speed this along," chimed in one of the men.

Ms. Mitchell shifted in her seat. "Fine. So long as we're all in agreement," said Ms. Mitchell. She looked at each board member and waited for a nod. "Okay, then. Let's get this over with." She smiled.

She could hardly contain her excitement. The measure would be her crowning jewel in the long years she'd given to Sweetwater as a public servant. She and her fellow board members walked in single file to the large public meeting room. Not many people attended this evening. *All the better,* she thought as she took her seat and gaveled the meeting's start.

Chapter 54

"Finally," Kari grumbled under her breath. The board members filed into the room. She had met several of them through her representation of Stacy Stadt and expected alternates would fill in for Greg Stadt and Lori Spec. Instead, Lori took her seat with the other board members. She looked far more rested than Kari remembered from their short time together. Gone were the dark circles under her eyes and the sad downward gaze.

The meeting proceeded at a snail's pace. Finally, Margaret Mitchell called the zoning issue. After an introduction, the board asked for public comment. Kari went to the lectern, pled her client's interests, and then thanked the board for its consideration. On her way back to her seat, the door to the room opened.

Stacy Stadt and Ryker Jones walked in together, drawing everyone's attention as they laughed, still mid-conversation. Stacy's hand went to her mouth and then into the air as she waved a silent apology. Stacy turned to Kari, smiled, and nodded.

The zoning issue passed unanimously, yet Kari remained seated. She had planned to leave immediately following the vote but decided to stay. Curiosity burned in her as she waited for the next matter. She cracked her knuckles and tapped her pen on her thigh, unable to sit still. The pit of her stomach tightened upon seeing Ryker. During their last encounter he had threatened her with professional ruin. Mack had warned her to stay clear of the dangerous man for good reason.

Finally, after the agenda matters had been addressed, Margaret Mitchell spoke: "I'd like to propose the addition of one final matter to tonight's meeting. Whether Sweetwater Downs should be permitted to offer slot machine gaming in its facilities. Do I have a second?"

"I'll second it," said Reed MacIntry. Reed didn't look up when he replied.

"With the addition of the issue on the agenda, the board shall now vote. All in favor of the addition?"

One by one each board member approved the addition. Then Margaret continued, "Let the record reflect that this board has had four public meetings regarding the measure, has received numerous letters from interested parties, and has taken all those comments into consideration. Is there anyone present who would like to speak?" She waited for a moment, assessing the crowd and then her fellow board members.

Stacy Stadt stood and walked to the lectern. She cleared her throat and said, "As the new owner of Sweetwater Downs, I cannot overestimate the importance of allowing our establishment to include slot machines as entertainment for its customers. The Downs has seen a steep downturn after the other casinos in Maine installed slots. Not only has the Downs suffered, but the entire town has felt the impact of reduced traffic to the area. Our hotels and restaurants have suffered alongside the Downs. Look, if the board values everything the Downs has meant to Sweetwater all the years it has served our community, then it will allow the slots. It's the only way the Downs will continue to operate into the future."

Kari listened to Stacy going on and on about the impact of the slot machines on the town. Stacy had purchased the property and chosen to run it as a casino instead of clearing it for housing, as Greg had wanted. Interesting. Once finished, Stacy walked back to her seat next to Ryker. He nodded and smiled at her.

One by one each member voted in favor of passing the measure. Lori cast the final vote in favor of the measure. After adjourning, the board members walked out of the room in single file, just as they had entered. Margaret Mitchell smiled from ear to ear, obviously pleased.

Kari stood to leave, then glanced toward Stacy and Ryker. He shook Stacy's hand and then patted her shoulder. Ryker turned to Kari and winked at her. A chill ran up her spine.

Once in her car, Kari locked her doors, something she had rarely done in Maine. Ryker had a way of making her paranoid. Lori's statement to the police had unraveled the case against Stacy quickly, as Kari had anticipated. Ryker had seemed to fade away with the closing of her file. She'd even moved back home, freeing herself from Jimmy's worn-out couch. Seeing him again tonight had been unexpected. Heat in her body rose as she turned the ignition and blasted the air-conditioning to cool off. A tendril of sweat rolled slowly between her shoulder blades.

Kari's phone buzzed: "Caller ID Unknown." She took a chance to answer. "This is Kari Sharpe."

"Ms. Sharpe, seeing you tonight was an unexpected bonus." Ryker's words oozed out of her device. Her breath hitched in her throat as her mind reeled.

"I can't say the same. Thought you would've left town already, back to whatever hellhole you spawned from," she said. The raw edges of a panic attack licked her thoughts. She struggled to maintain her cool, unwilling to let him know the effect he had on her.

He simply laughed in reply. "Come now, Ms. Sharpe, is that a way to talk to a fan? I called to congratulate you on your success in finding who murdered Greg Stadt. My hat goes off to you." He paused, then added, "My work in Maine is finished, but I plan to keep your card, just in case I need a good lawyer."

Balling her toes and free hand, she clenched and unclenched, trying to relieve her panic and anger. "Don't ever call me again."

She moved the phone away from her ear to hang up. His cruel laughter finally cut off when she disconnected and threw the phone in her cup holder. She sat for a moment, trying to reclaim her calm. Anxiety caused her mind to bounce between unrelated possibilities in a futile attempt to gain control. After a few more rounds of breaths, her thoughts drifted gently down like the settling of a shaken snow globe.

Kari's phone buzzed again. "Damn it! Leave me alone!" she shouted at the phone. Then she saw the caller ID—Bill.

Relieved, she picked it up to answer.

"Hey there," she said. Her voice sounded rung out, exhausted. A perfect mirror image of how she felt.

"Hi, please tell me you're leaving the town meeting and not just on a break. Municipal stuff always seemed to drag on longer than imaginable. It's why I won't touch that sort of work," he said.

"Oh yeah, I'm leaving. You won't believe what happened," she said.

"Your zoning amendment passed? You won, like you always do?" he joked.

She told him everything that had happened at the meeting and with Ryker.

"Geez, that guy is unbelievable. I haven't felt good about you returning to your place even after the case against Stacy resolved. Maybe you should go back to Jimmy's or my place? It'd be fun to have you bunking with me for a while," he said jokingly.

She turned on her blinker as she navigated onto her street. Running her hand through her hair, she said, "Nope. I won't run from him anymore. He won't bother me. This is over. He said his time in Maine is finished. I assume that means he's heading back to Jersey. Hopefully for good," she said, trying to sound more confident than she felt.

The TV played in the background as Bill took a minute to speak. Finally, he said, "Okay. Maybe you're right. Who knows. In any case, you can't be chased out of your home forever." He paused and added, "We still on tomorrow?"

"I wouldn't miss it for anything."

The next afternoon she joined Bill at his yacht club. They had planned to go sailing for the day, maybe even stay the night on one of the islands in Casco Bay. The sprawling club entrance overlooked the waterfront. The ocean sparkled a deep, dazzling, tranquil blue in the afternoon sunshine. A gentle ocean breeze caressed her skin as she walked down the path to the boat launch. She felt lighter and freer than she had in years. Her business was steadily growing, Jimmy had been sober for months, and she was in love. Finally in love.

"Hi, Josh, can you give me a lift?" she asked the launch operator.

Bill's boat had been moored far into the bay. The club placed the larger yachts on the outer rim of the field. Every boater who passed saw the largest, most impressive sailboats and motorboats placed in a protective half circle around the marine entrance to the club. Bill's forty-two-foot Sabre yacht certainly qualified to be in the prestigious outer rim.

"Sure thing, hop on board," said the launch operator.

Kari took the young man's hand to steady herself as she stepped onto the boat. The boat's teak glistened with fresh polish. Its brass fixtures shone from care as they sparkled in the sunlight. Thick cushions in nautical navy and white lined the bench seating. Folded wool L.L.Bean blankets had been thoughtfully arranged for members who required fortification against an evening chill.

Kari leaned back into the cushions and allowed herself to enjoy the luxury of the ride. The driver took his time navigating several large motorboats. One megayacht sat waiting to be taken out for the weekend. The lucky family had equipped it with Jet Skis and a slide for swimming off the side of the boat. Kari checked herself for a moment. She looked at her outfit, suddenly unsure of herself. Did she still carry the stench of poverty, alcoholism, and neglect? Would she ever fit into his life?

She had chosen what she considered a perfect sailing outfit—white capri pants, a pink polo shirt, and a white cashmere sweater tied around her shoulders. Exhaling, she adjusted her green Tory Burch ball cap and Maui Jim sunglasses, satisfied.

The loud engine quieted as they approached Bill's boat. As the wind shifted, the exhaust from the boat traveled toward them, making her cough slightly. She grabbed her canvas tote bag, ready to climb aboard the sailboat.

"Have a good sail," said the launch operator.

"Thanks for the ride," said Kari with a slight wave.

Bill came out of the salon just in time to help her climb aboard. He leaned down to take her hand in his, gently pulling her toward him into an embrace.

"You look beautiful, as always," he said into her ear.

She smiled, then said, "I feel bad that I didn't bring any food or drinks, but you said you had everything covered."

"I have tons of food and drinks on board. I bought all your favorites," he said with a smile and wink.

He took her tote bag as they climbed down the ladder into the interior of the boat. She followed behind him and asked, "Does that mean you bought the things I like to eat when I'm eating to be healthy, or the stuff I actually want to eat?"

He laughed and said, "Don't worry. I included a good amount of your weekend foods."

"Perfect."

A few minutes later, after returning topside, she dropped the bowline into the ocean as he spun the helm, navigating toward the center of Casco Bay. The powerful engine roared as the boat sliced through the calm sea. The sunlight bounced off the water, warming her skin. Once they cleared the mooring field, he cut the engine and hoisted the mainsail. The wind grabbed the sail, heeling the boat slightly on its side as they glided through the glistening ocean. The gentle sound of the water lapping against the hull mingled with the screeches of seagulls.

She sat back on a thick cushion in the topside seating area, watching him adjust the lines. He effortlessly moved his lean, muscular body through the necessary steps to adjust the sails to perfection. Once satisfied that they were traveling on course, he nestled in next to her.

He placed his arm around her, drawing their bodies tightly together. His steady strength and warmth held her in place. She exhaled, placing her head on his shoulder.

"I never want this day to end," he whispered in her ear. His voice husky with emotion.

"Me neither," she said as she lifted her chin to kiss him.

Epilogue

George McGovern sat on the deck of the club, overlooking the golf course. The vast greens had been expertly manicured to a perfect trim. Leaves on the wooded section swayed in the light breeze. The sun had begun its descent, coloring the sky in glory, its last gift of the day. He crossed his legs, careful not to wrinkle the freshly pressed linen trousers he'd chosen for the evening. Swirling his crystal tumbler of whiskey, he felt like he owned the world.

"I see him, thanks."

He glanced to the door to see Ryker Jones approaching. He reflexively made a sour face as though he'd just bitten into a lemon. The man was repugnant, but useful.

"Ryker, thanks for stopping by," said George. He never moved to greet Ryker or extend a hand.

"I'm always free for a celebratory drink." Ryker smiled as he sat on the deep-cushioned, down-filled chair next to George.

"Marshall, I'd like a refresh, and my companion will have . . ." He allowed his voice to trail off, not wanting to order for the man.

"I'll have the same, thanks."

They remained quiet while they waited for their drinks. A few minutes later Marshall returned with two crystal tumblers of whiskey on a silver tray. His white-gloved hands never smudged the crystal, something George had insisted upon at his club. He simply would not tolerate fingerprints on the Baccarat.

"Here's to a job well done," said George. He held up his glass for a toast. They clinked glasses.

George leaned back into the cushions. He sipped his drink, then said, "This couldn't have been better. Everyone received something they desired out of this little venture. Everyone." He paused for a moment and then added, "You see, the trick in life is giving people what they want, while *always* getting what you want."

Ryker smiled and said, "I'll have to remember that." Ryker took a long sip of his drink and said, "You were right. Kari Sharpe never wavered in her representation of the Stadt woman, even when threatened. She's one tough broad."

George looked at Ryker as though he saw him for the first time. "Successful people who came from poverty can be dangerous. They've seen the bottom and climbed out. It makes them tricky to deal with."

Several ladies in tennis whites chatted and laughed as they walked past. George nodded to them. His eyes trailed to their asses. "I'd say it worked out perfectly for everyone."

Ryker leaned over to clink glasses again. "Yes, it worked out perfectly."

"We can thank my son. Bill played his role beautifully."

"I'd say so," said Ryker.

"Once everything settles down, I'll need you to handle something for me. Nothing big, just an itch that I can't scratch. An itch and a new business opportunity."

"Sounds intriguing."

George held his glass to Ryker and said, "To new beginnings."

Ryker smiled, leaned in to clink glasses, and said, "To new beginnings."

After taking a warming sip of the expensive whiskey, George glanced at his watch and said, "Speaking of Kari Sharpe, she and Bill are meeting my wife and me for dinner soon. It would probably be best if you left through the service entrance."

George stood and walked away.

Acknowledgments

Writing this novel was not a solitary endeavor, and I am deeply grateful to the many people who guided and supported me along the way. My heartfelt thanks go to my editor, Jessica Tribble Wells, whose keen insights and thoughtful feedback sharpened every character, bringing an idea to life. I am amazed by the work you do. Your commitment to excellence and your ability to see beneath the surface inspired me to push my boundaries and strive for something greater.

My humble gratitude to my developmental editor, Clarence Haynes, for gently nudging me to find my voice as a writer. Your patience and expertise helped me see the nuances of my story long before I would have otherwise. Thank you for never giving up on me and for reminding me that each draft brings me closer to my true vision.

To Grace Doyle and the entire team at Thomas & Mercer. I greatly appreciate your hard work, professionalism, and kindness as you helped me along the way. Your dedication to nurturing new authors and creating a supportive environment made this experience truly memorable. It has been an honor to work with such a talented group.

About the Author

K. T. Konkoly is a practicing attorney who started right out of law school as an officer in the US Navy Judge Advocate General's Corps, where she served as a criminal defense attorney at the naval base in San Diego, California. Upon leaving the navy, she moved with her family to Portland, Maine, where she rose to partner in one of the city's biggest and most respected law firms. Konkoly has always been a litigator, staying close to the courtroom action as both a JAG and private attorney. Outside of work, Konkoly enjoys spending time with her family and her dog, Tony—not necessarily in that order. She also enjoys sailing, traveling, gardening, reading, cooking, and spending time with friends. *Undertow* is her second novel.